He wanted to know her

He wanted to watch her with her children again.

God, she was beautiful. She must have men beating down her door in this frozen town. However many single women Oro held, there couldn't be another who looked like her.

She had fallen silent. She must want an explanation for why his partnership with Victor had ended.

You asked if she wants to sell the shop, after telling her the one lie she'll find out if, for some reason, you decide to buy it. He'd given her the wrong name.

The only thing to do was to artfully back out of that lie, to escape what he'd already said by uttering a soul-baring truth.

He stared at the cabinet. "I didn't know what to expect when I came here. I introduced myself as Joseph Thomas, and I think I misled you." *As Victor did.* "My name is Joseph Thomas Knoll. I wasn't just Victor's business partner. I was his brother."

Dear Reader,

To me, as a writer and a person, few things hold the importance of place.

As an adult, I've lived on the ocean in a building that was little more than plywood walls plus electricity. I've lived in Utah's canyonlands, in high desert and now in the county with the highest average elevation in the United States. For me, place is the great things of nature, such as mountain peaks, and the small things—lichen on a rock. Place is buildings; place is wilderness; place is civilization and place is people. In *A Family Resemblance,* Sabine Knoll is linked to place through a long love of mountains, through friends, through the comfort of the familiar, through history. She and Joe Knoll, the hero, share unusual experiences of place that allow them to transcend the gap of being strangers, and to know and understand each other fully.

I address you as writers, too. Who of us does not find personal expression in letters, in poems, in journals, in words that record what we choose to set down? Again and again, as writers and as people, we return not just to other people and to love but to place. I hope you enjoy the mountain town of Oro, Colorado. Thank you so much for joining me in this place.

Best wishes,

Margot Early

A FAMILY RESEMBLANCE
Margot Early

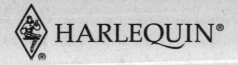

TORONTO • NEW YORK • LONDON
AMSTERDAM • PARIS • SYDNEY • HAMBURG
STOCKHOLM • ATHENS • TOKYO • MILAN • MADRID
PRAGUE • WARSAW • BUDAPEST • AUCKLAND

ISBN-13: 978-0-373-71357-8
ISBN-10:   0-373-71357-6

A FAMILY RESEMBLANCE

This edition published by arrangement with Harlequin Books S.A.

® and TM are trademarks of the publisher. Trademarks indicated with
® are registered in the United States Patent and Trademark Office, the
Canadian Trade Marks Office and in other countries.

www.eHarlequin.com

Printed in U.S.A.

Books by Margot Early

HARLEQUIN SUPERROMANCE

HARLEQUIN SINGLE TITLE

For Rodent
with much love
from Maggot

Special thanks to the administrators and instructors of the Silverton Avalanche School (silvertonavalancheschool.com) in Silverton, Colorado. I highly recommend their excellent program, which is taught by nationally recognized members of the American Avalanche Association and highly trained and experienced mountain rescue specialists. Avalanche education can increase the safety of mountain dwellers and winter recreationalists, particularly those who venture outside ski resort boundaries. Interested readers will enjoy visiting the Colorado Avalanche Information Center on the Web at http://geosurvey.state.co.us/avalanche. Incorporated into this work is information gathered from individuals, books and personal experience. A mountaineering book that has become my hands-down favorite is Jennifer Jordan's *Savage Summit;* this book about the first five women to summit K2 is a must-read for women because it is first about us, about being women, and Ms. Jordan portrays each of these climbers with compassion and insight. Finally, all gratitude to my friends and loved ones from the mountains to the sea who contribute each day to my joy in work and life.

All technical errors in this fictional work are mine.

CHAPTER ONE

Oro, Colorado

THE SLEDMAKER'S SHOP sat on the uninhabited south side of the Eureka River. Joe used his gloved hand to push snow off one windowpane, then scraped at ice beneath until he could see in.

An unfinished flyer lay upside down and runnerless on one side of the worktable. Kicksled parts hung from a pipe overhead. Boxed segments leaned against a wall. Saw and plane lay uncovered, shavings curling beneath four years' worth of dust blanketing everything. For Joe it brought to mind Dickens's Miss Havisham; the shop just needed a similarly cobwebbed female, waiting for the sledmaker's return.

Stepping away from the shop, he dug into the snow with his poles as he made his way back along the river, over a track as yet uncleared of its fresh, still-falling snow. The afternoon turned dark blue, edging toward the dark of solstice and the year's longest nights.

Lights from windows, Christmas lights on eaves and fences, sparkled across the river, making Oro come alive.

Only one house sat on this side—against dense trees and away from any avalanche path, which wouldn't have been the case if the house had been built a few hundred yards to the east or west.

It was a cabin constructed in the Arts and Crafts style, possibly from a kit. It was handsome and undoubtedly warm, sound and practical. As well built as the sleds.

Although it was five-thirty, no lights burned in that house. A bank of windows glowed at the only other structure on this side of the river, the Gold Mountain Community Center, a ski-lodge type of building, steeply roofed with jutting decks. Cars were parked outside. Others drove up, their headlights illuminating the slow snowfall, as Joe shoed past, and he heard a dance band playing inside. He remembered a sign he'd seen that day at the tiny Oro Market. Oro Family Dance, All Welcome.

Curiosity drew him toward the building. He loosened and kicked off his snowshoes and carried them across the parking area, moving behind the blinking lights of a small plow clearing the lot.

A six-dollar cover charge, according to the sign outside.

And he was not a member of this community. He was an outsider.

A small boy, accompanied by a woman with short light-brown hair, attractive with the kind of health that enough money and leisure could provide, took his ten-dollar bill and carefully counted back four ones.

"Thank you," Joe told him. "Well done."

The boy grinned. Missing two front teeth.

The band, with a saxophone, lead and bass guitar, keyboards and percussion, called themselves The Montangnards. On the hardwood floor, a couple in their fifties two-stepped to a Beatles song, while a young and extremely striking blond woman danced with a boy who looked about five while holding a younger girl in her arms.

She was unmistakable.

The white-blond hair in two braids, the arched black eyebrows and heart-shaped face and deep red bow of a mouth, coloring from a fairy tale, all of her surprisingly small and powerful. Again he knew astonishment that she had loved and married Victor Knoll, a man twenty-five years her senior.

So those were two of the children. Where was the third? He thought he'd been told that the oldest child was a girl. He could not take his eyes off the woman. Envy, mingled with bitterness, stung his ever-suppurating injury, the wound Victor had so calmly dealt.

First, Teresa—the woman *he* loved—had loved Victor. Then this woman had. The sledmaker had not been, in Joe's opinion, a handsome man. However, he'd been one of the most lovable, magnetic people Joe had ever known. Balding, beaky nose, a sense of humor, a smile like the sun, kind. He had married this woman, who was at the time perhaps all of twenty-three or twenty-four years old.

She had married him, and those were their children, two of them anyhow.

She owned his shop and the land on which it sat.

For a hard-felt, hard-swallowing moment, Joe wanted that shop and everything in it. He wanted everything he could get that had once been Victor's.

A tall man with long jet-black hair joined her on the floor and began dancing with Sabine Knoll and her children. She gave him a look that was only polite, turning away and smiling at her son.

Joe had never met her. He hadn't come here to have anything to do with Victor's widow or his offspring—not really. Victor had been his brother, sixteen years older, and more like a father to him—once. Had Victor ever mentioned his younger brother and onetime business partner to Sabine? Impossible to say.

It didn't occur to him to approach her then, and he definitely wasn't asking her to dance. There was a time for everything.

This was the time for him to remember the reasons he'd come to Oro.

And all the reasons he *hadn't* come, all the things he wasn't here to do.

AGAINST SABINE'S SHOULDER, Tori said, "There's Daddy."

This had become an irritating trait of Tori's. Victoria knew perfectly well that her father had died before she was born—as perfectly as an almost-four-year-old could understand the concept of death. *I wish it was your daddy,* Sabine thought, not even bothering to turn around to see who had inspired the remark this time.

Strange how someone could be gone for four years, and— It wasn't precisely that she still *mourned.* But she knew perfectly well that Victor Knoll had been the love of her life and she was unlikely to love that way again.

"Daddy's *dead!*" Finn yelled at his sister. "Stop being stupid! We don't have a dad."

Sabine said, "Be nice, Finn." She hated refereeing between these two. Maria, the oldest, was uncommonly sane and mature for a nine-year-old. She'd always been an easy child. Finn and Tori were not easy. In fact, they seemed determined to present a picture to the world that suggested their mother could not raise them successfully without the help of the husband she'd lost. About once a week, Sabine asked her sister, Lucy, *It's me, isn't it? I'm not strict enough, am I?*

Her sister generally declined to give an opinion. And Lucy was hardly an authority on mothering.

Yes, Sabine missed Victor, and not just—or mostly—as the father of her children.

"It's Daddy," Tori insisted. "It's Daddy in the picture."

"What picture?" The band started another song, Van Morrison's "Brown-Eyed Girl." Sabine peered into Tori's small face, which had Victor's brown eyes rather than her own blue ones. But Tori was pointing over Sabine's shoulder, and Sabine turned with her daughter in her arms.

The man was staring at her. His expression was not that of a man admiring an attractive woman. It was different. Deliberate, yet without sexual meaning.

He was dark-haired, dark-skinned, with five o'clock shadow and the nose of an eagle. He reminded Sabine of black-and-white photographs of polar explorers—or the first men to climb Everest, though why she should romanticize *those* men she didn't know. The family in which she'd grown up had been Himalayan mountaineers; from personal experience, she knew mountaineering to be something different from what the uninitiated perceived, both for the loved ones waiting at home and for the mountaineers themselves. Sabine had been both and—in a snow-buried, ice-locked part of herself—still was and always would be.

In any event, she'd never seen this man before, he bore no resemblance to Victor, and, as usual on this subject, she had no idea what Tori was talking about. Sometimes, when she was tired or annoyed, when ice had caked beside her car and one of the children fell, when she needed just *one thing* from the store and discovered it had closed three minutes earlier, when she'd been up shoveling at thirty degrees below zero since three in the morning, and Tori said something like this, Sabine almost believed her daughter did it to torment her, which was ridiculous.

But what she would give for one glimpse of Victor, even as a ghost.

And not be able to touch?

"That's not your father," she said matter-of-factly. Perhaps simply hearing the answer had been Tori's objective. Like in the book *Are You My Mother?* Although Tori's question was, *Is that my daddy?* A game.

It wasn't a game Sabine enjoyed, nor did she particularly mind. If Maria had suddenly burst out, *There's Daddy!* it would've been different. She was the only one of the children who had any real recollection of Victor. Probably Finn remembered a little—impressions.

But Tori wouldn't know Victor if he walked into the Oro Community Center.

Sabine turned away from the stranger, trying not to remember, trying to remember, moments of jumping into Victor's arms, wrapping her legs around him. Feeling so exquisitely *loved* and loving him, eager to make up for the long years of imprisonment in his previous marriage.

Except that Victor had always refused to consider himself a prisoner, just as he'd refused to turn his back on a situation everyone else had judged impossible and un-workable.

"In the picture!" Tori said again. "Daddy in the picture!"

What was she talking about? "Where's Maria?" Sabine asked Finn, ignoring Tori's outburst. "We should go home and bake those cookies, so they'll be done by bedtime."

"Yes," Finn said.

"Mommy, *look!* He's Daddy in the picture!"

"Quiet, Tori. Stop yelling." Sabine put her down, unwilling to let her daughter shriek in her ear. Tori was getting louder by the minute. "It's time to go home." Others were just arriving.

"I want to see Aubrey!" Tori screamed.

"Tori, I am so not in the mood for this. If you want to stay until Aubrey gets here, you need to lower your voice and be pleasant. Do you want to dance?" Aubrey went to Tori's preschool and was her favorite playmate.

Tori shook her head, brow furrowed, an expression of stubbornness crossing her features. She tugged on Sabine's hand. "Mommy. Mommy."

Sabine crouched down to hear her.

"In the picture."

"What picture? Sweetie, tell me what picture you mean."

"In the attic!"

The attic of the house Victor had built the year after they'd moved to Oro from Minnesota was now the children's favorite play area. It had been Victor's place at home, a den of sorts where he'd done some of the paper-work for the business. The rest of the family had always been welcome to join him. There was no part of Victor's life that he had closed off from her.

He used to carry Maria and later Finn up into the attic with him. The children had sat on the floor looking through old issues of *National Geographic,* playing with wooden blocks he'd cut and finished for them or with Maria's dollhouse, a Second Empire Victorian, like many of the homes in Oro; Victor had planned to wire it for electricity when Maria was older.

There were many pictures in the attic. After Victor had died, Sabine wished she'd taken the time to ask him to identify every single person in every single photo. She wished she'd asked more questions about his life before she'd met him.

But what had it mattered? She'd known the key parts, and she had simply wanted him back.

She supposed she still did, but accepted that it wasn't possible.

He'd been only fifty-six when he died. That was *nothing.* Nothing. She'd counted on having him much longer—as though that would've made it easier when he finally died before she did. Ironically, he'd died in a way he probably wouldn't have in old age—avalanche burial while cross-country skiing.

"Oh," Sabine said. "He looks like someone in one of Daddy's pictures?"

"Daddy," Tori said again, in a tone that implied her mother was impossibly stupid.

Of course, Tori probably didn't know which man in the

pictures was her father. Tori had seen photos of Victor but not recently. "When we get home, you can show me. Believe me, Tori, the man over there is not your father."

Tori's bottom lip stuck out, but then she spotted someone on the opposite side of the room. Freeing herself from Sabine, she sprinted across the floor in her black patent leather shoes and black velvet dress, the Christmas dress she wouldn't be able to wear for more than this one year. It had been Maria's.

Finn said, "Mom, I want to go home and make cookies."

"We'll go soon. Aubrey just got here. We'll stay for a little while so she and Tori can play."

Maria, with her blond braids—flaxen blond, white-blond, like Sabine's—came to join them. She wore a pair of sheepskin-lined pink suede boots that Sabine had bought secondhand, white corduroys and sweater, and a pale pink ski jacket.

I am lucky, Sabine reminded herself, as she often did. She was thirty-four years old, owner of her own house, mother of three beautiful children. Between the homespun yarns she sold in Oro's shops during the summer, the two jobs she held during the same season—waiting tables, selling clothes for a Front Range designer—and her and Lucy's winter snow-shoveling business, she made enough money to support herself and her children. They'd done better when Victor was alive and making sleds, but even alone she seemed to make a little more money each year. She could spin faster all the time, particularly with Maria carding the wool. Maria earned a percentage of the profits from each skein of yarn. Maria saved her money, too, and she had knit sections of the sweater she was wearing, made of white lambswool.

Yes, I'm lucky.

She was happy, and she'd known more love in the five years of her marriage to Victor than most people knew in a lifetime. And she *had* taken one lover since his death, but she regretted it. It had made her sadder than ever, as though she'd violated the sacredness of the love she'd shared with Victor by sleeping with a man who wasn't his equal in any way.

Maria said, "Can we go?"

"In just a few minutes. After Aubrey and Tori have some time to play."

It was seven o'clock when they reached home. Sabine lit a fire in the woodstove with Tori tugging on her leg, saying, "Mommy, come see the picture," and Finn saying, "Can we make the cookies yet?"

Maria said, "I put on water for spaghetti, Mom," which was the kind of thing Maria did.

"Thank you, Maria. I'm just running up to the attic with Tori."

The framed picture hung on the wall beside the old desk Victor had used. He'd never bought anything new for himself, but had showered her with gifts and given generously to other people, too. No wonder Sabine hadn't remembered the picture and Tori had. It hung slightly lower than Tori's eye-level.

"That's your daddy," Sabine said, pointing to Victor. She didn't know the identity of the other man—but Tori was right. The other man in the photo might be the same man they'd seen at the community center that night—

though the photo showed a younger version. The man at the dance was in his forties, she guessed. The photo must be twenty years old.

Who was he?

It probably wasn't the same man.

Yet Sabine remembered turning and finding his eyes on her with a predatory expression that didn't seem to have anything to do with desire.

She studied the photo, studied Victor's bright familiar smile. Back then, he'd had more hair, black that'd gone silver as he lost it. His smooth olive skin was like that of his companion, who was a bit taller and perhaps fifteen years younger.

Curious, Sabine took the photo off the wall.

"What are you doing, Mommy?" asked Tori.

"I want to see if Daddy wrote anything on the picture."

The frame was inexpensive, the back easy to remove.

There it was, like pain. Victor's familiar scrawl, his messy male writing. *The sledmakers.*

He'd had a partner in the business before she'd known him. Joe? Yes, that was his name. "I think that's Joe," she told Tori, reassembling the picture in the frame and pausing to study Victor's eyes, that clear brown, like cognac, with a long thick fringe of lashes and whites whiter than snow. Her lover's eyes. God, how she'd loved him—and still did, wherever he was.

His companion was brown-eyed, too, Sabine thought though she couldn't be certain. Their mouths were similar, his and Victor's. And their chins. Strong. Good chins.

What had Victor said about his business partner? Very little, as Sabine recalled. There'd been so many other things to talk about. He'd been immersed in caring for Teresa. What had happened to Teresa was so horrifying. And Sabine—at first all she'd been able to think about was the fact that Victor was married, married to Teresa.

With simple loyalty, he'd refused to leave his wife, refused to speak words of love to Sabine or to make any overtures toward her, always denying with his actions what she saw in his eyes. When she quit working for them, quit because temptation seemed too great, she had seen a brief dampness in his eyes that he quickly both hid and denied.

He had never cried in front of her. Ever.

Then, Teresa had died.

He could abandon the dead.

Finn came up to the attic, dressed as Blizzardman, a superhero he'd invented. Lucy had sewn a pale-silver satin snowflake onto the back of his white satin cape. "Can we make cookies yet?"

"Yes. We'll start them. And dinner."

She picked up Tori and carried her downstairs, following her superhero son. Finn had begun kindergarten this year, and it felt to Sabine that she'd had nothing but problems with him—and Oro's tiny school—ever since. His teacher, who also taught the first-, second- and third-grade students, including Maria, did not want Finn wearing his cape to school, which he chose to do every day. But there was no rule against it, and Sabine was strongly in favor of capes, strongly in favor of a six-year-old boy who spent hours imagining himself gathering into the force of an avalanche or freezing villains with a look from his eyes. And Finn was a loner. He was different.

He had no father, and she believed he needed one. But nowhere could she find a man whom she could love and respect as she had loved and respected Victor.

The children were in bed when Lucy finally came in, flushed, the blue shell she wore over her other ski clothes steaming. Lucy was an ultrarunner and adventure racer. Sabine envied her the freedom of long workouts; her own often consisted of skiing while pulling Tori on a sled or dragging the children's sleds up to the top of one or another of their favorite sledding hills—or, of course, shoveling, her main outlet for activity.

Lucy was Sabine's height but of stockier build with a broad freckled face and the same white-blond hair as Sabine's. She had once told Sabine that it was no fun being "the ugly one." Sabine hadn't known how to react, except to deny Lucy's claim to ugliness. Now Lucy said, "I think we've got to get up on the Independence."

The Hotel Independence, one of the buildings they'd contracted to shovel.

"I saw Mac at the rec center just now," she continued, "and he said there's three feet on the north side of the roof. By the way, he says there's some guy in town asking questions about you and Victor."

Sabine didn't believe in coincidence.

It had to be the man she'd seen earlier that night, which meant that man must be Victor's former partner, Joe.

"Like what?" She didn't know why she shied from telling Lucy about Tori's confusion; she probably didn't want to admit that Tori couldn't pick Victor out of a photograph.

"Mac thought he sounded interested in the shop."

She didn't say, *Interested how?* Interested in buying, undoubtedly.

"Don't you want to sell?" asked Lucy. "This time, maybe?"

How odd to see her younger sister, twenty-nine, who hadn't blanched at paddling some of the most dangerous rapids in the world, who had run a hundred miles through lightning and hail, who possessed Sabine's own fearlessness in the mountains, quail at asking this question.

They had argued about it in the past.

Now Sabine just shrugged. What if the man Tori had noticed *was* Victor's old partner? What if he did want to buy the business?

Later that night, when she finally lay down in the four-poster hickory bed Victor had made for the two of them, the bed in which he had finally come to her, finally become hers, Sabine again pictured the man standing on the edge of the dance floor. She remembered how, when she'd turned, he'd been staring at her. At them.

Had he heard Tori shriek that he was her daddy?

Sabine didn't think so. She fell asleep wondering if the stranger was merely passing through and if he'd known Victor. If, by some chance, he was the mysterious "Joe" who'd made sleds with Victor twenty years earlier.

HE RETURNED to her house the next morning and saw that she was home. The chimney breathed wood smoke. A Subaru station wagon sat outside.

Joe parked his truck, a green Toyota with a camper shell and Alaska plates, on the snow-packed dirt street and switched off the engine. Was this the way to do it?

Why do it at all, any of it?

He'd come to Oro. He'd seen the shop. He'd seen the house. He'd seen Victor's wife and children.

He'd even visited the cemetery and seen his grave.

He'd seen everything he'd come to see and done everything he'd come to do. He didn't need absolution any more than Victor had.

And it was too late in any case.

But he did want something here, and what it was he couldn't articulate. Years ago, he had lost something—many things. He wanted those things back, wanted himself unchanged by the events of that period, the period that had severed him from Victor. Other trials that had led to maturity he could easily accept. He had never expected a life without hardship.

But somehow, back in those weeks when things went so wrong, he had learned bitterness. He wasn't sure he'd ever unlearned it, and he'd begun to believe his only hope for salvation lay in those faint cracks through which sentiment for Victor sometimes leaked.

The day had dawned icy with a wind blowing sleet. Now, at 10:00 a.m., the grayness remained.

She'd already shoveled her drive, he saw.

Or perhaps someone had shoveled it for her.

He couldn't remember who had sent him the wedding photo. Not Victor. He'd learned about the children's births from his aunt, who had lived across town from Victor and Teresa, then from Victor and Sabine, in the brief time they'd stayed in Minnesota after marrying.

She's quite young, but they seem very happy, his aunt had written.

He'd pondered that clause often. *She's quite young.* Why not, *He's old for her?* Why not, *There's a twenty-five-year age difference?* The blame, expressed this way, seemed to lie with Sabine.

His aunt had forgotten about Teresa, forgotten how she had come to be Victor's wife, forgotten that Teresa had loved another man before Victor.

Joe, of course, never would.

The porch steps were swept of snow, as well. Yet everywhere, he saw prints of small boots and other evidence of children.

Two Nordic-style children's kicksleds, undoubtedly made by Victor.

A Minnesota Flyer—that was what he and Victor had called the model when they'd built sleds together in Minnesota—leaned against the side of the house beneath the porch awning.

Did Sabine know what had happened to reduce Teresa to an idiot, something between vegetable and madwoman? She must have. It had been no secret.

Well, sleds weren't inherently dangerous. But how had Victor felt about his children using them?

What had Victor really felt about anything?

Joe had believed he knew him. Once.

He felt little inclination to speak with Sabine, yet he'd seen the shop last night, and he'd made a decision. A decision to *ask,* and there was no one to ask about the shop but her.

He knocked on the door, his knuckles striking the wood beside the four small windowpanes.

After a few seconds, he heard soft footsteps inside.

When she answered, he saw she was wearing mukluks, which had padded quietly over the hardwood floor. But what struck him, more forcibly than it had last night, was that she was beautiful.

It was one of life's rules, he had once believed, that like inevitably mated with like. Yet several women had told him they loved Victor for his goodness and found him handsome because of that goodness.

One of life's other rules was that women who looked like Sabine Knoll were shallow. Even when they appeared at first to be deep, their sorrows turned out to be of the kind that had been bred around their beauty.

Today her platinum hair was woven into one ropelike braid, but strands had come out, as though she'd been outdoors. Her eyebrows were surprisingly dark, yet delicately shaped. Her eyes reminded him of a fall sky.

He tried to read their expression. She'd seen him the night before. Had she recognized him from a photo? Perhaps. And if Victor had told her about him, that might be cause enough for trepidation.

Or wariness....

"Yes?" she said.

He decided to give away as little as possible until he could determine what she knew. "I'm looking for the widow of Victor Knoll."

"I'm Sabine Knoll," she said, opening the door wider. "My daughter actually thought she recognized you from a photo the other night. Did you know my husband?"

"Yes." *My whole life.*

Her voice surprised him. It seemed mature, experienced, almost businesslike, issuing from a face and body profoundly young—and also, to his eye, both fragile and strong.

"Were you the Joe who was his partner for a while?"

Like that, she revealed how much she knew. And how little. Like that, his impression of her as mature, experienced and businesslike vanished. She was naive, unintelligent or both. "That's me," he said. "Joseph Thomas." It was the wrong name and the right name. His father used to call him this; Victor occasionally had, too. First and middle name. What was to be gained, he wondered, from deceiving Sabine Knoll?

Satisfaction—a satisfaction that had nothing to do with her and everything to do with what Victor had done to him.

Revenge?

He wouldn't have put it in such crude terms.

And revenge wasn't precisely what he wanted.

More a leveling of things—an even score.

As though being loved by the woman a dead man had loved in life was equal to a guardian taking what had belonged to his ward. Not that Joe had been Victor's ward at the time, or that Teresa had been a possession. But Joe had loved her.

She had learned—readily, as readily as people always did—to love Victor.

"Would you like to come in?" Sabine asked. "I have to pick up my daughter at preschool, but not for an hour."

He wanted to warn her that she shouldn't invite strangers inside, and the instinct shocked him. He wasn't interested in protecting her. He had no concern for her at all, less than for any woman on earth.

That was bitterness, the indifference of the truly self-interested, speaking again, and he did not like himself for it, for his sudden intention to be nothing good in this woman's life. It wasn't why he'd come to Oro. And he hadn't come to stay or even to linger. He'd come to look, to see, and to move on and quietly rebuild himself into an older version of someone he used to be and had lost along the road.

To create a better life.

The old life seduced, calling to him from halfway around the world. Climbing. Climbing was what had restored his manhood, permitting him to move beyond Victor and Teresa.

But had he really put it behind him? Ever?

"Thank you," he told Victor's widow, following her into the kitchen.

They sat at a maple table with four mismatched chairs, one holding a child's booster chair. Before she sat down, she said, "Can I get you anything? Tea? Coffee? Cookies?"

"No, thank you."

So she sat and peered at him, waiting.

That impressed him, that she didn't rush to fill the silence. He felt her wariness return, but he no longer worried that Victor had spoken of him.

"A friend of mine told me that Victor's old shop is sitting equipped and unused. I went over and looked in the window."

"Yes," she said, the word slow as a breath.

"I wanted to ask if you're interested in selling the business."

"It's hardly a business anymore. Not after four years.

He had almost no sleds in stock. I've hung on to the last ones he made."

The last ones he'd made were sitting in the shop gathering dust, as far as Joe could see.

"Other people," she said, "have offered to buy the business. I—" Hesitation. "I'm protective of Victor's vision for it."

He didn't ask her to describe that vision. He thought he could guess much of it, and he remembered some.

"And I don't know why your partnership ended," she added. "I can't recall what he told me. It just seemed very much in the past."

Gazing through the open arch into the next room, he saw, in a nook by the fireplace, three spinning wheels, baskets of wool, bobbins, other wooden spinning accoutrements, all in a happy and rustic disorder. It looked as though she'd been spinning when he knocked at the door. A hobby? What was important to her?

He wanted to know *her*.

He wanted to watch her with her children again.

His curiosity displeased him.

God, she was beautiful. She must have men beating down the door in this frozen town. However many single women Oro held, there couldn't be another who looked like her.

She had fallen silent. She must want an explanation for why his partnership with Victor had ended.

You asked if she wants to sell the shop, after telling her the one lie she'll find out if, for some reason, you decide to buy it. He'd given her the wrong name.

The only thing to do was to artfully back out of that lie,

to escape what he'd already said by uttering a soulbaring truth.

At least part of it.

He stared at the cabinet. "I didn't know what to expect when I came here. I introduced myself as Joseph Thomas, and I think I misled you." *As Victor did.* "My name is Joseph Thomas Knoll. I wasn't just Victor's business partner. I'm his brother."

CHAPTER TWO

I'M HIS BROTHER.

Anything so appalling, so horrifying, so totally unknown, must be true. She didn't say, *I never knew he had a brother.* This man must already recognize the extent of her ignorance.

And of Victor's lie.

Victor never lied to me.

No. He'd just neglected to mention that his former business partner was also his brother.

Gazing at Joe Knoll—and she had no doubt he was who he said he was, the truth was in his eyes—she thought, *I hate this man. Why did he come here? Why did he ever tell me this?*

And what else would he say before he left?

She would listen.

She couldn't stop herself from hearing about the things that had made Victor into Victor.

But could anything justify her husband's never once, in five years, mentioning that he even had a brother?

Her mind searched for excuses. Trying to pretend that she'd never asked Victor if he had brothers and sisters.

She had asked.

He had shaken his head, staring at a point she couldn't see.

Had he explained when she wasn't listening?

But those times were rare. The sledmaker's shop had always been a place for those who needed to talk, and Victor had listened, saying the right things, always comforting, loving, appropriate, down-to-earth, often funny. She, in turn, had been Victor's listener, a role she'd cherished from the beginning, before she realized with horror that it was too late and she was in love with him.

"He was sixteen years older than me," said Joe. "Our mother died when I was seven. Our father died three years later, and Victor raised me."

Good God. Because of the way in which she and Lucy had been orphaned, Victor's failing to reveal this seemed an even greater lapse of candor. "Do you have other brothers and sisters?" Her face heated as she asked, flushing at a question like this about the man whose children she'd borne.

"No."

This was Victor's brother, and he wanted to buy the business. Perhaps.

Sabine studied his face as she asked, "Why did your partnership end?"

Hesitation—just a beat. Abruptly, she knew he'd lie.

"I decided to go to Alaska. I became a climbing guide. Then I started a business guiding in the Himalayas. I've been doing that for fifteen years."

Her heart pounded.

The Himalayas.

Not such a coincidence. Many American Himalayan climbers made their homes in Colorado's San Juan Mountains. So why did this seem more than coincidental to her?

The symmetry, its fitting with her life, with her life

before Victor, troubled her. And it explained some things about Victor that she'd never understood. But as an explanation for Victor's never saying he had a brother, for his having a brother who never called or wrote, this was so inadequate that Sabine simply stared.

Joe's eyes were shaped like Victor's. But they weren't warm like Victor's.

They weren't Victor's eyes, yet reminded her of Victor and so, subtly, angered her.

"In retrospect," Joe said, "I regret...not ending our partnership but just—cutting myself off from him—for so many years. Not forgiving." As he spoke, the eyes changed, did become like Victor's, conveying some of the humor, some of the good will toward people and life in general. "He—well, he married my fiancée."

Sabine did not let her eyes go wide, did not reveal any of her shock. Given what had happened to Teresa, this news was— "Teresa?" As though Victor could have been married to someone else, before Teresa, and never mentioned her, just as he'd never mentioned this brother.

Joe nodded. "I was twenty-five. Teresa was two years older."

"Did you ever see her—after—" Sabine faltered. "After—"

"The accident? No."

"How did you know about it?"

"Aunt Faye."

Sabine blinked.

"Aunt Faye took against Victor a long time ago. Because he didn't move in with her, bringing me along,

when our father died. She lived three miles from you and
Victor. Anyhow, she was my godmother. She often wrote
to me after I left town."

Sabine could not address or care about this new revelation, an aunt she'd never met, Victor's aunt, living three
miles away back in Minnesota. "You're telling me that
Victor stole your fiancée?"

Another pause. "They fell in love. Victor was—charis-
matic."

Teresa.

Sabine had never known the woman this man had loved,
the woman with whom Victor had fallen in love. She had
known someone else. Someone who slurred her words,
who was given to violent outbursts, her beauty lost to the
half life of changed existence. Did Teresa know the difference?

Yes. She had said so.

I used to be beautiful and smart.

And Victor, so patient, so devoted, so thoroughly living
the words "in sickness and in health." He was faithful
even when Sabine began to have long talks with him in
the kitchen, even after the moment she fell irrevocably in
love—in a single look across that room as he turned from
the coffeemaker. Even after she understood that he liked
her, that he found her attractive, even as he tried to hide
that he was tempted.

He was always so good. Touch had been fleeting,
stolen. Briefly, his hand on hers, but only to thank her for
her work cleaning the house. Never anything inappro-
priate.

Which had made the attitudes of a *few* people strange.

Shrugs about Teresa and him. Someone saying, *After the way they got together*... As if there was a story there.

Sabine hadn't listened, believing the people were criticizing some past behavior of Teresa's. How could people be so petty, she wondered, as to gossip about the past behavior of a couple who had suffered such a tragedy, changing their marriage and their lives? She hadn't listened at all. Sometimes she'd said coldly, *Victor is extremely devoted to her,* making it clear that she wouldn't participate in the conversation.

Devoted. Faithful.

The embrace had happened when *she* had needed comfort, when she'd cried in his presence and he had listened.

After that, they both knew.

The next day she told him she was quitting.

He didn't ask why. They both knew.

Eight months later, she heard about Teresa's death.

A month after his wife had died, Sabine saw Victor in the local market. He said the house was a mess. He asked if she was still cleaning—she'd cleaned house and done some cooking for him and Teresa, as well as waited tables and tried to participate in the community while she sorted out her own life, her goals, even her values.

Later, he said he'd worried that she would think he was a dirty old man if he showed how he felt.

That had never occurred to her.

Sabine finally said to Joe Knoll, "That's the entirety—the whole story—of the end of your business relationship?"

"You don't think it's enough?" Amusement in his voice.

She thought it was plenty. "I just prefer to have all the facts. You aren't the first person asking to buy the business. I've never been tempted to sell."

"Why not?"

She saw it again in his expression: a subtle scorn for sentimentality, for feeling, for holding on to the trappings of something that was gone—her marriage to Victor.

But he probably didn't understand, probably had never experienced what she and Victor had. And he didn't know the sorrow she felt—and the self-blame—after she'd taken a lover who wasn't, for her, Victor's equal.

But how pure and true was it really, Sabine, if he failed to tell you any of this? The brother, the stolen fiancée?

On the other hand, she knew nothing about Joe Knoll. He could be lying about what had happened with Teresa. He could've invented his engagement to her. He could have loved his older brother's fiancée—loved his wife. How was Sabine to know? Living with Victor, loving him, she'd accepted in a way rare for her that he was what he seemed to be. But certain experiences since his death had reminded her that plenty of people went through life re-inventing themselves and their pasts to create the impressions they wanted.

Nothing to be lost by saying some of this. "Why should I believe you? I believe you're Victor's brother, but I never heard any hint that Teresa had been your girlfriend first."

Was that true?

Only because she hadn't known that Victor even *had* a brother. Otherwise, the suggestion was there. People had dropped hints, words that took for granted that she knew what they knew.

And I stopped them talking. Didn't I want to know?

Because part of her *must* have known that there was something askew about Victor's marriage to Teresa—that there had been something not to be proud of. But why listen when the man's present reality was tending to a head-injured woman who, from time to time, lashed out at him physically, sometimes drooling and spitting like a perfect nightmare of the madwoman in the attic?

"You don't have to believe me. You asked a question— why our partnership ended. I answered it."

Sabine did not like him, did not like his coming to her home, the home she'd shared with Victor, and upsetting her memories, upsetting everything. She yearned for Victor, Victor whom she'd loved, Victor to whom she'd been profoundly attracted, intellectually, spiritually, emotionally and physically.

Instead this dark stranger had come with tales from the past, a past that had nothing to do with her. So what if Victor had fallen in love with his brother's fiancée and she with him? He had suffered since.

He had told her once, *I don't think what happened to Teresa happened as a punishment for anyone. That's not the God I believe exists. I just think this is the way it is.*

She'd never asked what he or Teresa had done that might have deserved punishment.

"Can I ask you something?"

She started out of her reverie.

"You're very attractive," Joe said, "and you've got to be about three decades younger than my brother was. Why did you marry him?"

People had asked her this before. Two people. She

didn't like either of them, although she hadn't minded a lady from church telling her, *Sometimes marriages with big age differences work out well.* A European woman had told her that the French believed a good age difference was for the woman to be half the man's age plus seven years. Victor hadn't lived long enough for the two of them to experience that magic time.

Sabine didn't mind the question from Joe Knoll. There had been no disgust or censure in his query, nor voyeuristic curiosity, just a trying to understand, as though her answer might help him resolve mysteries in his own life.

"I was completely, totally, in every way, in love with him. Which isn't to say I thought he was perfect. He could be passive-aggressive, insensitive. Sometimes he'd say and do things without having a clue how they'd affect someone else. I just loved him."

"Did you meet when he was married to Teresa?"

"Yes." She didn't like that question, didn't like the questions it could raise. And *had* raised. The first question was whether she'd made love with Victor while Teresa was still alive.

The second question... Well, since a bad reaction to medication had contributed to Teresa's death... Since Victor had been in charge of her medication...

But Victor would never have done that.

Joe gazed thoughtfully at the kitchen cabinets, which Victor had built.

Sabine said, "I'll have to think about your offer. When it *is* an offer, that is."

In other words, when he'd told her how much he was willing to pay.

She should think about it this time. Think about what Victor would want. Her refusal to sell up until this point wasn't a way to keep Victor's memory alive, whatever Lucy thought. Anyone who bought the business, Joe Knoll included, would change it. But she intended to handle the sale of the business as Victor would have wanted. And possibly he would've wanted his brother to have it.

And if Victor had indeed married the woman to whom his brother had been engaged, Victor might want the business to go to that brother now.

How can I find out the truth? From the aunt she hadn't known existed until today?

And was it really *necessary* to know?

Even if it was true and she did know, that knowledge wouldn't make anything clearer. She had no doubt that Victor had changed because of Teresa's accident, just as she had no doubt that he'd been a good man before it happened.

So who needed a voice whispering to her that a man who could rationalize marrying the woman his younger brother loved might also be able to justify a more serious crime?

Victor would never, ever have murdered Teresa. His commitment to Teresa had been part of who he was. He'd found his attraction to Sabine as horrifying as she had found hers to him.

He'd said later, when Teresa's death had made it possible to say things left unsaid until then, *It would've been wrong to tell you how I felt.*

Victor was not responsible for the death of his disabled wife.

And if Teresa had really meant so much to Joe, why had he never tried to see her after the accident?

Well, by then she was Victor's wife.

"I assume I can review the books, from the business," Joe said.

A reasonable request, one she should have expected. But she wanted him to leave, to be gone. It would be so much easier to simply say no, that she wouldn't sell to him.

But she had a feeling that wasn't what Victor would've wanted.

There was another side to the Teresa story—two more sides, if you included Teresa's.

I always trusted Victor, trusted him and trusted in his goodness, and he never let me down.

"I haven't said," Sabine told Joe, "that I'm interested in selling. And I'm not convinced you're interested in buying." Because what mountaineer ever stopped climbing? They were addicts. She should know.

What mountaineer, indeed.

I stopped.

But would she have started again if not for Victor, Victor who seemed to have an unreasonable dislike for the sport? He'd derided its selfishness to a degree he seldom criticized anyone or anything. Of course, he'd finally confessed with a rueful smile that she was so strong, so athletic, that he wondered if he could keep up. After that admission, she'd found it easier to avoid climbing.

The books for the business… She could hardly recall where they'd be; she could only remember a day two months after Victor had died, when she'd left the shop and locked the door, swearing she'd stop going out there, stop visiting and trying to be with him, trying to call him back.

She had not kept that vow.

She'd thought of cleaning the shop, perhaps using it as a studio for spinning, but it had all been too hard. It had seemed that if she left it as it was, maybe he'd reappear, looking up from wood he was sanding with his smile like the sun.

I don't want to sell it. I want Victor back. I still want him back.

To cover her feelings, she rose and took a piece of scrap paper from a pile it was Finn's job to cut or tear to note-size. She took a pen from a jar against the wall. Her throat had swollen, knotted. *I want Victor. Why did we have so little time?*

Grief felt different after four years, but longing didn't change. Not really. No one else's arms would feel as safe, no one's skin as perfect, no one's scent as attuned to hers. Victor had been like the sun, and who could compete with the sun? Not this dark brother of his with the face of a mountain man, of a veteran, the brother who still had plenty of thick dark hair, who was three inches taller than Victor had been, who reminded her firmly that she did not like tall men, that they frightened her, that she could never feel safe with one.

Victor had been strong, yes, but not tall, not like Joe Knoll.

Joe reminded her that without Victor she was alone and vulnerable. She did not appreciate the reminder and wondered why she'd let this man into her kitchen at all.

I can't sell the business.

She also knew what Victor would say, knew so strongly that she could hear his voice, deep, warm and comforting, her favorite voice in the world, saying, *See what he offers.* A touch of humor in the words and in his tone. And always practical. *How much?* Thinking it over, thinking his own thoughts, eventually sharing them with her.

Levelheaded, sensible and mature.

"Do you have a local phone number?" She did not look up.

"I'm staying at the boardinghouse."

Sabine nodded. One of Oro's less expensive accommodations for guests and long-term residents was a renovated miners' boardinghouse. It stood on the other side of the river and three blocks down.

In her silence, Joe felt his own unanchored life. At the boardinghouse, he had a bed to himself in a room shared with an otherwise homeless local, a drifter who seemed to have floated in and out of Oro over the last decade and was presently doing some kind of work online.

If he bought Victor's business, Joe would be committing himself to something permanent. That unsettled him.

"I'm not at all sure I want to sell." Speaking, Sabine realized that never before had she gone as far as assembling the business records for someone else to view. This man, with his surprises, had drawn her out of her safe refuge. Or, rather, he'd come to her within it and taken her unawares.

Sabine had moved to Minnesota, seeking a refuge of sorts—deliberately stepping back from the world of high-altitude mountaineering. Victor, who had applauded that step, had taken her to other mountains, although he'd discouraged her from climbing them. Had he been afraid that the small world of climbing, let alone the smaller world of Himalayan mountaineering, would bring her into contact with Joe? Now it seemed more than likely.

Victor, why didn't you tell me? What was your relationship with your brother like?

But the most important question was one to which she doubted she'd ever receive an answer: How would Victor explain the triangle involving Teresa, whom he had married? What would his side of the story be if he could tell it now?

But the money from the business… In Oro's present real estate market, land was worth more and more every year. Just the land on which the shop sat could change her life and that of her children.

But we don't need *more than we have.*

Yet just to be able to hire a sitter once in a while so she could go skiing alone instead of so she and Lucy could shovel. Maria was mature enough, in many ways, to watch the other children for short periods of time, but Sabine sometimes longed to have a whole day to herself. Occasionally, she found herself horrified by longings to revisit the places of her childhood and teenage years, those kingdoms in the sky—the Himalayas. Out of the question, that ultimate evasion of responsibility, yet mountaineering in the highest realms of the earth had once been her addiction and she'd believed it would be her whole life.

It had stunned her to find anything she could love as much, let alone more.

But she had.

Victor.

Her children.

Yet sometimes she felt as though she'd put part of herself aside, tucked it away in a drawer where she could ignore its existence, and even those closest to her never knew of its presence—*especially because Victor hadn't wanted to know.* Disloyal thought.

Victor had saved her, saved her from that reckless need to climb, to climb the highest peaks in the world. She'd never wanted to live only for herself. High-altitude mountaineering needn't be that self-serving and wasn't always, yet it could be. At the end of her life, how much would her summiting Cho Oyu or Annapurna matter?

She was glad of the things she'd done, the things she'd seen, but her present existence—picking up her children after school, baking cookies with them, teaching Maria to spin, cutting out paper dolls for Tori, taking them skiing and sledding in winter, hiking in summer—this was the full moon of life. As tired as she often was, these days would go by too fast. She'd been told so by women older than herself, told often enough to believe it.

Treasure each moment and be thankful.

"You'll want the real estate, too," she said to Joe Knoll, although it was a question.

Joe thought about this. He didn't intend to buy Victor's shop or the business. But real estate in Oro was a good investment. "How many acres?"

"Roughly ten." Sabine subtracted two, automatically, to surround the house. "Tell me more about your guiding. Did you guide treks or mountaineering expeditions?"

"The latter."

Though it was the answer she'd expected, it chilled her.

Had her past found a way to follow her through time, to trail her like a ghost into the different life she'd made for herself, a life removed?

She still had questions for Joe. Where had his money come from? "How did you get into outfitting expeditions?"

"Financially?"

"Yes."

"I started in a partnership and bought out my partner."

"You can't possibly run this business *and* that business. You can't be two places at once."

"I sold that business earlier this year."

Sabine badly wanted to ask why, but it wasn't relevant. Not really. Death could have decided him. Or deaths.

Most likely, he simply preferred more freedom to climb without having to care for clients.

"If I decide to sell," she said. "I'm not prepared, if you know what I mean. So I'll need a little time."

"I'll call you tomorrow afternoon, then?"

"Actually—" She was getting used to being cool and aloof, to shutting men down, turning so cold she stopped anyone who pushed her, stopped them like a wall they hit, a barrier that would not give. "My attorney will call you tomorrow with the details." Because she could not deal with this man herself. She didn't want him to know that, but already he'd set her world tilting the wrong way.

He's not a thing like Victor.

Yes, she could see family resemblance now. But this man lacked Victor's warmth, his easy sense of humor. He was just a difficulty, and his presence and the things he'd told her this morning were like a glass sliver pressed into hcr foot—or into the wound of her husband's death, of his absence from her life.

The phone rang. She turned the handset of the cordless so she could read the caller ID. It was the preschool.

"Hello?"

"Sabine? Tori's not feeling that great. She has a little fever and says her throat hurts."

The exhaustion of single motherhood flooded over Sabine. *Victor, I need you. I've needed you every day.*

But the cruelty of death was the continued silence, the ongoing nonanswer, to such pleas.

"Tell her I'll be right there to get her."

Sabine hung up the phone and said "Goodbye" to Joe Knoll, even as she hurriedly gathered her coat and Sorel-style boots and began pulling on the warm clothing.

She knew men, men in Oro, who would drag their feet leaving, seemingly to enjoy just a few more minutes in her entirely hostile presence.

Joe Knoll was on his feet and at the door. "Thank you. If I don't hear from your representatives, I'll check back."

"Fine."

Then, he was gone and she was left with the new reality he had created with his revelations.

NORAH MORRIS HAD worked as a partner in an Aspen law firm for twenty years before semiretiring to Oro. Norah had first met Victor and Sabine and one-year-old Maria on top of fourteen-thousand-plus-foot Uncompahgre Peak in the San Juan Mountains. She had become a frequent dinner guest at the Knoll home, Finn's godmother, Victor's and Sabine's attorney and finally Victor's executor.

Norah was unafraid of chicken pox, which was what Sabine thought Tori must have. It had been going around the preschool and the grade school. At least if Tori had it, the children would likely all get it and be done with it. After Sabine had gotten a feverish and restless Tori to sleep, she sat in the living room with Norah and Lucy, newly arrived home from running, in snowshoes, one of Oro's backcountry trails. For both of them, Sabine repeated everything Joe Knoll had told her.

"Did Victor tell you any of this?" she asked Norah. "Did *you* know he had a brother?"

"No."

"What do you think?" she asked her friend, whom she sometimes regarded as almost a mother substitute because she'd lost her own mother when she was so young. She and Joe Knoll had that in common.

"About what?" Norah asked and didn't wait for an answer. "Whether Joe Knoll is who he claims should be easy to determine. I'll research the matter if you like."

"Thank you. *You* didn't know, did you?" she asked Lucy, who'd only come to live with her after Victor's death.

"Of course not."

"What I don't understand is why this—Joe—" Sabine said "—would choose to buy a defunct business rather than start one of his own. It's not like there's huge name recognition, especially when no sleds have been made or sold for four years. Other manufacturers, many better known, make kicksleds. Why not just start out for himself?"

"I have the same question," Norah said. "Not that the answer should have any bearing on your decision."

Lucy frowned. "I think it might. I mean, there was bad blood between him and Victor. *If* he's who he says he is. None of us know him, but we all knew Victor."

Sabine was intensely grateful for this point of view.

Lucy continued. "Say it's all true and they cut their ties because of Victor's first wife, Teresa. If his brother has bad feelings about that, if he feels Victor wronged him, why would he want to move to a place where everyone thinks well of Victor's memory? People *loved* Victor."

"It is odd," Norah agreed. She looked at Sabine. "What's he like?"

"Who? Joe?" The first name by itself sounded too familiar. "Victor's brother? He's not like Victor."

Norah lifted neatly groomed eyebrows. She had been black-haired when she was younger; now her hair was silver. At sixty-four, she kept it short, almost crewcut, but her features were so feminine that it in no way detracted from her looks, which remained striking. "Well, I wouldn't expect him to be like Victor. Brothers and sisters often *aren't* alike. And you say he's much younger than Victor and that he's done different types of work."

Sabine said, "Why do I feel as though you're trying to make me like him?"

"Me?" Norah seemed aghast.

Lucy, on the other hand, looked intrigued by the question.

Norah said, "I couldn't care less if you like the man. I don't even care whether or not you sell the business, though it might be a good move for you and the children. I'm always surprised that you choose to stay here at all."

"Where would I go?"

"Somewhere with an opportunity to meet men."

This time Lucy nodded emphatically. Of course, she had a man in her life, a fellow adventure racer named Greg Lord.

"There are men here," Sabine told both of them. "And I have met them."

"If you could pick from, shall we say, a more diverse population, you might feel differently."

"And I might not. I loved Victor. He was one of a kind, he was himself, I'll never find another man like him, and if I did it still wouldn't be the same."

"Why would you want it to be the same?" Norah asked sensibly.

Because, Sabine thought, *I can't imagine both different and better.*

But today the standard against which she judged all men had changed. When someone had told her that Victor wasn't what she'd always believed him to be.

He was, instead, a man who could marry the woman who'd been engaged to his brother, a brother to whom he'd been more than a brother, more like a father.

He was, in fact, a man who could fail to mention that brother to his second wife, fail to mention him at all, except as Joe-who-used-to-be-my-partner.

What would have silenced Victor on the subject?

Sabine knew. That much she did know.

Shame.

Shame would have kept him quiet.

And possibly remorse.

Norah said, "Don't think for a moment that I'm saying you should get over Victor's death or move on. I don't think anyone has the right to say that to anyone else. But you've got three small children, and I suspect you're not the sort of woman who's entirely happy without a partner."

The sort of woman... But there were women like that. And Norah was right; it wasn't her.

"You think if I sell the business it'll help me let go." She spoke to Norah but stole a look at Lucy, who kept her eyes down, staying out of it.

"It might. But I'm not telling you what to do. I will tell you only one thing: If you do sell, get every penny you can out of that real estate."

"Yes," Sabine said. "Yes."

CHAPTER THREE

"SHE'S STILL IN LOVE with her husband, man." Jason Botts, Joe's roommate, had spent his usual half hour in the shower at the end of the hall, warming up after a day spent using the high-speed Internet at a barely heated coffeehouse. "Won't look at anyone else."

Jason, Joe had discovered, was a mine of information about Sabine Knoll and everyone else in Oro. Whether the information was accurate Joe couldn't be sure. But Jason's sister, Karen, was a friend and running partner of Sabine Knoll's sister; she also took care of Sabine's children while Sabine was working. Jason frequently qualified his disclosures with, *That's what Karen says, anyway.*

Joe had noticed that Karen Botts seemed to say a lot—doubtless far more than her employer knew. He'd also noticed that a few of Karen's statements seemed to carry a bite of jealousy. There were women, he knew, virtually incapable of uttering a positive word about others of their sex. Jason had said that Sabine seemed like a good mom. Karen had some complaints, but…

But Sabine was stunning, beautiful.

"Hasn't looked at anyone else since he died?" Joe repeated, challenging this statement, which he found incredible.

"Oh, she was running around with Hart Markham for a while, but it didn't last. Hart said he couldn't stand up to Saint Victor. No one can."

Joe didn't laugh. He hadn't yet dropped the news that he was Victor's brother. Doing it later would be awkward.

"I always felt that way about him myself," he said. "Saint Victor. He was my brother."

Jason neither blushed nor answered, just pulled on long underwear over winter legs. He was a couple of years older than Joe, overweight and out of shape, but smart and funny. He read science fiction and wanted to have a sci-fi Internet bookstore. "You remind me of him a little."

"The saintly quality?" Joe murmured.

Jason laughed and didn't answer. "Good luck with the widow," he said instead. "If that's what you're after. You'd probably have a better chance than anyone, being related to him."

"It's not what I'm after." He lifted *Flannery O'Connor: The Complete Stories* off the battered, scarred nightstand, which had once been painted blue like the inside of a swimming pool, giving the room the look of a historic hospital unit.

"Did you see his shop?" Jason asked.

"Yes. I used to work with him, actually. Making sleds. In Minnesota."

He didn't particularly miss Victor, had stopped missing him after he'd seduced Teresa—*stolen* her, Joe still thought occasionally. Also, he *was* interested in the widow, for what she represented—Victor's last prize—and because she was beautiful.

But she wasn't his goal. His goal was intangible, born

of something destructive inside him, something that took pleasure in darkness. But also born of a desire for good that came and went like wispy clouds. He had loved other women since Teresa. How long could anyone mourn the betrayal of someone totally faithless? Not indefinitely.

Yet he'd never stopped mourning Victor's treachery.

He'd never stopped mourning the downfall of the brother he did not miss. And it was partly in hope of some kind of salvation that he'd come to Oro, to observe Victor's widow and children. That the shop was there gave him hope, too, for goodness and innocence gone.

But he wouldn't buy the business. He had wanted to see if Sabine cared to sell. He'd wanted to see the extent of her devotion to a dead man's memory. He'd heard of that devotion before Jason told him. Everyone in Oro seemed to know.

"You can really make those sleds?" Jason said abruptly.

"What sleds? Which ones?"

"The kicksleds. But all of them."

Joe nodded. "I can."

Jason studied him. "I thought you were just a climber. Most climbers aren't into anything but climbing."

That wasn't exactly true. More true was the fact that many climbers he knew loved being in the mountains more than anything. More than love. More than sex. More than their own offspring.

Was he any different?

He'd sold Himalayan Caravan, but hadn't he done that, in part, to escape the responsibility it represented and the unwelcome notoriety he had earned himself and the company?

He hadn't done it to put the money back into a different business, his brother's dead sled-making business in a sleepy and not particularly accessible Colorado mountain town.

Even to be near the most beautiful woman he'd ever seen.

But he suddenly wasn't content to sit and read, just as he knew he'd never be content living month after month in Oro. He stood up and slipped on his parka, hating and loving the addiction spinning through his veins again, to return to the highest mountains.

THE CHILDREN WERE ASLEEP, Norah had gone home, and Lucy had left to spend the night at her boyfriend's house. Sabine tried not to think ahead to the ordeal of having three children with chicken pox. Maybe it *wasn't* chicken pox.

Sabine sat on the floor in the attic. Not once since Victor's death had she bothered to go through his belongings up there, photos and letters tossed carelessly in the desk drawers. He'd thrown things out when they'd moved from Minnesota—he wasn't much of a pack rat—but rather than sort out the rest, he'd dumped everything in boxes, moved them and, as far as Sabine could tell, never looked at them again.

She didn't know what she hoped to find. He'd always been willing to answer every question she'd asked about Teresa.

Except I didn't know what to ask.

She didn't know now, either.

Teresa had come from a wealthy family. She'd been a downhill skier and a mountaineer. She'd been recovering from a broken femur at her cousin's place in northern Minnesota when Victor met her. Or so he'd said.

To Sabine it had always sounded as though Teresa didn't belong in Minnesota. She'd always sounded like a woman who would've been more at home in the Alps— or in Aspen.

Joe Knoll, like Victor, didn't seem the kind of man more at home in an atmosphere of wealth.

Sabine was familiar with his world. There were few Westerners who'd grown up closer to high-altitude mountaineering than she had. She and Lucy had waited at one base camp after another while their parents pursued one more summit.

Sabine couldn't remember a time when she hadn't known that people died climbing mountains. She did, however, remember the shock she'd experienced at the age of eleven when an overheard conversation between several people at one of those base camps made clear that her parents didn't *have* to participate in this activity, that they chose to risk their lives, to risk making her and Lucy orphans. When she'd told Lucy of her discovery, her sister had seemed as dumbfounded as Sabine by the revelation.

She and Lucy had climbed, too, and Sabine had been the youngest person to ascend one of the lesser known Himalayan peaks. Her father had told them proudly, *You could do this, you know, either of you, both of you. You could become the greatest women climbers in the world.*

Sabine did not believe that, although she'd believed it then.

Believed and wondered why she'd want to be the greatest woman climber in the world.

The next year, her mother died on Annapurna. Her father died of pulmonary edema the year before she moved to Minnesota.

She'd gone there on the advice of a friend, a former climber, who'd seen her and Lucy rushing to sign on to an expedition to Nanga Parbat, as though determined to follow their parents to death in the mountains. He had said, *Sometimes it takes more courage to live with the rest of the world.* And he had offered them his cabin in Minnesota. Lucy had declined, but Sabine had accepted.

The choice had forced her to live with loss and to exist in a world where people were not measured by how they functioned—and, to a lesser degree, behaved—in air with very little oxygen.

She had waited tables at a diner where she wore a polyester uniform. She'd produced a radio show for the local public radio station. She'd cleaned houses, including the house of a man whose wife had been badly injured in a sledding accident and now acted, said one local, like Mr. Rochester's wife. Teresa Knoll had gone from wealthy beautiful socialite athlete to crazed hag.

And she knew it.

Not always, but sometimes. More than once she'd said things to Sabine showing just how much she remembered…and felt.

I used to be more beautiful than you, she had said once. *I could have married anyone.*

Sabine, young and inexperienced when it came to marriage, had said, *I think you chose well.*

Teresa had let loose with one of her insane laughs. That had been after Sabine had realized, with horror, that she herself loved Victor; she thought the laughter must mean that Teresa knew.

Not that Teresa ever said. To Sabine, Teresa had seemed more unlikable than pitiable. Sabine had partly feared Victor's wife, partly felt revulsion in her presence.

But the biggest part of her had felt awe, awe at the tenderness with which Victor cared for Teresa, a tenderness that had seemed all the more angelic when it occurred in the face of such offensive behavior.

Had the pre-accident Teresa been so lovable that not one man but two had wanted to marry her and that one of them, a good man, had risked a permanent rift with his brother to do so?

Yet beautiful and charming could be enough.

And Teresa *had* been beautiful. Everyone agreed on that. Beautiful and as magnetic as Victor. Beauty had allowed her to retain a childlike quality that people mentioned almost as often as they did her. Sabine had returned to Asia just once since Victor's death, with Lucy, taking her children places she'd known as a child, to see if she could find a trace of the person she'd been before she became wife, mother and widow.

There, she had twice run into people who had known Teresa Leed—Teresa as a long-legged, red-haired climber, "the best-looking redhead I ever saw," claimed someone who recalled her success on Cho Oyu. On those occasions, the world had seemed very small indeed.

What happened to her anyway? one man had asked. *God, we were all in love with her.*

The encounters had left Sabine with a bigger question than who Teresa had been before Victor married her: How had *he,* a Minnesota sledmaker, attracted this exciting woman?

It was the same question plenty of people had asked in relation to her. How had Victor been able to attract her?

She didn't know. If there was a magic formula to Victor, it wasn't one she'd been able to put her finger on. She'd loved him. Simply, truly and completely.

She dragged out boxes stacked against a flat interior wall of the attic. Some of them were labeled. *Taxes. Photos. Receipts.*

The tax records from his years as Joe's partner would be gone, long since discarded, but they weren't what she wanted. The recent business records were readily accessible. As Sabine found the box of receipts and other tax records from the year before Victor died, she set that aside.

A box promisingly labeled *JUNK* was still sealed with packing tape.

Sabine opened it.

What did she hope to find? More photos of Victor and his brother together? Were there family photos from Joe's childhood? If so, who had them? If not, where were they? Had someone destroyed them? Lost them?

There was still a framed photo of his parents, young and probably newly married, downstairs on a shelf by the woodstove.

Victor, why didn't you tell me you had a brother?

What had really happened? Surely it was Teresa who'd chosen Victor. Why hadn't Joe's anger been directed at her?

No, it would be even stronger toward Victor.

The shoe box was at the bottom, beneath an ancient pair of cross-country ski boots. Labeled Photos.

She lifted the lid, and there it was.

The photo on top.

A group of people around a table, probably at Thanksgiving. The house in Minnesota. A younger Joe Knoll seated beside a beautiful woman with curly red hair, prominent cheekbones like a model's, chocolate-brown eyes and a healthy vibrancy that leaped out of the two-dimensional medium.

Teresa before.

Sabine had seen photos of Teresa from before the accident. Tall, athletic like a colt, laughing, joking, beautiful, but more than that. Alive with personality.

The woman Sabine had known had been, while not grossly overweight, out of shape. Her skin had sagged where cheekbones and smooth jaw used to show. There had been no beauty to eyes that always seemed either clouded by apathy or sick with unfocused violence. Her ambulatory status had never translated into exercise. Victor had taken her for walks as one walked an aged dog with bad hips, patiently and slowly.

Sabine had understood how it must have seemed to him, her appearing in his life, healthy and whole, young and clear-headed, happy to have the job of test-riding new sleds, even learning to harness his friend's malamute to new dogsleds.

She used to ski out to his house. The cleaning supplies were already there. On the days she was going to cook for him and Teresa, she brought food in a backpack.

He'd said that he and Teresa used to ski to the store to do their shopping.

Then he'd looked as though he regretted even mentioning it, as though it was a sin to mention a past that might seem happier.

In the photo, Teresa sat on Joe's left. She wore an engagement ring.

His fiancée.

So that much was true.

She leafed through other photos from that period. Sled photos. Joe pushing Teresa on a kicksled. Teresa pushing Joe, running, laughing, strong.

She paused, listening for the children. She should go down and check on them soon.

A newspaper clipping about Teresa winning a speed-skating race. A photo of her skiing.

When had Victor fallen in love with her? And how?

For Sabine herself was not his first illicit love; Teresa had been. Twice he'd fallen in love in situations that weren't viable. First, his brother's fiancée. Then, falling in love with someone else when he was already married.

But in both cases he had eventually gotten what he wanted.

Maybe the strain of being so good the rest of the time, in other situations, brought it out.

The proof of Joe's identity rested at the bottom of the box: it and the photo of Teresa as fiancée were as bookends on Victor's untold chapters. This shot showed Victor's father, a nineteen- or twenty-year-old Victor and a serious-looking boy younger than Tori. Each wore the same face, showing solemnity, loss, determination to carry on. On the old man and the young man, it fit. But the third face belonged to a three-year-old, and Sabine wanted to pick up that small boy and hold him, let him cry for his mother who was gone.

The boy was gone now, turned into a man. Why not sell the business to Joe Knoll? People kept telling her to let go of Victor, to move on with her life. People who hadn't lost a spouse, people who'd never lost anyone, who had no clue.

But weren't they right?

Then I wouldn't be sitting up here in the attic alone, thinking about waking up every single night until all my children have gotten over chicken pox. I would have a partner.

That was part of the trouble. She knew no single man who would be a responsible father to her children. None of them could do half the job Victor had done and would have continued to do.

Which is why Norah thinks I should sell the business and move away from Oro.

But would Joe Knoll actually buy the business?

Sabine doubted it. And really, she didn't *want* to move away. She loved the mountains, loved Oro.

She loved her memories, too.

And here she could do the things she most enjoyed, when work and the children allowed—climbing, skiing, running, hiking. Here, she could enjoy those things safe in her role as a mother, untempted to venture back to the land and life that had killed her parents.

Because sometimes it was tempting. She remembered, and she was still young.

Joe Knoll had been a climbing guide. He probably knew at least a couple of the people she had once known.

She placed the lid on the shoe box and cleaned up the area. When she left the attic, she took the box with her, to explore at leisure. But she was glad she'd come upstairs.

Victor would not return, would never return, and what she missed, suddenly, was not her husband but the feeling of being her own woman, someone she used to be before she'd become half of a pair.

JOE CROSSED THE BRIDGE that spanned the river and made his way toward the property that had been his brother's. The house sat by itself against the trees, the shop some distance beyond.

The downstairs lights in the house were on, and as he neared it he saw her pass a window, her blond hair, in two braids again, easily visible. He imagined what Victor must have felt, knowing that she was his and loving her. He must have felt his unreasonable good fortune.

Joe watched her put on a stocking hat and her coat, and then the door opened, and he thought he should flee but he couldn't move. He stood in the falling snow, which crept up around his Sorel boots, as she came out onto the porch and grabbed a shovel.

She saw him. She froze.

He felt guilty as a Peeping Tom. "I'm sorry," he said at once. "I got restless, decided to walk and found myself wandering this way again."

Without answering, she began shoveling her drive, with strength and energy born of practice, using only the light from her windows, not even bothering with the porch light. After a few moments, she said, "Tell me about your life in the Himalayas. You were a guide yourself?"

"Yes." He came over to join her. "Give me that."

For some reason she laughed, then murmured, "Thanks, but I can handle it."

"What do you want to know?" he asked.

"Why you sold your business, actually. Not many people turn away from climbing." She tossed another shovelful of snow beside her.

"Have you ever climbed?" he asked.

"Yes." Giving the same answer he'd given her, an uninformative *Yes,* she felt she understood something about him. Mountaineering—each moment of each climb—was more than could be expressed in a whole conversation or in an eighteen-volume set of books. "My parents were killed on mountains. My father was John Ingram, and my mother was Betsy Sikes."

In the snowy night, Sabine saw his eyebrows lift slightly.

Joe said, "I had no idea. Then—isn't your sister...?"

"Lucy Ingram. Yes." Lucy had won two of the most difficult adventure races in the world.

Her parents were not famous climbers, per se, but they had been mentioned in many mountaineering books, her father for his repeats on K2, her mother for a first female ascent on one of the Himalayan peaks just under 8,000 meters and for her repeats on Everest.

"So I grew up climbing," Sabine said, wondering again why he'd sold his business, why he wasn't still in the Himalayas. She had always understood choosing to allow the mountains to take you because you chose to climb them. And she'd understood the belief that one would always make the safe choice, would be smarter and luckier than other people.

"But you were Victor's housekeeper in Minnesota," Joe said. "How did you end up there?"

"A friend persuaded me that I might want to look at life away from the mountains and see if it was worth staying alive for." That sounded stupid. She wished she could have phrased it better—less melodramatically—but it was the truth.

"You knew Teresa," he said.

They had already covered this ground, so she said nothing.

"Victor must have been attracted to you before she died."

If he dared imply, in any way, shape or form, that Victor had been responsible for Teresa's death... It was an insult she didn't have to take.

She had checked on the children before she left the house, but she was conscious of how much time she spent outside, out of earshot.

She gazed at Joe Knoll, then resumed shoveling. "I don't understand why you sold your guiding business. Or why you came to Oro. It's not as though Victor is here. If he were alive and you wanted to make peace with him, I could understand it more easily, I think. And you could make sleds anywhere. So why *did* you come to Oro?"

The forthright question, reaching through the snowy night, interested him. But even more, he desired her. She was an athlete, genetically, historically. She had climbed big mountains. She was like him in ways she could never have been like Victor. He wanted her to love him and desire him more than she had Victor. He wanted to regain what Victor had taken from him, and he recognized this as childish.

He could not tell her why he'd come to Oro or why he'd

sold the guide service. A selfish decision of his, high on a mountain though not within the Death Zone, had caused a tragedy and rendered him unlovable to the one person who had really loved him. She had realized that he was made of selfish choices.

He'd seen it, too.

So many things he couldn't tell Sabine.

But he had learned to thrive by being as candid as possible about what he could discuss. Trust, once broken, couldn't be reforged. He wished Sabine would trust him. He wanted her, and wanted her for reasons that felt largely physical, largely aesthetic—or else were linked to a kind of revenge, a payback. It was a safe type of attraction.

Also, she represented a challenge. He was attractive to women, yet she seemed indifferent.

But she loved Victor.

He could seduce her for that reason alone.

He said, "I came to Oro because I wanted to see you. And my nieces and nephew."

"Why?"

The cool reply cracked in the night, sharper than snowflakes.

"They're the only family I have." That was true, but it wasn't the reason he'd come to see them.

"What about your aunt?"

"She passed away."

Sabine considered that. Except for Lucy, her family was all dead. She said suddenly, "Have you ever been married?"

"No."

She imagined his life with, she was certain, great

accuracy. A series of girlfriends, to whom he was probably unfaithful, when he wasn't away climbing mountains—and when he was. Not an empty life, because for a climber, the mountain was divine and to climb mountains was to be one with the Beloved. Some wouldn't have put it in such terms but simply said they couldn't stop or they loved it or it was the only place, the only time, the only way they felt alive.

No, his love life didn't interest her. Nor did his supposed longing to meet his family—her family. No. All that interested Sabine was how many feet of snow would fall. The Avalanche Forecast, which provided the most accurate weather predictions, had promised twenty inches, with thirty-mile-an-hour winds. Wind, Sabine knew, could deposit snow ten times faster than precipitation did. High winds meant increased avalanche danger—and more shoveling.

Now the snow began falling harder. She and Lucy needed to work two of their most difficult shoveling contracts the next day. But if Tori was sick... Well, Lucy could do it alone—or with Greg, who was always good about working for them when there was too much snow to handle.

If I sold Victor's shop, sold the real estate...

She hadn't spoken to a Realtor, hadn't tallied anything, yet she knew roughly the value of the equipment in the shop—and of the building—and of the acreage. She knew because an adjoining property had sold the previous summer. "Four hundred thousand dollars," she said.

Through the fast-falling white veil, Sabine could no longer make out his features. At first, she was sure he didn't know what she meant. He had no serious interest in buying the shop or the land—valuable real estate—surrounding it.

She was wrong.

Joe understood. She was offering to sell Victor's business. She was letting go.

He had money. Money to fund expeditions. Money to find new avenues for commercial Himalayan expeditions, ways to climb mountains without having to look after people who probably shouldn't be up there—that is, without agreeing to guide climbers who could pay for his services yet weren't ready for high-altitude mountaineering.

Buying the shop and the land would mean forfeiting the level of financial freedom he'd gained. In Oro, he could, conceivably, become land poor.

She had stabbed her shovel into the snow. She stood hugging herself, trembling.

Joe knew then that what Jason, his roommate, had told him was true. She was still in love with Victor.

But she was willing to let go a little bit. He could make that happen.

"What would you do with the money?" he asked.

"I would spin," she said without hesitation. "I might open a yarn shop, sell looms, wheels, things like that."

"Here?"

"Actually, Oro is growing. In summer, tourists come. On the train."

The narrow-gauge railroad.

"But mostly," she said, "I would spin." *And go for runs,* she thought, *and hire a babysitter just so I can go climb*

a mountain. No Himalayan peak. But one of the thirteen-
or fourteen-thousand-foot mountains around Oro. In the
winter, she could ice-climb.

And she could spin. And spin.

Joe wondered how she would react if he agreed.

Like him, she wanted freedom, if only the freedom to
sit at a spinning wheel for hours. But he wasn't going to
give it to her at the cost of his own.

Yet he sensed his brother's presence. Not as a ghost or
a spirit—just an impression of Victor. And Victor seemed
to be urging him to help Sabine.

Candor? Was that the way?

"I would buy the business and the shop," he said, "but
I don't need the acreage."

She shrugged. "Well, that's how I'm offering it. Good
night." Collecting her shovel, she turned in the falling
snow and trudged back to her porch.

CHAPTER FOUR

"YOU THINK HE COULD come up with the money?" Norah asked. She stood on a shoveled section of the Hotel Independence's southern sidewalk while Sabine worked beside her, and Lucy cleared the far end.

Sabine knew Lucy was champing at the bit to leave and ski the fresh powder.

They'd been working since 4:00 a.m., Sabine with her cell phone on her waist. Her sitter, Karen Botts, a running friend of Lucy's, was reliable and used to showing up hours before dawn. For these reasons, Sabine kept her on; for reasons unrelated to the way Karen cared for Maria, Finn and Tori, Sabine would've liked to let her go. Karen could be an appalling, no-holds-barred gossip, and Sabine would bet every one of her spinning wheels that Karen did plenty of gossiping about her. But beggars couldn't be choosers, and Karen *was* responsible, trustworthy in the area that mattered. When Sabine woke that morning, Tori's fever had gone down, so she'd left Karen with instructions to call if Tori felt worse.

Of course, she couldn't get cell phone reception from just anywhere in Oro. So every half hour, she went to the northwest corner of the roof, held the phone out over the edge, and checked her messages.

"I don't know." Sabine shook her head in response to Norah's question. The wind tugged at her braids. "I don't know what a guide service would sell for. I don't know if he operated only in the Himalayas or where his base was. I got the impression he went to Nepal and never came back till now. Anyhow, I suspect it's moot. I think he has the money and doesn't want to spend it. I know climbers. He wants to be able to pick up and go climb a different 8,000-foot peak every year."

Norah gave a nod of assent. "For future reference, it's usual to take further counsel when you come up with a price. A Realtor? Me?"

"Point taken. I was worried about Tori being sick and having to go to work, and suddenly it seemed like the most brilliant plan in the world to sell to this guy. Anyhow, he's not going to go for it."

"Don't be so sure. But I was just encouraging—you know—everyday prudence."

"You're right." Sabine stopped shoveling to gaze through the still-falling snow at her friend. "Norah, can you take it from here? I mean, if anything happens with this. And he'll approach us if he wants to do it. Which he doesn't."

Norah patted her shoulder. "I'll run by the house now and see how Tori is. If I don't come back or send word, assume all is well."

"Thank you." Sabine hugged the older woman, catching a whiff of a distinctive perfume that she would smell nowhere else in Oro. She kissed Norah's cheek, skillfully made up with Elizabeth Arden products. "You are a gem."

Lucy had reached the end of the sidewalk. As Norah headed across the street to get into her Saab and drive the half mile to Sabine's house, Sabine walked down the sidewalk toward her sister. "I'll finish," she told Lucy.

"Sure?"

Sabine nodded. She liked working alone, it was already afternoon, and all her shoveling here was on the ground. She wouldn't have to do another roof until the next day. "He'd heard of you," she blurted out. "And Mom and Dad."

Lucy's face revealed absolutely nothing, and Sabine could imagine why. Lucy probably wondered if she, Sabine, was interested in Joe Knoll as a man but wouldn't ask for fear of discouraging Sabine if that was the case, discouraging her by even mentioning the possibility of Sabine's ever loving anyone but Victor.

How would Lucy really feel if Sabine fell in love again? It was strange, but Victor's death had brought the two of them closer. Sabine had wondered if sibling rivalry had been lessened by her own suffering, if Lucy had begun to feel that things were more equal. Lucy thought Sabine, "the pretty one," had everything. But Lucy was a celebrity, an elite athlete. *I'm the one who should be jealous.*

And she was.

Lucy said, "So he still didn't say why he'd prefer to buy Victor's business instead of starting his own? He didn't say why he came back to Oro?"

"I don't believe he really wants to buy the business. But his agenda doesn't matter to me. If he has some vendetta, it's against Victor or his memory, not against me. Not that I'd want to help him get even with Victor."

"If he *has* come to even a score with Victor," Lucy said, "I think he'd do it through you or the kids. Don't you? He can't hurt Victor now. But Victor lives in you guys."

"Payback after twenty years?"

"It does sound improbable when you put it like that." Lucy raised her shoulders in a shrug. "More likely he wants to make peace with Victor's memory."

Victor would want me to help him do that, Sabine told herself.

"So—" Lucy changed the subject "—I'll see you at six tomorrow to work on the courthouse?"

"You're going to Greg's after you ski?"

Lucy nodded.

"Okay." Sabine hugged her quickly. "Have fun, and be safe." Though how could she be, except at home by the fire? Victor had been skiing a flat riverside trail and triggered a slide above him that hadn't run for a hundred and fifty years. It took down trees three times the thickness of his body. Bad luck.

"Yes, yes. Relax." Lucy tossed her shovel in the back of Sabine's station wagon and repeated, "I'll see you tomorrow."

"Ski low-angle," Sabine called. A slope less than thirty degrees wouldn't slide; less than twenty-five degrees was even safer. But Lucy knew that, and Sabine heard the wind devour her warning.

"Always am. Even when I'd rather not be." Lucy winked and tossed her shovel in the back of Sabine's station wagon.

THAT NIGHT, Joe sat at the bar of the San Juan Saloon with Jason. Norah Morris had called him to discuss the possible sale of Victor's business and the attached real estate. By the end of the conversation, he'd been tempted—more than tempted—and, after making clear that he was far from a commitment, had said that if she put something on paper he would consider the proposal. He had no Colorado attorney and would have to find one, preferably with a real estate background. He figured that wouldn't be too difficult.

"Hey, Jason." A tall, very attractive brunette, her skin ivory-white and flawless, her hair falling in a smooth pageboy, slid onto the bar stool beside Joe's roommate. Snow flocked her hair and her red Gore-Tex jacket. She had the bones of a model. "I'm Karen," she said, thrusting her hand toward Joe.

He shook it. "Joe."

"Victor's brother."

Joe had a feeling he was about to hear things. It wasn't as simple as just hearing things, either. A person who would speak freely to someone she'd just met about other people was a person who would also broadcast that man's affairs to anyone who'd listen. Or she'd find her own explanations for the unexplained and advertise those as fact.

Jason said, "I'm surprised you're here. Isn't Sabine still shoveling?"

"Of course not. Even she has to see her kids sometimes. I guess she just got too tired to work anymore. I don't get it. There are plenty of men in Oro willing and able to shovel."

"Maybe she likes the activity," Joe said. He now understood why Sabine had laughed when he'd demanded her shovel of her. *But she'd rather be spinning.*

He'd been thinking about that all day. He'd been thinking of maidens told to spin straw into gold and thread from nettles. He'd imagined filling the great room of the Craftsman house, the room into which he hadn't been invited, with wool and flax and silk and whatever she could spin, making a pile to the ceiling and telling her that if, when she was done spinning it all, she no longer loved Victor, he would buy the shop *and* the property. Though for every flight of fancy like this, he'd fallen prey to about ten of a more intimate— and generic—kind.

"Well, I understand it with Lucy," Karen continued. "I understand her wanting to shovel. She's young, she's an athlete and she doesn't have any children." Karen eyed Joe. "But I can read your mind. She got your attention. She's pretty, of course. She doesn't have to *prove* anything." After a pause she added, "You must have known her before she and Victor moved here."

He decided not to answer. Karen herself was extremely attractive, a type he had met before. He was sure she'd modeled—probably very successfully. Being pretty had opened her to opportunities her peers hadn't known—but she was jealous of attention given to other women. Or something like that. He'd never understood why some women could love the friendship of women more than the love of men and other women were ready to claw out the eyes of their rivals—over nothing.

"So what brings you to Oro, anyhow?" Karen asked.

"Victor's family." A simple answer. He hoped she wouldn't ask how long he was staying. He didn't know and didn't like revealing that uncertainty.

"Jason says you made sleds, too."

"Victor and I were partners. Many years ago."

"I never really got the relationship between him and Sabine. Not that I knew them when he was alive. But he was so much older than she is. Some women marry older men because they've never known their own fathers or else they were obsessed with them and have to relive it somehow."

Joe didn't comment. He doubted utterly that any kind of father fixation lay behind Sabine's love of Victor.

"So, do you have a family?" Karen asked. "Kids?"

"No."

She nodded, and already he could see she was filling in the blanks with whatever story most pleased her.

"What do you do, Karen?" he asked. "Besides care for my nieces and nephew?" And criticize their mother.

"Well, I'm a Realtor. But this isn't the busy season, so I do a bit of work for the county attorney."

He wondered if Sabine used her as a Realtor, if Karen Botts would handle the sale of the property....

But he wasn't buying that property. He wasn't tying himself to Oro, Colorado.

Why not? It was a reasonable place to live between expeditions. If he bought the shop and land...

"What's wrong?" Karen asked.

"Nothing."

Sabine wouldn't sell the house. She hadn't said so, but Joe knew the answer. Victor had built the house.

And did he really want the house Victor had built for his second wife? No.

Its presence would in no way devalue the land, if he

bought— He shoved another dollar across the bar for the bartender and stood up. "See you back in the room," he told Jason and smiled briefly at Karen. "I'm glad to meet you."

Outside, he started back toward the boardinghouse. But he was restless, the walk suddenly too short. He stayed out in the falling snow, heading up to Gold Mountain Road to cross the bridge that would lead to the sledmaker's shop and, incidentally, Sabine's house. Did she know how Karen talked behind her back?

In a town this size, she probably did.

He had barely crossed the bridge when he saw through the snow that the lights in the shop were on.

Sabine must be out there.

And he should stay away.

But he could see her face in his mind's eye, and his longing to know, to see her in this setting where Victor had worked, overcame prudence.

The wind silenced his footsteps as he moved toward the building, his legs sinking to his knees in the snow.

Sabine sat at the workbench, sat staring, her face a picture of sadness.

Receipts and folders lay spread out before her, but she seemed to have abandoned them.

Go away, he told himself. *Leave her.*

Instead, he made his way to the door and knocked. Another deal had occurred to him, another proposal, one she'd be as unlikely to accept as agreeing to spin straw into gold.

But many people thought climbing mountains was crazy, too.

THE KNOCK, she thought, belonged to a man. *It will be him, and he's the last person I want to see, this person who tarnished Victor's memory for me.*

But wasn't it Victor who'd done that?

She got up, went to the door and turned the knob.

Joe Knoll stood on the other side, snow dappling his black ski hat, hood and parka.

Again, she felt ridiculous anger, absurd anger, anger that he wasn't Victor. "What do you want?" she said.

Joe studied her. At other times he'd seen her tired, wary, doubtful. But now she looked as though she hated him.

The suggestion he intended to make was a gamble. Her dislike made it interesting—and somehow easier.

"I saw the light on," he said, entering the shop. "And came to suggest something. You're not including the house in the sale," he observed.

"No." She sat down on the stool at the workbench and resumed looking through receipts, sorting, working with an adding machine, recording a figure in the ledger beside her.

"Is it because you don't want to lose that connection to Victor?"

"Actually, the reason for it is none of your business."

"Of course it is. Maybe you want to rent out the house to a bunch of degenerates."

Sabine snickered, not kindly, and not at the thought of renting her home to degenerates. Rather because Joe Knoll provoked a private meanness in her.

She didn't like herself for it.

Joe heard no meanness in her laughter—but she definitely wasn't falling over her feet trying to please him.

He was used to being wanted by women. Lovers had begged him to marry, to let them move in; women fell over themselves to compromise, make sacrifices for him, forgo the chance to have children because he'd told them he wanted none. Not Sabine. Not only could he sense no attraction in her, she seemed indifferent to him. He sensed that she regarded him as a nuisance. Or worse.

She preferred the memory of his much older, shorter, less handsome brother, felt passion for a man Joe knew to be ordinary, a man who'd never summited an 8,000-meter peak, who'd never lived anywhere more exotic than Oro, Colorado, who made sleds, occasionally watched televised sports, read murder mysteries and political science, had never fought in a war, had experienced nothing in life that should have made him so attractive to women.

Joe couldn't remember the last time he'd had to put himself out in order to attract a woman.

"What do you want?" she asked, not looking up. "Your suggestion?"

Candor. He chose candor. "You have three children, a babysitter who is less than loyal and you shovel snow for money. My buying this shop, the business—and the land—could make a huge difference to you financially."

"Obviously." Sabine wanted to ask about her "less than loyal" babysitter. But what could he tell her that she didn't already know? Karen hid her fangs behind a veil of concern, but the fangs were there.

"I will do it," he said, "if you agree to let me live in your house with you for a year."

"What?" She gaped at him. "Why?"

"Part of the reason is that there's no shower or kitchen in here."

"There's water, and a propane hookup. There's even a futon in the loft upstairs." The loft... *Don't think about it, Sabine. Don't remember.* "Anyhow, you said *part.* Why else?"

"It appeals to me." He grinned, a grin of both amusement and appreciation. He seemed wolfish, devilish, sexy. All of it surprised her, most of all the fact that she found him that way.

"I won't insist on sleeping in your bed," he said, with an air of tremendous generosity and benevolence.

Sabine decided to ignore his considerable charm—and the flirtation. "It would be adequate," she asked, "for you to be allowed to sleep in the attic, for instance? That was the space Victor used as his office."

"Sounds fine."

"All right," she said. "I'll have my attorney contact you, and we can draw up a contract." After that, there'd be thirty days till closing, *if* it closed, which was always a big if in Colorado real estate. That would give Joe time to research the title and do whatever else was involved. "When we close, the year will begin."

"And while we wait," he said, "I'll be allowed to live here. In the shop. There's a bathroom." The door, beneath the stairs, stood open.

She shrugged. "All right."

"Then may I stay and look over the place?"

He knew she wanted to refuse.

"If you like."

Joe pointed to a sled, a Minnesota flyer hanging from

the wall, without the runners attached. "Will you keep this one?" he asked.

She glanced at it. Victor had used rosewood. For whom had he made it? It must've been an extra, to sell if someone stopped in, requesting one for a birthday. He'd died in late January, after the Christmas rush. He'd had time to get caught up on special orders. Did she want the flyer? *I want everything he made, everything his hands touched or formed.*

Or at least, that had been true once. No need to consider whether it still was. After all, she had things he'd made for her, her sleds, her own kicksled, plus one with a bigger seat that he'd given her after Maria was born.

"No," she finally said.

"The others?"

"They can go with the shop." She didn't raise her head.

"So." He leaned against the workbench. "You loved my brother and now he's dead, so you're never going to love again."

"If you're really interested in buying this property," she said stiffly, "and if you want to look around right now, why don't you stay away from that topic. It's none of your business."

"I'm sorry. I'm just curious."

"About what?"

"Why you love him. What was special about him?"

"He was good."

It seemed she didn't have to think about her reply. But she kept speaking.

"He cared about other people. He *did* things for other people." Sabine knew she should stop. But she couldn't.

"And when he touched me or kissed me, he made me feel as though I was the only woman he'd ever known or ever loved. He made me feel that he considered himself the luckiest man in the world, luckiest simply because I loved him, because I was in his arms. He loved with a very pure, very sincere, very total love."

How hopeless, Joe thought, the dream of any man who had the misfortune to fall in love with this woman. "Did you never wish," he asked, "for someone young and handsome, someone fit—"

"No," she said. "I think every man in the world fails to understand that what you've just described isn't necessarily what women want."

"Alas," he said. "The curse of the godlike."

Sabine eyed him, apparently unsure whether or not he was making fun of her. He was—and of himself.

She did not smile.

It occurred to Joe that perhaps Sabine Knoll, strong and beautiful, wasn't such an interesting woman. That perhaps she had little to bring to a relationship.

If she'd been a nice person, that would've been enough for Victor.

This woman would bore me, he thought, telling himself it was true. The fascination she held for him was based on her love of Victor, a love that had not died with Victor's death.

She said softly, "You'd be surprised at what I really want." How could she love her children and yet yearn to be out doing what Lucy was tonight, or something similar? On those rare, very rare occasions, when she had a few hours to herself, one of her favorite things was to take one of the kicksleds and run and kick up the Oro Mountain Road, all twelve miles to the top—then sled down. She had done it when Victor was alive, and he'd always given her a half-anxious smile, not his usual fully focused smile, and said, *Be careful.*

She was. And she wore adventure-racing shoes with cleats on the bottom, good for braking.

Good for pushing off, for speed!

Other women told her it was okay and natural to feel trapped by her children. It didn't mean she didn't love them. It didn't mean she was a bad mother.

Just as her wanting to sit and spin—or stand and spin, with a spindle—for hours without talking to them or giving them any attention, just as that didn't make her a bad mother. After all, she didn't *behave* that way; she simply wanted to.

But her children didn't know her. They didn't know that sometimes she craved thin air, craved danger and speed. She did not crave the company of men like Joe Knoll. It wasn't enough for her that a man be handsome or a famous climber or guide. So many climbers, in her opinion, were screwed up. *Like me.*

Or why would she still feel as though she had to work hard at being a woman who would decide *not* to climb another Himalayan peak, and another, and another, until she died on one? How could the desire to return to that world live within her after all this time?

But she would settle for spinning herself into a Zen trance, a Sufi whorl.

"Tell me," Joe said. "Tell me what you really want."

"Something I can't have, not for years to come."

"Freedom," he said abruptly. "From your children."

She turned on the stool, looked up at him, but said nothing.

"You shovel snow for a living," he said. "You grew up climbing in the Himalayas. I imagine that at some point, probably even when Victor was alive, you woke up and realized you were a wife and mother and that you used to have another kind of life and you miss some of it, anyway."

"What are you? A mind reader?"

"A mountaineer."

It sobered her—that this man could possibly know her soul. But he couldn't. He couldn't know the desperation that came with her certainty that she'd already experienced the most she could ever expect of love—more than she'd been given any reason to expect. She sometimes felt she'd been blessed with too much of everything in life. Too much of beauty, too much of brains, too much of wealth and, with Victor, too much of love. With this suspicion came a private unspoken certainty that it would have to be paid for—with comparable loss, with comparable loneliness, with comparable dissatisfaction.

She also had the sense that there was something unnatural about her. How could she have three such wonderful children yet sometimes long so fiercely for freedom that she fantasized about simply abandoning them? Not more than a brief thought here or there, a wish for a distant relation who would take them off her hands for a month or two now and then—or for a husband who would care for them and let her do the things she wanted.

If she could've had Victor back, it wouldn't have mattered; she wouldn't, she felt sure, want anything more.

When he was alive, the entirety of her situation, adored wife of adored husband, mother of their children, had pleased her. She'd felt secure, useful.

But now, as a mother alone, she noticed her emotions surrounding guilty thoughts. That she wasn't doing a very good job on her own, without Victor. That she lost her temper too often. That other people in the community believed she wasn't a good mother and that they were right.

Joe Knoll couldn't fix any of that for her. He might make it even more attractive to turn her back on her responsibilities—which she never would. He might encourage her to do the selfish thing, whatever that was—and she would not. What he wasn't was Victor, the one person who could help her be truly happy with her life as it was now.

"I don't miss mountaineering," she said, and that in itself was true. There'd been plenty of times, however, when she'd wished Victor had been more ready to go for hikes with her and the kids. Of course, he *had* gone occasionally, even to mountaintops, but she knew he'd known internal doubts then, comparing himself to Oro's younger, more athletic men.

Despite Victor's apparently unassailable self-confidence, she'd known she held great power over his self-perception—and she gave him no reason to doubt, her heart so full from the disbelieving way he sometimes said, as if making a discovery for the first time, *You are beautiful.*

But Sabine had always perceived him as the more desirable one. He was good; she, merely beautiful.

Joe watched her. He didn't consider himself a kind

man. He'd learned courtesy as a child from his parents and later from Victor, forgotten the lessons learned, then re-learned them in order to make the most money possible as a guide.

Right now, he knew he was pestering Sabine and that he was in no way winning her over—not even close. He wanted her to be attracted to him but even more, he wanted her to like him, although he wasn't sure why. Was it because he'd overheard her teasing one of the snowplow drivers in the market that afternoon, when she hadn't even known Joe was in the next aisle or in the store, giving the driver a hard time with a dry sense of humor Joe hadn't realized she'd possessed?

When it had happened, Joe felt he'd been given a glimpse into the person who had attracted Victor. No, not the person who'd attracted Victor, for Victor had liked people and liked women, but the person who'd been Victor's wife. She must have teased him, and Victor, so used to praise, would have taken the teasing as intimate affection, which it probably had been.

But maybe this was something Joe was making up....

Yet he wished Sabine would tease *him*, would give him a hard time, would pay him that compliment.

Could he make her laugh?

Could he even make her smile, with a real smile, one that was a precursor to mirth or joy?

The woman he'd left in Nepal—or rather the woman who'd left him before he'd left Nepal—had once said that his sense of humor was his best characteristic. She'd said that *after* telling him he had no sense of humor, that he was dull as a two-by-four.

Of course she'd been angry when she'd said it.

Joe still wasn't sure what to think.

Nothing had seemed funny after Victor had won Teresa, not at first, and later, for a long time, everything humorous that came out of Joe's mouth had ended up sounding sarcastic and bitter.

"You know, you really haven't satisfied my curiosity on one point," Sabine said unexpectedly.

"Yes?"

"If you plan to make sleds again, why don't you just pick a place you want to live and start from scratch? It would certainly be less expensive than buying this parcel of land from me in Oro. And I have the distinct feeling that you came here knowing nothing about the town or its real estate market or the local economy or anything. All you knew was that your brother had been living here when he died. And quite frankly—" Sabine realized she should stop talking but couldn't seem to control herself. Emotion burst out of her like water from a broken pipe. "Quite frankly, I think you took pleasure in telling me that Teresa used to be your fiancée. I think you might even have come here just to try taking some kind of revenge on Victor. He's dead, so you want to make me and our children miserable. I think you're still bitter and that you didn't come here for any good reason at all."

"You're wrong." It stung because he'd come to Oro for very good reasons; it was only since arriving that he'd felt again the old desire to get back at Victor. "If I'd wanted to hurt Victor, I would've done it while he was alive." He knew himself to be lying; part of him still wanted to hurt his brother and maybe always would.

"Then explain why you're doing this. Tell me the *real* reason."

For once, she looked straight at him, and the fire of her startled him. Startled, frightened and attracted him.

He couldn't tell her the whole reason. He wasn't sure he could tell her even part of it. When he did tell her, he sounded, even to himself, like the fifteen-year-old he'd once been, losing his cool with Victor, saying how he really felt, the way he'd been able to do with Victor and with no one since.

"I haven't liked myself, all right? What Victor and Teresa did changed me. I would've been a better person, maybe, if they hadn't done that. And I'm the only one who can control my life. I came here to try to remember what I was like before it happened."

He thought her face looked as it did because she was immensely, dreadfully sorry for him, seeing him for the pathetic, egotistical creature he was. He had just said, to her, the most honest thing he'd said in maybe twenty years, and she pitied him. How dare Victor's widow pity him for his courage in speaking?

"I never intended to make sleds again. I didn't plan to buy his business. You're looking at me like you feel sorry for me, Sabine. But guess what? I feel sorry for you. And maybe *that's* the biggest reason I'm buying the business and the land. Because you deserve better than what you're doing to yourself, burning yourself on Victor's funeral pyre. And that's also why I want to live in your house."

"Because you think I'll fall in love with you?" she exclaimed incredulously.

He shook his head. "I know you won't."

"Then why?"

Because if I share the house with you, you'll begin to live again. You'll have to. You will quit believing that memories are better than life.

"Maybe," he said, "my presence—not to mention the money—will give you freedom again."

"Do you know why I'm willing to sell?" she asked, speaking from spite. It was spite because his explanation for coming to Oro was the magic key; it was exactly what she'd needed to hear in order to be absolutely certain that selling the shop to Joe was what Victor would've wanted her to do. Knowing what Joe had told her, that he was trying to be a better man, she could be kind to Victor's little brother, which was how she perceived him just then, half forgetting that five minutes earlier she'd found him dark and disturbing. What would it have done to her if, say, Victor had been unfaithful? Would she have changed?

Oh, yes.

Because it was imperative that good people continue to be good. She hadn't put him on a pedestal, but for him to stoop, to fall that far…

I would've been so disillusioned.

Not just hurt.

Lost.

Few things were as troubling as that sort of profound surprise. And it would've been a loss, too. She would have lost Victor, lost the person she'd believed he was. He would've seemed like someone else to her—as, in some way, he did now, in light of Joe's revelations.

Yet Joe's pity wounded her.

"Because you feel sorry for me." Joe calmly answered her question.

Sabine didn't respond. She felt immature and small.

"I do want to keep the house," she said. "And not—" she laughed as though she couldn't help it "—to rent to degenerates." She laughed again. "I live there and want to continue living there. I want my children to grow up in that house. In my opinion, it's the best house in Oro. But I agree to your plan. You can live in the attic for a year. And as soon as we finalize the contract, you can begin living here." She indicated the narrow staircase that led to the loft. "If you open the two windows up there in the summer, it's quite pleasant."

The loft. The loft. She and Victor had made love there, with infant Maria asleep nearby.

What she did next was idiotic, and she did it because she still loved Victor, and for a moment she felt certain he was urging her in that direction.

"Actually, if you agree that we'll make this deal promptly, you can start staying here tonight. I mean—" she shrugged "—you're family." *Insane, Sabine. Insane. What are you saying?*

She tried to imagine Lucy's reaction, which reminded her that Lucy was out skiing. Then she remembered that her sister was staying with Greg Lord that night.

She should go to sleep. She must sleep before shoveling again. Eat, sleep, shovel, and try, desperately, to be attentive to her children and not resent them, all the while hating herself. Why couldn't she do *some* of the things she craved?

If—when—he buys the property, you can go. You can

*take them all to the Himalayas again. You can raise them
as you were raised. You could go off for the whole year
he's living in your house.*

Raise her children as she was raised?

To run wild around base camp? No, not wild—sober
and too old for her age. To be left with the base camp
doctor, with the cook, with their favorite sherpa, with one
climbing friend or another, with one parent while the other
risked his or her life.

No. Not as she was raised.

She could, however, take them trekking. They could
live somewhere wild. She could become herself again, a
different self.

Someone besides Victor Knoll's left-behind-on-Earth
widow.

She shrugged again. "I imagine Victor would have
wanted me to let you stay. Agreeing that we're going
ahead with the sale."

Her insides felt as though they'd been stung by nettles,
as though her heart had. This was just a shop and just a
shell, a shell with no Victor. Whoever Joe Knoll was, she
sensed he needed help. The help she could offer was to let
him get busy in Victor's shop. To that extent, she could do
for him what Victor might have, had he lived.

"I'm not giving you a key tonight," she said, "so don't
lock yourself out." She gathered the paperwork into a
stack, lifted it and stood. She still wore her coat. "Can you
take care of the stove?"

"Yes," he answered. "If I stay, I'll go back to the boardinghouse first."

"Good night, then."

She opened the door and stalked through the snow, angry.

Angry because Victor was gone and she had to be strong. Every day she kept having to be strong.

CHAPTER FIVE

HE HAD NOT MEANT to make her pity him. Joe wanted no one's pity, certainly not Sabine's. He had been truthful, so truthful it appalled him, and so she'd felt sorry for him and undoubtedly felt she should be nice to her dead husband's poor little brother.

He'd already paid for his night's lodging at the board-inghouse, but he packed everything in his room. Coming up with the financing wouldn't be a problem, because no financing was needed. He possessed the financial resources to buy Sabine's property outright.

Jason was in bed reading Robert A. Heinlein. "Where are you going?" he asked Joe. "By the way, my sister likes you."

Joe didn't answer. He hadn't cared for Karen Botts at all. The best he could muster was compassion. It *was* sad for such a beautiful woman to be so jealous, so unwilling to be generous. "I'm moving into the shop."

"Already?" Jason sat up, apparently stunned by Joe's success where success had seemed impossible. "She must like you. Or is it because you're her brother-in-law?"

"The latter." He shouldered his pack. "See you soon. Come down and say hi."

"Okay," Jason said. "Hey. Think you'll need a Web site?"

Right. That was what Jason did on the Internet.

"Yes. Come see me." He left, wondering why Jason was so easy to get along with, yet his sister had rubbed Joe the wrong way—wrong in *every* way.

HER CLOCK RADIO woke her at five-thirty with the Avalanche Forecast. Avalanche danger had risen from Considerable to High close to and above the treeline with increased natural avalanche activity and high likelihood of triggering avalanches in fresh windslabs….

Sabine listened with half her attention. She'd become an expert at taking the minimum amount of time to get ready for work. Grabbing clothes from the rocking chair at the foot of the bed. She yanked on synthetic long johns and worn insulated Carhartts, brushed and braided her hair in less than five minutes, then hurried downstairs to have four pieces of toast, an egg in a glass of orange juice and chai tea from tea bags. She started her car, scraped the windows and returned inside to wait for Lucy.

Glancing at the answering machine, she found a message waiting, probably left the night before, when she was out in the shop. "Norah here. He's who he says he is. A few extensive bios on the Internet, besides the usual sources. He used to run a company called Himalayan Caravans, and he's done some journalism and adventure writing, mostly in outdoor-type publications, although also one in *Psychology Today* of all places. 'The Mountaineer Mind.'" A small appreciative laugh. "Take care, dears. Love you all.…"

Just before six, Karen arrived. "Hi!" Karen said brightly. "It's cold out there. Are you going to be okay?"

Sabine nodded and sipped her tea. Part of the problem with no longer using Karen for a babysitter was that

Sabine actually liked her. Karen was friendly in the mornings and took good care of the kids, and the kids liked her, too. But Sabine knew, not just because of Joe's comments the previous night but also because Lucy had heard from other people and told her, that Karen had few kind words for her employer behind her back. Another factor was Karen's background. She'd trained in early childhood education before throwing in that towel for real estate. Sabine knew that Karen wanted children of her own—but it was getting late in the day.

"I met that guy last night," Karen said. "That guy Joe? Victor's brother?"

Sabine gave her an interested glance, unable to think of any reply at all. Finally she said, "He stayed out in the shop last night," she told Karen. "He's going to make sleds." That she was selling the business, the shop and the land were details her child-care provider didn't need to know.

"Oh." Karen's neatly waxed eyebrows drew together slightly above her high cheekbones, over the spectacular bones that had made her a model by the age of fifteen and kept her one until *she'd* tired of it. "Won't that be awkward for you? He's not much like Victor, is he? But won't he remind you of Victor?"

Sabine managed not to roll her eyes. *Everything* reminded her of Victor, but she didn't tell Karen this.

Karen spoke thoughtfully. "Everyone agrees Victor was a good man. I know it's true."

Sabine knew Karen said this as some sort of explanation for Sabine's attraction to him. It was on the tip of her tongue to snap that it was just as well Karen thought so, as she was now a chief role model in the lives of Victor's children.

By six-ten Lucy still hadn't shown up, so Sabine went out to the car by herself. Lucy knew they were supposed to shovel the walks to and around the courthouse this morning, and no doubt she was running late and would join Sabine there.

The snow fell, the flakes thick and fast. Sabine estimated that eighteen inches had fallen overnight. At least the snow was light and fluffy. She looked at the clock high on the courthouse building when she started shoveling and again sometime later. By six-thirty, she'd worked halfway down the sidewalk on the southern side of the building, but Lucy still hadn't come. She decided to shovel alone until seven and then call Greg's house. Possibly Lucy had returned late from her workout and decided to sleep in. That wasn't unheard of, but it didn't happen too often—and never before in weather like this, with so much snow on the ground.

At seven, the county attorney arrived and stood watching her shovel. He remarked, "You could get more done working with men. In fact, I hesitate to mention that this is traditionally men's work."

Sabine was on the point of asking if a person needed to pass the bar to practice law in San Juan County and if so, how had Simon gotten his job? He swung his briefcase and asked, "How many feet an hour do you do?"

"Never measured."

"I can't figure you out. You spin yarn, which is feminine work, and then you do this. I just don't get it. And your sister thinks she's a guy, too, but no one thinks *you* are, Sabine."

She said, "You know why I use a plastic shovel, Simon?"

"Well, I assume the one-piece construction is easier for a woman to handle."

She decided not to offer the reply she'd planned, that she used a plastic shovel so she wouldn't kill anyone if she felt compelled to hit him over the head with it. What really astonished her about Simon was that he'd been *elected*. Norah had a point. The single men of Oro were a pretty limited sample.

Until Joe Knoll showed up….

"Excuse me." The clock read seven-ten and Sabine took her cell phone from her pocket and walked away from him, speed-dialing Greg's number.

"Hello?" He sounded groggy.

"I'm sorry, Greg. Did I wake you guys?"

"Uh—Lucy's not here. She's at your house."

"Oh, I left. She hasn't gotten here yet."

"No," he said. "She stayed at your house last night."

Foreboding shook her, and her eyes strayed toward mountains she couldn't see, mountains completely shrouded by falling snow. "She didn't. She was going to stay with you."

The silence on the line told her that Greg was thinking what she was, that he was now alert. "Where was she going?"

"As far as I know, up Moth Mountain and into Hurricane."

"There's a hut back there," he said. "Look, where are you?"

"The courthouse." The county would, of course, understand if she had to abandon the shoveling to help find her sister.

But no one would want her to participate in the search. She knew that already. Avalanche danger. Her children at home. It would give Karen something to talk about for twenty years.

Lucy. She was so used to going anywhere and everywhere alone. She had an avalanche beacon, but without companions to find her and dig her out—fast—that was only for body recovery. Lucy never wanted to consider the possibility of being injured out where no one could help her. *I just have to rescue myself,* she always said. In fact, she'd done just that in a race two years earlier, hobbling over the finish line with a broken foot. The avalanche that had suffocated Victor had also broken ribs, vertebrae and a femur. A rescuer had seen the avalanche swallow him, bury him, two hours before they'd found him with probes. A beacon might have saved his life, but he'd seen no danger on his route. Neither had Sabine, until he died there.

As though to multiply the disregard for her own life and her loved ones' feelings, Lucy's dreams for the future pointed not toward greater caution but back to the Himalayas.

How can you blame her, Sabine?

Now, however, Lucy hadn't returned from a winter workout. A foot and a half of new snow in Oro, who knew how much up on Moth Mountain and in Hurricane Gulch. *Increased natural avalanche activity and high likelihood of triggering avalanches in fresh windslabs....*

"I'm going to call some people," Greg said. "If neither you or I saw her last night, she's missing, and it's time to start looking."

She'd never felt so grateful that Lucy had linked her life with possibly the only man in Oro capable of keeping up with her. If anyone could be trusted to organize the rescue effort and to find Lucy, it was Greg Lord.

If she's alive.

No, I'd feel it if she were dead.

She hadn't known when her father died. Her mother's death, however, she'd known as a wet-clay feeling in her abdomen, a heaviness, a certainty that something was very wrong.

Lucy's fine. She must be fine.

No. Not fine. Injured, at least. Maybe frostbitten. Not dying of hypothermia, not Lucy.

She put the phone in the upper pocket of her overalls, to make sure she'd hear it if Greg called, then carried her shovel back to the sidewalk. Okay, Lucy wasn't here, she'd have to shovel just one person's width on each of the walks. No, she'd finish this sidewalk as she'd started....

But her movements seemed ghostlike, as though she herself wasn't there. Instead, she walked into the past, into the last day during which she was the wife of a living Victor Knoll.

She remembered so clearly that it wasn't a memory. She was living it again....

That day

THE SHOP WAS EMPTY. His skis and poles were gone. Sabine glanced at the sky, cloudless and crisp. *Damn.*

She'd have to wait.

Again.

She'd come out twice that morning, and both times someone had been in the shop with him, confiding, pouring out troubles, Victor listening, listening and working. Sabine had said once that it reminded her of Samuel Hamilton in *East of Eden,* and Victor had said, *hardly,* and she'd asked what he meant. *He was an intellectual,* Victor had said. *I'm not. I'm just a sledmaker. A husband. A father.*

Sabine had rolled her eyes and told him to read the book again.

Today, she hadn't had him to herself. That morning, he'd taken Maria and Finn out to the shop with him and let her sleep in. She'd been so tired lately.

When would he get back? She couldn't go after him. Maria was in the house with a friend, and Finn was taking a nap.

It would have to wait.

A siren sounded from the east-west highway, the two-lane that eventually became gravel, then four-wheel-drive, the scenic route, the direction in which Victor would have skied, along the path that ran parallel to the river.

She grasped the worktable.

Knowing.

Knowing utterly.

And trying not to shriek....

BUT THIS WAS NOT that day.

One, two, three, four. One, two, three, four. Sabine switched to the other side, right leg forward. Shoveling was rhythm, and she found it comforting.

A Toyota pickup drew to the curb beside where she was working.

Joe Knoll climbed out and walked through one of the paths she'd cut to the shoveled sidewalk.

The expression on his face showed her that he knew Lucy was missing. "What?" Sabine said.

"Greg couldn't raise you on the phone. He came by your house to look through her clothes to see if he could tell what she was wearing."

"The blue Arcteryx suit." Lucy had so many sponsors, tested so many products, that Greg had been smart to check everywhere she kept clothes. The blue suit, which had been a gift from him, was Lucy's favorite. If only it were safety orange.

"He figured that out. I offered to go with him, but he said he thought you could use help here. Search and rescue is setting out, I guess." He glanced around. "Do you have another shovel?"

She didn't want him, not now.

My sister isn't dead. I would know. "I knew when Victor was dead," she said. "I knew. I don't think Lucy's dead."

Joe looked at her, giving one slow nod, the nod of one who's seen death in the mountains, as she had. "Shovel?" he asked again.

"I can do it myself."

"I'm sure of it." Joe couldn't understand the sudden surge of protectiveness he felt toward her. Was it what she'd said about Victor and his own realization that at some point she had faced the enormous quiet horror of losing the person she loved most in the world? For Joe had no doubt that Victor had been that to her. Husband, lover, best friend.

For just a moment, sardonic mockery swept through him, as though anyone being spouse, lover and best friend was impossible and only a subject for fantasy or ridicule.

The reaction shamed him.

"They could have used you looking for Lucy. You're competent in the mountains."

"I suggested that. But as Greg pointed out, I don't know these mountains. And he was concerned for you. So let me help you shovel. If you refuse I'll be emasculated."

Sabine laughed, or tried to.

That he'd persuaded her to do anything close to smiling made him feel strangely empowered, proud, manly in a way he wasn't used to feeling. Was it because she'd looked so terribly sad when he'd driven up? "So, do I need to go buy a shovel?"

She inclined her head toward the station wagon, then dug her own shovel into the snow. She and Lucy owned three one-piece plastic Remco shovels in primary colors, seventy-five dollars apiece, designed for toxic spill cleanup. Scooping and tossing another shovelful, she muttered, "Thanks."

When he returned with the blue shovel, he began cutting another path from the sidewalk to the street and they worked toward each other.

"Some time," he said, "would you tell me how Victor died?"

"I wasn't there. You'd do better talking to one of the search and rescue people who found him." An evasion. Of everything she couldn't stop thinking about.

"Which slide was it?"

She didn't find his questioning insensitive. Saying how he'd died or where wouldn't make him any more dead or her any more sad. "It's called the Miner's Daughter Slide." She told him about the big trees, more than a century old, that had come down.

Joe wondered whether she'd had to identify Victor. And if so, what shape had his brother's body been in?

"Is he buried here?"

"Yes. We had agreed that if…anything happened, it would be good for the children to have someplace to visit."

"And do they visit? Do you?"

"Yes."

This time, he heard her sigh, and it wasn't a sigh at his questions but because of some weariness she'd experienced, perhaps that of being a widow with three children.

Sabine thought of Lucy, trying to imagine and trying not to imagine what could have kept her sister from returning to Oro the night before. She worked through scenarios that would leave Lucy alive and unharmed. Shoveling faster, she noticed how quickly the snow, now blowing horizontally, gathered on the ground, on the sidewalk she'd already cleared. She gazed across Main Street to the old town jail, now just a tourist site. If the visibility was this bad, the snow falling this hard in town, what was it like up in the mountains? And what if the Colorado Department of Transportation closed the pass? Because, at this time of year, the trail Lucy had taken, up Moth Mountain and back to Hurricane Gulch, was accessible only from the highway.

But if CDOT closed the road, it would be due to avalanche hazard—or for blasting, avalanche mitigation. They would close it only if it was unsafe for the road to remain open.

Yes, if unharmed, Lucy could ski back to Oro without breaking a sweat, truck or no. If she made it as far as her vehicle, she could drive down to the gate—provided the road itself was passable—and use the emergency phone to ask someone to unlock the gate.

But if she could make it to her car, she would've done so already.

Sabine glanced at Joe. He wasn't bothering to reassure her, and she appreciated that. She knew he hadn't forgotten that her sister was out there somewhere. Like her, he knew Lucy could well be dead, and he didn't waste time with meaningless insistence that she must be all right.

They finished the sidewalk in another fifteen minutes, then cleared the long walks up to the courthouse steps. They were done by ten, and Joe said, "Where next?"

"The roof of the Independence."

"Lead the way. I'll follow in my truck."

They stopped at noon and went into the Wandering Elk for lunch. The elk head on the wall wore a Santa Claus hat over its ears and red tinsel garlands in its antlers.

They ordered at the counter, collected their own silverware, water and coffee and sat across from each other in a vinyl booth with turquoise seats and a red Formica table. Two CDOT workers came into the diner, and their eyes met Sabine's across the room. *No. No. No.*

One walked over to the booth where she and Joe sat. "We're trying to keep it open," he said. "But if we have to close it, we have to."

"I know. Oh, Bill, this is Joe Knoll. He's Victor's brother."

"Glad to meet you, Joe. We'll get in touch, Sabine. Or tell Greg, anyhow. We know the search team's up there, and we'll let 'em out when they come down in any case."

Obviously.

"Everyone," Bill added, "wants to find Lucy. She's our star."

She's our star. Yes, it was true. And Sabine had often envied her sister that stardom but even more, her freedom. Being an adventure racer also meant taking time alone day after day to train. Running, skiing, biking…

Now Sabine asked herself, *How would it be if you were lost out there?*

Which was why she didn't climb Himalayan Peaks, why she didn't ski alone in the backcountry, why she didn't do so many things she would have liked to do.

As they ate, Joe said, "What's next?"

"Oh, I can manage the rest by myself. Just write down how much time you've spent and I'll write you a check. Lucy makes fifteen dollars an hour. We split our fee."

She tried to interpret his expression and decided it betrayed something like astonishment. "What?" she said.

"How do you get by?"

"Well, I receive social security because of Victor's death. I sell yarns in the summer and wait tables and I sell clothing for a designer on the Front Ridge."

"But this sale will make a big difference to you."

"As it would to most people."

"I'm surprised you haven't sold it before, in light of that."

She had no reply.

He said, "So, where are we working this afternoon?"

"I told you I'll do it myself."

"You don't have to pay me."

Yes, I do. She took out her cell phone and checked for calls. She'd had none. Where was Lucy? If they found her alive, it would have to be soon. The day seemed to have grown darker since that morning.

Sabine couldn't think of life without Lucy—even the strictly practical elements of life. She depended on her sister in so many ways.

"Sabine."

She lifted her eyes.

"Let me help. Okay? I didn't talk to Victor for years. I think that by letting me stay in the shop, you're doing something for me on Victor's behalf. If Victor was here, he'd want me doing this for you."

Sabine knew he was right, knew it so well that she could almost hear Victor saying, *Let him help you.* Victor might tell her that sometimes it was a kindness to let someone do something for you.

"All right." She tried to smile but couldn't. "We've got a couple of residential roofs. Summer people. They're both Pro-Panel."

"And you were going to do it alone?"

She felt herself flush and hated the fact. "I *have* done it alone. But you're right. It's not smart. Anyhow, when we shovel, try to leave a base of about three inches. At least three inches. It'll keep us from slipping."

"Okay." Joe wondered what Victor would have to say if he knew his wife and the mother of his children had turned to shoveling roofs to make ends meet. Joe figured his brother would've objected. He put the question to Sabine.

She considered. "I just don't think about it. He wouldn't have stopped me. I'm sure he'd be proud of me. Of the fact that I'm strong. He used to tell me I'm strong, and it was a compliment. He used to tell me I'm a good mother." Her voice shook. It was a long time since anyone had said that. Victor had been the last person.

The sadness of her missing Victor was palpable. From across the table, Joe saw it and felt it. "Where do you think he is now?"

He hadn't meant to ask.

"With God," she said with certainty. "With a God who loves him."

Joe's eyes shifted downward slightly.

"What do you think?" she asked.

"I don't know. When people die in the mountains—especially if they're left where they fall—that seems most right to me. So many of them seem…as though that's where they should die."

"To you." It burst out of her.

"I can see how you might see things differently," he said.

"Oh, I wouldn't have wanted either of my parents to feel that Lucy and I imprisoned them, that they couldn't be or do what they wanted because they had children. But I did wish—well, it would've been nice…if they'd realized we needed them. And Victor certainly wouldn't have chosen to die in an avalanche that day. He loved me, and he loved Maria and Finn and would have loved Tori. He loved his life. He didn't want to die at all."

"I'm sure you're right."

"And I don't think his being dead is the way it's supposed to be. I think it's the way it *is*." She didn't know why she was trying to explain this to him, these things she'd said to no one but Lucy.

A weight settled in Joe's chest. What Sabine was expressing—was that how Chris Monegan's mother felt? It hadn't been Joe's fault that this very young man had died on Everest. Yet he should, somehow, have prevented it, which *did* make it his fault. It had happened, and it had torn his existence apart. The only comfort—or absence of discomfort—lay in believing that he hadn't been to blame, that it would've happened with or without him, with or without another guide, that it was cosmically slated to happen.

But that meant believing in fate. And Joe did not believe that fate was stronger than choice.

They shoveled until three. Sabine picked up Maria and Finn from school and returned home to find Karen with Tori, who mercifully showed no blistering spots, no sign of chicken pox. Tori was coloring at the kitchen table. Sabine started to fix a snack for Maria and Finn, and Karen said, "Oh, I can do that if you don't feel like it."

Not for the first time, Sabine sensed that Karen was tempting her to choose an easy path—something easier than caring for her children. Sometimes Sabine even imagined that Karen did this in the hope that Sabine would leave her some dirt to spread around Oro.

Now Maria and Finn and Tori all wanted their mother's attention, Tori to show her what she was coloring, Maria to share her homework, Finn to ask if he could please watch the cartoon network. Sabine wanted to be with her family and wanted to feel that her child-care provider supported and believed in her as a mother.

"I'll do it," Sabine said. She knew her tone was sharp and didn't care.

"You must be worried about Lucy."

"Greg hasn't called or come by?"

"No. Do you want me to find out what I can? I can go

see if any of the search and rescue people have come back."

"Thanks. That would be great."

But at that moment someone knocked at the door. Sabine glanced up and saw Joe through the glass. "Let him in, will you?" she said to Karen.

Karen opened the door. Her movement back from the door was delicate, ladylike, almost shy. She managed to look embarrassed, as though she felt she was intruding on Joe's surprise visit with Sabine. "Well, I'll go, all right?" she said in her little-girlish voice.

"Thank you," Sabine told her. "I'll have a check for you when you come back, okay?"

"Oh, thanks." Karen pulled on her leather coat, her pageboy swinging in artlessly perfect geometry against her china-doll skin. "See you." Again, she seemed to emphasize that she was leaving Joe and Sabine alone, although there were three children in the room, as well, two of them clinging to Sabine's legs and begging, *"Moom, look. Mommm, look."*

"Just a minute, Tori. Yes, Finn. You can watch TV. Have you three met Joe yet? Joe's Daddy's brother. Maybe that's why you thought he looked like Daddy, Tori. And he is in the photo upstairs."

Tori stared up with her large dark eyes, as though expecting Joe to do something frightening or something magical and spectacular.

"Joe's going to make sleds in Daddy's shop," Sabine told them. "Joe, this is Maria, Finn and Tori."

*"Victor*ia," said Tori. "I'm named for Daddy. Daddy's name is Victor, and I have his name."

"No, you don't," Finn said.

Don't start, Sabine thought, not because she minded them bickering in front of Joe but because she felt exhausted by their bickering at all.

"Vic*tor* and Vic*toria* are two different names," Finn insisted. "You're stupid."

"Your sister is not stupid, Finn. Victoria is the girl's form of Victor, and she's right—she was named for Daddy."

"I don't care," Finn said indifferently and went into the other room. A moment later the television came on full blast. Sabine walked in after him, took the remote and lowered the volume. "Finn, don't call people stupid. It's mean."

He didn't even look at her but sat with his eyes glued to the TV.

"Finn, did you hear me?"

"Okay!" he shouted.

"And don't shout at me."

"Okay!" he shouted again.

Sabine returned to the kitchen. Joe had dragged a chair out from the table and sat to examine the pictures Tori had colored. "And—well, that's a waterfall," he said. "Isn't it?"

"Yes. And that's a fish, swimming up the waterfall."

"Fish don't swim up waterfalls," said Maria.

Sabine decided not to get involved in this one.

"This fish is swimming up this waterfall," Tori told her. "Anyhow, I bet some fish do."

"You're right," Joe told her.

Sabine asked, "Did you learn anything? I thought that might be why you came by."

"It is. That CDOT fellow we met this afternoon told me they're going to close the road, but Greg and the others are still out, so they'll just have to use the phone and call to have the gate opened."

"No one's heard from them? Anything at all?"

"I don't know. I only talked to that one man."

"What's wrong?" asked Maria.

"Lucy didn't come back from skiing last night, so Greg and some other people are out looking for her, in case she got hurt."

"Or died," said Tori matter-of-factly.

Sabine stared. "What makes you say that?"

"Karen said on the phone that Lucy might be dead."

"Well, it's possible," Sabine answered carefully, "but I certainly don't think Lucy is dead. Shall we sit together and ask God to keep her safe?"

"Yes," Maria said. She, of all of them, knew that people who didn't come home really might be dead.

As her father had been one afternoon.

While Sabine joined hands with her daughters, Joe walked into the other room, and Sabine heard him say, "What are you watching?"

She said, "God, please keep Lucy safe and help Greg find her, because we love her and need her and we want her to come home."

Though what had God done about Victor? Sabine had loved him and needed him and wanted him to come home, too. But he'd died, never to come home again.

"Okay, let's see your school folder, Maria."

The minutes crawled by.

Joe was back in the kitchen with Finn. "Finn and I

would like to know if it's okay for him to come out and help me clean up the shop?"

No, it's not okay! I don't know you, and I don't want you anywhere near my children. He reaction was unreasonable.

"Finn, I need to see your school folder first."

"Later," Finn said.

"Now."

"Later," Finn repeated, his face wearing an impish smile.

"Do you want to go up to your room for a time-out and *then* show me your school folder?"

"No. I want to go clean up the shop."

"Do what your mom says," Joe told him.

Sabine felt like snarling that she didn't need his help with her children. But there was no reason, because Finn completely ignored him and said to Sabine, "Shop first."

"Folder first."

"Shop first."

"Time-out."

Finn left and got his backpack and hurled it down as hard as he could on the kitchen table. There was very little in it, so the pack made almost no impact, but Maria pulled her homework folder clear and said, "Finn, don't be a jerk!"

"I'm not a jerk, but you're ugly!"

"Thanks, anyhow, Joe," Sabine said, "but Finn's got to stay inside this afternoon."

Finn burst into tears and began screaming incoherently. He lay down on the floor and kicked the wood and banged his fists, and Joe mouthed, "Sorry." He waved and, looking pained, slipped out the back door.

CHAPTER SIX

"WE HAD TO STOP because of avalanche danger." Greg sounded as though he hated himself for having heeded warnings and acted to preserve his own life. He also sounded as though he wanted to be alone with his misery. "We couldn't get back to the hut. Avalanches. The last one almost caught us. We had to come home. We didn't know what else to do. I started her truck to make sure it was running all right. I put a full first-aid kit in it and left another in a cache near the Basin Trail. I wanted to stay in the truck, but I guess it's illegal."

"Oh, Greg." Sabine felt almost as bad for him as she did for herself. Her sister couldn't be dead. *But if she wasn't dead last night, if she was only injured…* Yes, time was running out. Lucy could not be expected to survive in this weather. Injured. Alone.

And tomorrow I have to shovel again. Yes, most of the people who wanted her to shovel could find someone else to do the job on this occasion, but Sabine felt there was a perception that she was less reliable because she was a woman and a mother. Therefore, she must be more reliable.

Besides, not working wouldn't help. Shoveling would keep her hands busy, at least, even if it wouldn't completely occupy her mind.

She put the children to bed, trying to remember when she'd last gone this long without talking to Lucy. Even when Lucy was out of town racing, they talked on the phone. When Karen had returned later that afternoon to pick up her check, Finn had been shrieking in his bedroom, Tori had been whining and Maria was curled up in the window seat with her nose in *Pride and Prejudice,* as though all around her was blissful silence instead of tension-fraught din. Sabine had paid Karen, thanked her and seen her out the door with the distinct feeling that Karen's disapproval of her mothering would make itself known throughout Oro within hours.

Alone in the house, she gazed out the window. Snow was still falling. Lights were on in the shop. She could see them from her spinning area in the living room, the place Victor had designed with her in mind, envisioning her spinning and watching their children play. It had been like that for a time. *For a long time,* she told herself again, as if she hoped to convince herself she hadn't been cheated.

But why did he never tell me that Joe was his brother, that he had a brother, that Joe had once been engaged to Teresa?

Teresa had died because of a bad reaction to her medications. Two medications that shouldn't be mixed, that could, in some cases, cause death. That was what Victor had said. Once, Sabine had asked what the medications were, and Victor had said, *Oh, I don't really want to talk about it. I killed her by giving her the medicine prescribed for her.*

He had felt that he'd caused her death, but he hadn't expressed much guilt. Some. He had said, *Part of me thought it was a blessing. She wasn't happy.*

Sabine had never suspected Victor of murdering Teresa and didn't even now. But concealing his relationship with Joe, Joe's engagement to Teresa—all of that made her feel she'd never known him. If he wasn't the person she'd always believed, then who was he?

Sabine pulled a coat from the coat rack by the side doors, French doors, part of the whole Craftsman-style house Victor had built. She shoved her feet into her Columbia boots, rated to forty degrees below zero. She had shoveled at thirty below.

It wasn't that she particularly wanted to talk to Joe.

She wanted to talk to Lucy, but if Lucy was here, Sabine knew she'd never speak to her about the feelings she was having. She wouldn't talk to Joe Knoll about them, either. It was just too hard to sit there in the house, wondering where Lucy was, picturing her dead in an avalanche— highly possible—or with a broken leg, dying slowly, freezing to death. Anything could have happened.

Checking her watch, she promised herself that she'd spend no more than fifteen minutes out in the shop. In any case, if Maria woke up, she'd know where to look for her mother.

Sabine went out, on the path she used to take so often, sometimes with a baby in her arms, sometimes with two children, to see the man she'd loved.

She took the path to speak with the brother he'd never told her he had.

JOE HEARD HER FOOTSTEPS, knew it was her and opened the door. There was snow on her hair, which she'd worn down, as he rarely saw it.

At once, Joe said, "I'm sorry about this afternoon. I thought it would be fun for Finn. I didn't mean to cause a problem."

"No. It was fine. I'm sorry it didn't work out. He just... does that. The tantrums, the screaming. I'll let him come out another time, but I couldn't today. It's hard to keep him on task with school."

"It all looks hard to me. A single mom with three children."

The sympathy surprised and touched her. She hadn't expected it from him, had thought he wouldn't care about another person's small logistical problems or appreciate how much work three children could be.

"I hope I'm not disturbing you." He'd been cleaning. He'd put up sled parts, moved things she had felt too sacred to touch. She was glad the person who'd moved them hadn't been her.

"No." He paused. "You must be worried about your sister. It's not easy to wait alone."

"Yes. And there are things I—" Sabine stopped herself. "I want to talk to you about certain things. I've never wanted to talk to anyone about them. I want to say they don't matter, but now my brain won't let them go."

His eyes, the brandy shade of Victor's, the same shape as his, studied her. He didn't speak.

Sabine rushed on. "I know Teresa was hurt sledding. I know she hit a boulder. I'm familiar with the run. It's long, so you could go very fast. And Victor was with her, and it was just the two of them."

"Yes."

"They'd been married only a short time. A couple of

years," Sabine said. "What was she like? Was she good, like him? I only knew her after. She could be...monstrous."

"She was an imp. She played hard. She was an athlete and absolutely certain she was the cutest woman ever born. She was right, too. Other women intensely disliked her. Jealous, I suppose. But one of our friends, a married woman, said Teresa was a man's woman. She devoted a lot of time to flirting, seduction. Even when we were engaged, she'd flirt with anyone and everyone. It didn't bother me."

"Victor?"

"She was different with him, and that should've been a clue for me. She settled down and tried to be steadier for him, more serious, but later— You know, I think he liked her as she was. Playful, making life hell for every man she met."

He suddenly turned to her, then backed away to sit on a stool, offering her another, the more comfortable one. "Now, I want to ask you something. What was she like when you knew her?"

Sabine gathered her thoughts. He'd lit the woodstove. It was warm in the shop, burning her cheeks, giving her an odd sense of safety. With Joe she felt an enforced intimacy she didn't understand, as though they alone were caught in the mystery of Victor's—

Deceit.

"Sometimes she seemed almost—like a normal person. She wasn't beautiful anymore. Her jaw was a little slack on one side from the accident, and she didn't do anything with her hair. She had some gray, and I asked her once if

I should take her to get highlights, that it would be fun. She laughed at me—or laughed, at any rate. She called me the foulest names. I mean, she had a mouth on her. She'd forget things. She also had a twitch that was like a tic. And she occasionally drooled. Victor used to take her for walks, and sometimes she'd fight with him. Once, when I was there, she hit him and made his nose bleed. We thought she'd broken it. She was really difficult."

"I heard her meds killed her."

"Yes."

"That must've been hard for Victor. I assume he gave them to her."

"He did."

Joe rose from his stool.

When he stood in front of her, it didn't frighten her. She knew what he intended, as though his body were part of hers and she directed his limbs. She knew what he'd say— not the words, but the idea.

He touched her face with one big hand. His hands were like Victor's, huge, beautiful to her. She missed Victor's hands, and yet who had her husband been?

Joe said, "You are beautiful, Sabine. You're one of the most beautiful women I've ever seen. Men would kill to have your love."

"Well, he didn't." Her voice shook. *I have to believe that much. I knew him. I knew him.*

Joe stepped back, dropping his hand, all emotion or tension gone as he turned from her with a shrug. "I'm sure you're right. But I thought I knew everything about him before he and Teresa—"

"How did you find out?"

"She told me. And Teresa was not subtle. She handed me—well, we were out in the yard at the house, under that big oak—"

"Yes."

"—handed me the ring and said, 'I don't love you anymore. I'm in love with Victor.' That was it. I thought she'd had a psychotic break. I thought, *This can't be true.* I said something, I don't even remember what, and she said, 'I'm going to marry Victor.' I said, 'He's asked you?' and she said, 'Pretty much,' and I asked what that meant, and she said, 'Well, that you and I had to have this conversation. Then *he* and I could talk about the future.'

"When I went into the house, he was in the kitchen, sitting at the table, waiting, looking at me, looking as if he'd been waiting, and I knew it was all true. He said, 'I'm sorry. It just happened.'

"Was she 'good, like Victor'?" Joe repeated, throwing a glance at Sabine. "Was Victor good? I'd always believed so, as you do. No, Teresa was never good like Victor. I was surprised he loved her, although I did. I'd always thought he disapproved of her and half pitied me for wanting to marry her. I'd always thought he felt I was making a bad choice. Then…he wanted her." Joe hesitated before he spoke again. "She was unadulterated selfishness. Highly lovable, annoying, playful and childlike. But I don't associate goodness with her. She was generous with her money, interested in charities that benefited children, interested in making the world better, but that didn't translate into action in her personal life. I think probably *you're* good, Sabine, in the way you mean."

"No." She shook her head. "No. I'm selfish. I wanted—

I always wanted to be out doing what Lucy's—" She stopped, started again, told him about her envy of her sister's freedom.

"So, that makes you a bad mom or something?" Joe cocked his eyebrows. "If you were selfish, you'd actually be doing those things."

"But I think about it and dream about it, and sometimes I nearly go for it. Drop everything, tell the kids, 'Okay, this is how we're going to live.'"

"Oh, you're going to hell for sure," Joe told her dryly.

A feeling of relief washed over her, and she realized that he'd said what Victor would have. Not in the same words. But that comfort and acceptance was there. It frightened her, because this man was in no way Victor. It could be dangerous, a psychological and emotional disaster, for her to count on him.

"My kids are unmanageable," Sabine said. "But really, I didn't come out here to find someone to boost my self-esteem. I just wanted to know…the things I asked you."

"Would you like to see what I'm doing?" he asked, and she knew he'd ask her up to the loft, up to the loft where she'd made love with her husband, his brother, his brother who'd betrayed him and lied to her. Her husband had been dead four years, which should've been more than enough time for longing to fade and was not nearly enough.

"Okay." *What will I feel going up there, seeing his things up there, seeing it different from how it used to be?*

But first Joe showed her that he'd been using the shop vacuum to clean the tools and sweep the sawdust from the floor. He showed her how he'd hung the sled parts Victor had made on the walls, made an inventory of the wood supply still left.

As he put a foot on the bottom step of the narrow staircase, he said, "I'm using the futon up there. I hope it's okay. I've folded your linen, but I haven't brought it down yet."

I don't want to see it, she thought. Flannel sheets. And an afghan crocheted from yarn she'd spun.

Yes, those were folded on the trunk at the top of the stairs. It was an old shipping trunk, in which they'd stored extra pillows, sheets and blankets for the futon, for this bed, for when guests came to stay. But more often, it was she and Victor who'd rested together on the futon, when she came out to visit and he took a break from work.

It was what should have happened that day, the day he'd died.

How she'd been looking forward to it. To what she had to tell him, to the delight he would feel and show.

She stared at the futon. Joe had thrown a sleeping bag over it, and somehow that saddened her. Somehow it emphasized Victor's death, his never returning, this brother of his being there instead.

Sabine stared at Joe's backpack in the corner, to keep her gaze off the futon. "So—you must have stuff in storage somewhere?"

"Well, I shipped a few things back from Nepal, some things that are special to me. But I live pretty light."

"No high school yearbooks? Photo albums? Collections of books?"

"No." He looked almost sheepish.

"What?" she said.

"I threw out a lot of stuff when I left Victor's house. I wanted to sever my ties with the past. You know what I mean."

She supposed she did. And she knew what it was like to live light. Her parents had always been in financial trouble, or so it seemed to her in retrospect. They were always trying to finance one climbing expedition or another, and she remembered how often she and Lucy had been told that her parents couldn't afford to give them something they'd wanted. They'd learned not to ask and to be content with the kind of food the sherpas ate, lentils and grains. Living with Victor, she had felt very rich indeed. In fact, her whole adult life she had felt that abundance surrounded her.

When her children wanted something, she never said she couldn't afford it. Never. Because everything was a choice. None of her children had ever asked for anything truly unaffordable. Sometimes she preferred to spend money on something else. If that was the case, she just said, *Not this time,* because she believed that when her parents had said they couldn't afford something, they'd really meant that they'd chosen to afford something different.

Sabine gathered the sheets and afghan in her arms, almost as though she was gathering up her children. But really, she was plucking up her memories of Victor, precious memories of laughter, of how boyish and playful he could be with her, revealing a side of himself so private and delightful that it was as intimate as their love-making. With her, he became someone others rarely saw. A tender prankster and lover. A man who'd once confessed with something like chagrin that he could spend most of every day in her arms and had rued the impracticality of that scenario.

She felt Joe looking at her and wondered, irrationally, if he knew her thoughts or her feelings.

He said, "Thank you for letting me get started here."

He did know, then. Well, he must guess, guess that the shop and the loft and the futon and the sheets and the afghan were full of memories for her.

But she understood now, more keenly than ever, that she didn't want to live with memories. That had never been what she'd wanted. She'd only wanted the joy that was lost.

She said, "I'm glad you're doing this." She couldn't be more articulate, say that it was good for the shop to be used, good for sleds to be made or healthy for her to let go. Instead, she turned with her armload of sadness and walked back down the stairs. He followed. She heard him behind her, sensed him as a presence so much taller than Victor had been.

So different.

Victor…

Joe said, "I spoke with Norah earlier this evening."

"She called. She told me." They were supposed to sign the paperwork the next day. Joe had done what he'd promised. As Norah said, they just had to wait and see if he could really come up with the money.

He asked, "Does anyone have more ideas about what we can do to find your sister?"

"No. It's snowing so hard. When so much snow falls this fast, they close the roads because of avalanche danger.

Greg and the search-and-rescue people couldn't continue for the same reason." Sabine decided to say it out loud, or perhaps her voice decided to speak without her permission. "I can't imagine…her being alive. But she's resourceful. I can't imagine her being dead. She's done incredible things. She's very tough."

She turned to look up at Joe and saw the sober eyes of a man who knew that very tough people still died.

He chewed his bottom lip and for just a moment looked like Victor. She knew he felt helpless, helpless to comfort her, unable to promise her that Lucy was alive. "Will you be able to sleep?" he asked.

"I'll have to," she said, which wasn't really an answer. She had to shovel the next day, and she could not go on and on with such physical work in the face of exhaustion and without rest.

"I'm reading Flannery O'Connor's short stories," he said. "Have you ever read them?"

She shook her head.

"Would you like to hear one?"

She could spin while he read to her—as Victor sometimes used to and as Maria sometimes did.

"Okay. I need to go to sleep soon, though. Can you come in the house, so I can spin?"

He nodded. "Let me get the book."

The snow seemed to be falling even harder, if possible, as they made their way back to the house.

In the great room, Sabine cleared some of Maria's books off a window seat to make a place for Joe, but he settled himself on the floor near the hearth with its copper hood.

The hood was engraved with a quotation of Victor's choosing: *There is no fear in love, but perfect love drives out fear.* He'd told her it was from the Bible, but Sabine had no idea of the context. She'd thought it was a strange selection for the hood of the hearth. In Craftsman houses, these hoods sometimes bore a legend about life being short and craft long to learn. That would've seemed to her a more fitting choice from Victor.

She'd asked why he'd chosen the words he had, and he'd sat on the stonework beside the fireplace, read the words himself, then said, *Because they're true.*

Sabine hadn't argued. Perhaps it had come from his past, from Teresa's accident or Teresa's death. She was sure it spoke of the love Victor shared with her, Sabine.

Now Joe studied the words. He made no comment but opened the paperback he'd brought as Sabine sat at the Louët. She had three wheels. One was a Saxony Victor had made. She liked it, but the making of spinning wheels was an art, and his was not as finely balanced as the other two. The Louët had two wheels. It was the one she liked best. The third was a very portable traveller.

She was working on a worsted. Few hard spinners could create a good worsted wool, but she'd done them for years, and hers were superb.

The story Joe read was called "Revelation." He read effectively, and she found herself completely absorbed, lifted into another world, amused and aghast, sometimes laughing out loud, sometimes mesmerized.

By the conclusion, she was winding a skein of yarn, and then abruptly remembered the storm outside and that Lucy was missing.

Sabine glanced at the clock on the mantel, which had been a wedding gift. It was ten-twenty.

"I really do need to sleep," she said. "Thank you for reading. It was nice. I like to be read to. We're quite a family for reading aloud."

He stood and collected his jacket. Sabine rose to her feet, as well, to show him out.

At the door, Joe said, "My roommate at the boarding-house said you did see someone after Victor's death. That you dated someone for a while."

Sabine shrugged. She felt she shouldn't answer, that to do so would open doors she had deliberately shut. But she said, "Yes. Why?"

"It didn't work out?" he asked.

Sabine answered simply. "He wasn't Victor. No. It didn't work out."

Joe gazed at her until she felt that her answer had been both childish and naive.

"Some people never do get over it," she said. "And even you will admit that he was remarkable."

Joe nodded.

Waving, he slipped away into the falling snow, carrying the book that had done more than take her mind from Lucy for a moment.

The story had been about expectations, about who goes to heaven and what's expected of those on earth. At least, if she'd had to say what it was about, she would have said that. It had given her things to think about through the night, other than Lucy, lost in the storm.

But she would think about Lucy, about Lucy being dead or alive. And what would happen to her if she died.

And what had happened to Victor.

And what was in store for her, Sabine.

The freedom to live selfishly didn't seem so important anymore; the freedom to try harder was all that seemed to matter.

CHAPTER SEVEN

FOR THE NEXT TWO DAYS, Joe helped Sabine shovel. She had stopped refusing his offers of help, and she had stopped trying to force him to accept payment. Perhaps he felt he was paying off some private debt, doing a self-imposed penance. Anyhow, she didn't care enough anymore. Just after noon on the third day, the department of transportation reopened the road that allowed access to Moth Mountain and Hurricane Gulch, and the search-and-rescue team, with Greg accompanying them, set out again.

This time, Sabine felt certain they would find Lucy—dead or alive.

She can still be alive. Colorado was full of stories of people walking unexpectedly out of avalanche country after being lost for a week. And Lucy hadn't been gone that long. Lucy had taken avalanche courses, but in Sabine's experience that didn't keep a person safe from avalanches. Three of the people she'd known who'd been killed in avalanches during the time she'd lived in Colorado had been avalanche experts. Victor was the only victim she knew who'd never had any avalanche training.

She and Joe quit shoveling at three as usual, so she could pick up Finn and Maria after school. Finn had been promised that today, after school, he could go out to the shop with Joe and start "learning to make sleds." Joe pulled into the drive right after Sabine.

"Hey, buddy," he called to Finn. "Ready to help me?"

"Yeah! After my snack!" Finn answered. "Come in the house."

Karen sat at the table with Tori, coaching her as she wrote some of the alphabet on a piece of paper in different colored crayons. Tori said, "Mom! I can write my whole name now!"

Sabine leaned over the table and saw that Tori had written something that looked a lot like "Victoria Knoll."

"Good girl!"

"Are they searching for Lucy again?" Karen asked.

"Yes."

"I hope they find her." She threw a look at Joe and told him, "It's nice of you to help Sabine with all the shoveling. I'll bet it's nice for you, too, Sabine."

There was an undercurrent to Karen's words, and Sabine wondered, as she had many times, why this woman who would probably be happier in the city, with a wide selection of male admirers, had ever come to a small former mining town that most sensible people deemed too cold and remote for winter habitation. But that was easy; she'd come to make money in real estate, and she'd already made quite a bit.

"It would be nice for me if my sister was home," Sabine said. "*That* would be nice."

"Sorry," Karen said. "You know I care about Lucy, too. I didn't mean anything like that."

Finn said, "Joe, come see my room," and Joe followed the little boy upstairs.

"I just meant," Karen said, "that it must be nice for you to have a guy to hang out with. And he *seems* nice." Only Karen could drench that word in so many meanings. "You must be happy. I mean, Victor was a lot older than you."

"Your point?" Sabine snapped and wished she hadn't. She couldn't afford to lose Karen as a day-care provider— particularly not if Lucy…if Lucy— And there would be repercussions from her hasty retort. She might not hear them, but Karen would take her revenge one way or another. She was an unhappy woman with too little to do, so she made mischief. Offended by Sabine, she would make her mischief at Sabine's expense. Immediately, Sabine said, "Look, I'm sorry. I loved Victor profoundly. I'll never love anyone like that again. His age is immaterial. He was extremely attractive to me, and I miss him every day."

"I didn't want to upset you," Karen said. "I just meant that Joe's nice-looking. He *seems* okay, although you don't really know much about where he came from or anything. Still, he's Victor's brother. And it must be nice for you to have someone to date."

"We're not dating!"

Tori looked up from the table. "What's dating?"

"When Barbie has dinner with Ken," Sabine explained. "You know, when Barbie goes on a date."

"Oh. Dressing up in pretty clothes. You don't have any pretty dresses."

"I do," Sabine told her. "I'll show you later."

Maria had gone to her room, and Tori was the only witness to Sabine's and Karen's exchange.

"So what did he do before he came here, anyway?" asked Karen.

Sabine was sure Karen knew as much as she did, but the question was innocuous. "He was a Himalayan guide."

"For what company? It would be fun to check them out on the Internet."

Sabine didn't even have a computer. She didn't need one. But she knew how to use the Internet at the library. Why had she never done this herself? She could've found out more about Joe Knoll by researching his guiding company. Obviously, Norah had seen something about it, but Norah, whose private fantasies involved becoming the next Danielle Steel, had been more interested in Joe's writing credentials. "His outfit was called Himalayan Caravan."

"I'll look it up. Want me to print off the page for you?"

"Sure." Sabine shrugged. "If you want. I don't care." She did care, but she wasn't about to tell Karen that.

"So, he owned the company?"

"Yes."

Karen pulled on her sheepskin coat. "I'll let you know. And I'm praying for Lucy."

"Thank you," Sabine told her sincerely. "Thank you very much."

Joe and Finn came down the stairs as Sabine was slicing cheese and apples for snacks. Joe, who sat at the table with the children, borrowed crayons from Tori and drew a primitive-looking figure with large teeth and a hairy, human-shaped body.

"What is it?" Tori asked. "I like it. It's cute."

Sabine looked over. "I know what it is."

"What, Mom?" asked Maria.

"I'm going to let Joe tell you."

"You don't really know," Finn accused.

"It's very rude to accuse your mother of lying," Sabine told him. "I do know what it is."

"I'm sure she does," Joe said, confirming that she was right. How odd that he had brought back her childhood with that figure. It made her feel close to him in a way she hadn't felt close to Victor, and that unnerved her. It wasn't that Victor hadn't cared what her childhood had been like. He had listened whenever she'd spoken about it. But he hadn't questioned her. Sometimes she'd had the feeling that he felt intimidated by her past, a past in which she'd climbed such high mountains, rubbing shoulders with famous mountaineers.

And there was also the way he'd felt about mountaineering.

Undoubtedly, Joe was the reason for that, and he'd just drawn a picture of a yeti for her children. But had Victor ever been jealous of Joe?

Sabine picked up a brown crayon from Tori's pile. "I always drew him like this." And she drew her own version of a huge furry being. Hers was taller than Joe's and had toes you could count and a snout like a bear's.

"What is it, Mom?" Maria asked again.

"A yeti," said Joe.

"What's a yeti?" Finn demanded.

"The abominable snowman," said Maria. "Isn't it." Not a question. Just insistence on confirmation of her guess.

"Not exactly," Joe said. "But close. They live in Tibet."

"Do you think they really exist?" Sabine asked. "Isn't it supposed to be the case that they're really Tibetan bears?"

"That explanation never satisfied me," he answered.

"Have you seen one?" She remembered something from her own past, remembered it in a way that felt as though it was happening. Suddenly she didn't hear anything in the room. She was running along a path of stone and dirt. She didn't know where it was, only that she was in the Himalayas and she was running ahead of Lucy, winning a race. Suddenly it was in front of her, tall, like a hairy shadow but more than a shadow. Her heart pounded, and she came to an abrupt halt.

Then it dropped to all fours and ran.

But not like a bear. When Lucy ran past her, Sabine grabbed her sister's sweatshirt, stopping her.

"Sabine?"

She blinked. "I'm sorry. What did you say?" She had never in her life had a memory like that. It'd been as though she was there, back in her childhood, and she wanted to return to that place, to experience that wild freedom again.

Joe Knoll gazed down at her. "I said I've seen one. Twice."

"I'd like to hear about it," she said, feeling distant, far away from both him and her children, "sometime."

Finn said, "I want to know what a yeti is."

"I'll tell you while we're working in the shop."

Half an hour later, Sabine went out to the shop to see what they were doing. She found Finn sitting on one of the stools at the bench, using a Phillips screwdriver to attach a runner to a sled, probably one that Victor had been working on before he died. She assumed Joe would tighten the screws afterward, and as she came in, he peered down at Finn's work and said, "Whoops. We got that one in the wrong way. We want the screw to point this way."

"Rats," Finn muttered, and started unscrewing the nut with his small hands.

"Boy, would your dad be proud of you," Sabine said. "I bet he can see you working in his shop, and I bet he thinks it's great." She did believe that, too. She still felt unsettled after her memory of the yeti, as though everything around her was slightly unreal. Even Lucy's absence had lost its immediacy. She found herself wanting only to dive back into that profoundly vivid memory. She had heard of people having extremely vivid childhood recollections but had assumed those sorts of buried memories were always of trauma, and the yeti incident hadn't been traumatic at all. She had returned to that trail alone, looking for the creature. Why had she forgotten that she'd once been so obsessed with the yeti?

Joe asked, "Heard anything from Greg yet?"

It was growing darker. Again, Sabine had the sensation of almost floating, of being vaguely unconcerned about Lucy's absence. "No."

"Want me to put you to work?" he asked.

"No," she repeated. "I just came out to see what Finn was up to. I'm going back to the house." She wanted to be alone to think about the yeti, about everything that had happened after she'd seen it. *If only I'd seen it again.*

But it had happened just once. It *could* have been a bear.

Tori begged for pancakes for dinner, so Sabine made pancakes and bacon and a fruit salad and invited Joe to join them.

Finn brought in a "boat" he'd constructed from part of

a two-by-four. A long nail served as a mast and small plugs of wood for a crew.

Greg didn't call, and Joe, without asking, picked up the cordless phone and called Lucy's boyfriend's number.

Sabine didn't ask who he was calling. She knew. Joe and Greg were already becoming friends. She thought about the yeti instead. It *must* have been a bear, though her lingering impression was of something like a hairy, over-sized person. Well, not a person but human-shaped, comfortable walking on two legs, more comfortable than she thought a monkey or even a gorilla would be.

As two pancakes sizzled on the skillet, Finn said, "Tell my mom about the yeti stories."

"I think she's busy."

"But you have to tell her about Harriet and the yeti."

Joe leaned against the counter, close to Sabine. "When I was in junior high school, I used to write stories—actually sort of graphic novels, because I did it in comic-strip form—about a yeti named Migo and a girl named Harriet."

"Had you been to the Himalayas then?"

"Not yet. I used to read about it, though, and cut out pictures from *National Geographic* and hang them all over my room."

"What did Victor think?"

Joe shrugged. "I don't know if he paid too much attention, actually. He always wanted me to have dreams, but I don't think it mattered to him what they were. And he liked Minnesota. I think he was threatened by the thought of mountaineering. He loved making sleds." He stared at the windows. "Will they stay out all night?"

"Greg will stay as long as it's safe," Sabine said with certainty.

They sat around the table and as they ate pancakes, Maria said, "Yetis don't really exist, do they?"

"I've seen them," Joe said. "I don't know what they are. Maybe they're bears."

"I don't believe you," Maria said matter-of-factly. "I don't believe they're real."

"Bears are real," Joe reasoned.

Sabine couldn't tell her children about the yeti she'd seen, although she wasn't sure why, so instead she listened to Joe. He told them about sleeping outside in Tibet, sleeping in a tent and hearing a horse in the middle of the night and unzipping the tent to see the tall hairy creature standing in the moonlight.

"Either it was a bear, or you dreamed it," Maria told him.

"Either is possible," he replied politely. "But I don't think I was dreaming. And in the morning, I found footprints. I took photos. I have them."

"Where? I want to see them," Maria said.

"They're out in the shop. I'll bring them in after dinner. They're just of the tracks."

"Someone could have faked tracks," Maria insisted.

"Well, it would have to have been me, because there was no one else around. But I'll show you the photos. I saved two. One's from that yeti. Another is from a different one."

"They *are* real!" Finn exclaimed. "I am Blizzardman, and I have fought the yeti and won him to the forces of good."

Sabine felt it before it happened. Finn was going to lose control, throw a tantrum or do something else antisocial. She got up and walked behind his chair, on which he was now standing. "Finn, sit down. Finish your pancake."

"If they're real, how come they're not in the zoo?" Maria said. "If you want to pretend they exist," she told Finn, "there's nothing wrong with that, but they're not real."

Finn threw his fork at his sister.

Sabine hefted him off his chair. "Time out."

He screamed and kicked at her. She carried him to the staircase. When she set him down, he turned and pummeled her thighs with his fists.

Joe came around the corner. He scooped Finn into his arms and said, "Up to your room, sir."

Sabine frowned, watching as Joe carried a startled and suddenly docile Finn upstairs.

She listened, hearing Joe's voice. She couldn't catch too many words.

After several minutes, Joe returned downstairs. Sabine stood at the kitchen counter, eating two pancakes. Tori had finished eating, and she and Maria were watching a DVD, *Willy Wonka and the Chocolate Factory,* in the living room.

Joe said, "I told him he should come down and apologize to you. He hasn't said a word to me since."

"That sounds like Finn. His teacher's beginning to hint that he's ADHD. I don't think it's true."

"I don't think so, either."

Without consulting her, he began clearing the table and running water in the sink for dishes.

"Don't," she said. "I'll load the dishwasher. It takes about two seconds."

Joe noticed that she appeared to have stopped watching the clock, that she appeared less worried about Lucy. For some reason, this made him uneasy. She didn't seem like herself. Yet to ask her if anything was wrong would be asinine. Something was dramatically wrong. He said, "Do you mind if I come back to the house later? I—I'd like to check on you."

Just twelve hours before, she would've told him to suit himself or even said that she didn't want him checking on her. But now the thought that he was coming back to the house pleased her.

"Maybe after the children are asleep," she said.

"So I won't get them riled up?"

"Something like that," she admitted.

And then, instead of wondering and worrying about Lucy, she began watching the clock again, waiting for the children's bedtime.

After they were asleep, she cleaned up the kitchen and went into the downstairs bedroom, where she brushed her hair and put on waterproof mascara, the only kind she ever bought, and lip balm. *This is silly,* she thought. *I'm not attracted to him.*

But she liked him, and liked his way with the children.

She was spinning when he knocked at the door. She was working on the wheel Victor had made, spinning a bouclé, working on the first plying. Enjoying the slower speed of his wheel, she remembered the pleasure he'd had in making it for her.

But somehow the desperation to see his face had lessened, dimmed.

"Any word from Greg?" Joe asked when she let him in.

"Nothing."

Sabine returned to the spinning wheel. She had turned down most of the lights, except in the nook where she spun. The kids had left pillows on the floor near the fire, and Sabine hadn't picked them up. Now Joe sat on one and gazed up at her.

"I was worried about you," he said. "I still am. You seem a little—unfocused."

"I am. Just this afternoon, I remembered something I'd forgotten for twenty-five years." Her hands moving as automatically as her feet on the single treadle, she told him about the intensity of her yeti memory. "It felt so joyful that I just want to go back into the memory, if that makes sense."

"It does," he agreed.

"But I also wonder…"

"What?"

"I keep getting anxious—thinking there might be other things I've forgotten, bad things." She stopped the wheel.

He eyed her thoughtfully. "Is there any reason to think something bad might have happened?"

"I don't know." She couldn't put her finger on the reason for her doubt, yet it existed.

"After my parents died," Joe said, "I became obsessed with yetis. I don't know why. I read everything I could about Tibet and Nepal. I loved drawing them—and Harriet, the blond girl who was Migo's friend."

Sabine had been a small blond girl who had seen a yeti. To her, it seemed more than coincidence—destiny. "My father told me," Sabine said, "that the people of Simmek believed the yetis only revealed themselves to…well, the faithful, I suppose. They had religious significance, yetis."

"Did your father consider you a good girl?"

"Oh, I've always been a good girl."

Joe thought she sounded sad.

"Oldest child, all that," she explained.

"Lucy was the wild child?"

"Yes." *Was.* "Yes, she is."

Joe heard the superstitious correction. But perhaps it was just proof that sibling rivalry could outlive parents.

Sabine peered toward the window, watching the snow drift down outside, as if someone had ripped apart a feather bed. Abandoning her spinning stool, she sat on another of the pillows on the floor. "I think it's good news," she said, "that they haven't come back. At least they're still looking."

"Yes. That's true."

Sabine said, "I think I'd go…numb…if anything happened to Lucy. When Victor…well, I wasn't numb. It was a nightmare. An absolute nightmare. I…I was pregnant." She'd never said this next part to anyone. Joe Knoll was bound to be the wrong person, was bound to have an insensitive reaction, and that was the reaction she wanted. Indifference. "I was pregnant with Tori, and I had just found out. I was going to tell him. That day. But I never got to."

Abruptly, she was ashamed of having said it. It sounded maudlin, appallingly so.

She wanted to discount her own emotion. She wanted to say, *Not that it matters.*

But of course it had mattered. It had felt, still felt, as if Tori wasn't Victor's daughter at all but exclusively hers. That made it seem even more as though Victor had cruelly and knowingly abandoned her.

Which was ridiculous and untrue.

But how disappointing it had been to carry a baby and to never have the chance to share her joy with the baby's father.

"I don't dwell on it," she said quickly. "I'm lucky. I'm lucky to have these three children. I'm the luckiest person I know."

He didn't disagree with her assessment of her own good fortune. She was beautiful, her children were beautiful, she owned property in a beautiful place.

"When my parents each died," she said, "it was horrible. Particularly my mother's death. But Victor—I'd always believed I couldn't go on without him. Then I had to. And people *don't* understand. They understand if it's a child but not a spouse, because most spouses aren't passionately in love. But now I know a suffering I didn't know before."

Joe reflected on the disappointments to which he'd been exposed over time. The first that came to mind was the disappointment of clients who failed to summit Everest. He *had* made the summit, four times. It was hard to turn back without achieving it, and he'd done that twice, as well. But clients wrapped up so much of their identity, as though they somehow owned the mountain if they achieved their goal.

And, yes, he had fallen prey to those goals, to getting caught up in that dream, as if it was the only thing that mattered. It would've been easier to believe that he took joy in the achievements of his clients, but that wasn't it. His admiration was reserved for those who held a sane attitude toward the mountain, who were ready to come back another day—or not—and be happy. No, getting people to the top was about money and success, and it was determined largely by luck. By weather. Factors you couldn't control.

He had seen people suffer over their failure to achieve the summit the way others might over the loss of a child.

He reviewed his own sorrows. Like Sabine, he had lost his parents when he was young—younger than she'd been, in fact. Teresa had decided she loved Victor more. These things had caused him sadness of different kinds and in different measures. But Victor's deciding to love Teresa—that seemed to him the pinnacle of pain.

Until a year ago, in Nepal.

But that was nothing to share with Sabine.

"Your hands are like Victor's."

Startled, he glanced up.

"I loved his hands," she said. "He had the biggest hands I'd ever seen."

Joe put his own hand on the pillow where she sat, beside her hand. Hers was like a child's in comparison.

He touched her fingers, locked them with hers, and she accepted that touch, surprising him by not withdrawing.

"Sabine," he said.

"Yes." She did not look up.

"Sabine, may I kiss you? Or would it offend you?"

"It wouldn't offend me." *But—* She meant to say the words, yet couldn't.

But I don't know what Victor would think or feel.

Or what I will feel.

Every time I kiss someone other than Victor, I regret it.

And you're not Victor. You're not Victor. You'll be like every other man who is not.

So she wanted to stop before it started. She was afraid that she'd find him soft in comparison to his brother. Immature beside Victor's maturity. She was afraid his kiss would do nothing for her. She was equally afraid she'd like it, and what then? She wanted to say, *No, no, let's not do this, leave well enough alone.*

His hand touched her face, and the gesture, the cupping of her jaw, was eerie, because Victor had done it, too.

He is not Victor. He will never be Victor, and he will never be like Victor.

His mouth, his kiss, certainly wouldn't be. Victor's kiss had been measured. With Victor she had felt she was receiving what had never been given before. It wasn't true, of course, but she'd had that illusion, as though she was the first and last woman on earth and he the man privileged to know and love and taste her.

Joe kissed her.

Just one kiss. Very simple. Almost chaste. Almost familial. Thoughtful and tantalizing—which was the last thing she'd expected.

"Thank you," he said. He smiled, and the smile was more devilish, more rascally, than Victor's.

His kiss hadn't been like Victor's, and suddenly she was intrigued by Joe Knoll, not as Victor's brother but for himself.

Then, abruptly, he threaded both hands into her hair. This kiss was gentle but directed and certain, the kiss of a man pursuing what he knew he wanted.

She thought of Victor's hair, sparse and silver. She touched Joe's hair because it would be different.

His lips were not insistent but patient, knowing the kisses of many women, understanding and accepting that insistence could never bring him what he wanted.

She let her lips open, but her heart had already begun its too-familiar frustrated cry. *You're not Victor! I love Victor, and I'll never love you as much!* She felt her eyes grow wet.

He drew back:

"Sorry," he said, almost as though he understood where no other man ever had.

She waited for him to say something that would show he hadn't really understood, after all. *Sorry for coming on too strong.* Or, *I didn't mean to rush you.* Or something oblivious, as though he hadn't noticed her distress at all—which might be the case.

"Ah, Sabine," he said, leaning back on his hands. "Think you're doomed to it?"

"To what?"

"Never getting over Victor."

"Yes. I do believe that."

He didn't try to talk her out of it. Joe felt sorry for her. In his experience, people didn't get to pick who they fell in love with. She'd fallen in love with Victor and she loved him past death.

He said, "Did Teresa seem to still love him? After her accident?"

"I'm not sure. She was so…"

"Yes?"

"Well, she wasn't like any other wife I've ever met. I mean, she was a bit—crazy. Not like a mentally ill person. More like a Victorian idea of a madwoman. She seemed so very angry. Sometimes I thought she hated Victor."

"She may have."

Joe recalled his own flash of anger when he'd seen Sabine's tears a moment ago. It had dissipated almost at once. Anger had never won love, and he *wasn't* in love with Sabine, anyhow. He felt only pity for her, pity that she still missed Victor. Weren't such emotions supposed to wear out? How could she still recall his face or the sound of his voice?

"Why would she have hated him?" asked Sabine.

"For making sleds?" Joe shrugged. "Or just because he reminded her of when she was different."

Sabine thought about this. "I like talking with you," she finally said. "I've been lonely."

"I'm sure there are plenty of men in Oro who'd love to talk with you."

"No. I don't mean talk," she clarified. "I'm trying to say that you make me think. And you remind me of my childhood, of a time— I don't know, but I'd almost forgotten. There was a certain magic to it, and because Victor didn't love mountaineering, I tended to blot it all out or consign it to a back burner. Do you understand?"

"Yes." He'd consigned sled-making to a back burner, for other reasons. But now he was building sleds again. Today he'd had a young helper, as Victor once had. "Finn's a good boy," he said.

"You're one of the few who thinks so, believe me."

"Oh, he's wild. He came out of the womb as Blizzard-man, didn't he? Or that's my guess."

"Were you like that?"

"No. I doubt that I would have survived my parents' dying if I had been. I don't think Victor would've put up with it. He liked to wear the cape." Joe wished he hadn't said that. "In a different way," he added.

"Oh, I wasn't going to argue with you."

Her smile was wise, and he envied his brother not just this woman's love but the years they'd shared and the intimacy. Sabine had known that Victor liked to rescue others and perceived himself as someone who could remedy problems, could make everything better.

"Did he rescue you?" Joe asked her.

She considered what to tell him, how to explain. "No— not rescue. I tried to like Minnesota, but it— Well, it wasn't what I thought I wanted. I had about decided to throw myself at the mountains again, and I met Victor. He and Teresa were the first people I'd really felt for—felt sorrier for them than for me—since my father died. And I'd really never believed I could love a person more than I loved mountaineering."

"I don't think I can."

She looked at him. "Then, why did *you* come back? You don't want to make sleds more than you want to climb mountains, do you?"

"There are mountains here—and challenges."

That couldn't be the whole answer. When did you know a person well enough to perceive if he spoke the truth? Clearly, she hadn't known Victor well enough.

"Want to risk another kiss?" he said, and she wondered if she was one of the challenges he'd found in Oro.

She shrugged. "Sure."

He gathered her close to him.

Sabine liked the closeness, the touch. She liked everything about it, except that he wasn't Victor.

She knew, knew instinctively and deeply and also from experience, that it was a mistake to commit herself to, or go along with, a relationship in which she felt significantly less for the other person than he did for her.

However, Joe Knoll had not, so far, behaved in a way she found difficult to admire or accept.

So she kissed him back.

Her mouth opened, and he tasted her with his tongue.

She realized she couldn't remember Victor's smell. She realized again, again, again, that he was gone and would not return.

CHAPTER EIGHT

IT WASN'T LONG AFTER that kiss, when there'd still been no word from Greg or the search-and-rescue group, that Sabine had announced she should go to bed so she'd have energy to shovel.

Joe lay on the futon in the loft hours later. Sabine had seemed so delicate in his arms, better than anything he deserved. She didn't seem to find herself too good for him, though. Rather, she loved Victor or loved his memory and was deadened to desire for anyone else. She had spoken briefly of the man she'd dated, been lovers with, two years earlier. Hart Someone-or-Other. *I can't explain,* she'd said. *It's just that life has deeper meanings and some people don't get that. They want more money or a bigger house or to go to Europe before they die or...*

Joe had said, *What's the deeper meaning?*

She hadn't answered.

But he understood. Understood that Victor had known those deeper meanings, Victor with his gift for listening. Did he, Joe, feel that life held a meaning beyond the things that were supposed to be the hallmarks of a happy life— marriage and children and family? To love, to feel some grace in simply being human?

Was it something he had ever sought in his partners?

No. And in himself? His motivation, his *raison d'être* had been Joe Knoll.

What was it now?

The sale was going forth. He had chosen this life, although without forsaking the Himalayas, and from now on, this would be the place he called home.

He liked having Finn out in the shop with him when he worked. Victor's son was a handful, and more than once Joe had wondered how Victor would have managed being a father to this particular child. Finn wandered around the shop, climbing on things and jumping off. Joe had made rules and enforced them consistently, but Finn seemed to have a knack for getting into trouble. He'd banished Finn to the house after an especially dangerous breach—turning on a table saw. Finn had thrown a tantrum, and then after Joe had carried him, kicking and punching, back to the house, Finn had suddenly quieted and given him the silent treatment.

Did he now care about Sabine's children?

He was fond of them. Which didn't equal being willing to sacrifice for them or anyone else.

For Sabine?

No. Sabine wasn't interested in a relationship with him, was interested only in mourning Victor.

Move on, he wanted to tell her. *You love someone who's been gone from the planet for quite a while now.*

But clearly, for reasons he could know nothing about, she wasn't ready to move on. And he knew better than to become emotionally involved with a woman who couldn't return his feelings.

In the loft upstairs, he sat in the lotus position, trying

to meditate. He'd practiced Buddhism in Nepal, but he did not consider himself a Buddhist. In the mountains, he touched the divine, and the divine of the mountains was closer to him than a lover. Women said they understood this, even claimed to feel the same way, but Joe doubted them.

He emptied his mind. He had no idea how much time passed. A quiet peace came to him, and then headlights crossed the walls, walls paneled in pine by Victor, Victor who did nothing by halves. A moment later, he looked at the window. A vehicle had pulled up behind Sabine's station wagon.

No flashing lights. So not a sheriff bringing bad news. But another messenger, who could be bringing the worst.

Joe stood and descended the stairs. He yanked on his boots and grabbed his coat. He had no opinion about whether or not Lucy was dead. The human capacity for endurance frequently astonished him. He'd found himself looking out for Sabine these past few days. It was an instinct, perhaps filling a void left since he'd quit guiding. Maybe he had to look out for someone.

It was Greg's truck, and Greg left it running as he walked up to the house. Joe followed him toward the door, wondering if Sabine would want him there. He decided she wouldn't care one way or the other, as long as he wanted nothing from her.

Sabine and Greg came out together and walked toward the truck. The passenger door opened. Sabine called, "Don't get out! You're not supposed to be doing that."

The sigh, the bite within him, was a keen relief Joe

hadn't expected. A kind of joy. There would be no death here. Lucy was back.

He hadn't met Sabine's sister, although he knew her name because of her reputation as an adventure racer.

Sabine bent into the passenger door, hugging the person inside. "What *happened?* Are you going to Greg's tonight?"

Joe felt that he was intruding now.

Should he turn away and leave?

Sabine glanced up. "Joe. Come and meet my sister."

Again, relief. Relief at her kindness.

Lucy Ingram sat in the passenger seat, her arm in a splint, her face, round, broad, a face to match her stocky build, deeply windburned. "I broke a binding."

She told the tale of how she'd spent one night outdoors as she made her way to a hut, where she'd remained, living on her own supplies and water melted from snow, until this morning when she'd left her shelter on jerry-rigged skis. Joe stood in the shadows, slightly back from the open door.

Sabine finally said, "This is Joe, by the way. Victor's brother. He's living in the shop."

Lucy, her strawberry-blond hair awry beneath a close-fitting navy hat, squinted up at him in the dark. "Hi."

She was attractive, but not in a way that would attract every man, not like Sabine, who was beautiful, who was stunning, whom any man would desire. Lucy seemed strong and fierce as a woman warrior. He wondered if she'd become so successful, so famous, because she was the younger sibling and determined to prove herself. He wondered if he'd ended up climbing Everest—and other 8,000-meter peaks—for the same reason.

Greg climbed behind the steering wheel again, and Sabine hugged her sister once more. "Rest, and I'll see you tomorrow. I am so glad you're back. So glad."

Joe stood with her as Greg backed out of the drive through the still-falling snow.

Sabine trembled beside him until he finally asked, "Are you okay?"

"Yes. Yes, I'm fine."

But she wasn't. He could see that, and he wondered if she was remembering the day Victor had not returned to her.

"Do you need to talk?" he asked.

"No. I don't want to talk about it. Everything's fine."

He'd been right—or so he suspected. No one could talk Sabine Knoll out of her continued mourning. That would require a love that struck like lightning—which he, Joe, had clearly not inspired. He could be a friend to her, as a favor to Victor, the same reason she was being kind to him.

Still, Joe couldn't help noticing that he had progressed from wanting to hurt anyone connected with Victor to trying to help instead.

It wasn't what he'd intended. He'd envisioned many things when he'd come to Oro—but making life better for Victor's wife and children had never been part of the plan.

THE NEXT MORNING, Lucy sat cross-legged on the ugly plaid couch in the living room of Greg's rented house and told Sabine the details of her brush with death. Sabine listened with half of her attention, the rest focused on her own daydreams of a racing career like Lucy's or of climbing mountains as she used to. Daydreams only. The danger Lucy had faced was something to which she couldn't expose her children.

"You seem friendly with Victor's brother."

Sabine blinked, became alert. "Oh. Well, I thought Victor would want me to treat him nicely."

Lucy lifted an eyebrow.

No frostbite, even. Sabine was surprised at herself for a bitterness mingled with jealousy. Was it the same voice that spoke next, spoke too sharply? "I'm not falling for him or anything, if that's what you're implying."

"He's nice-looking."

"You can have him," said Sabine, knowing perfectly well that her sister was completely committed to Greg. "I'm never going to fall in love again. Not like before. Whenever I try and get involved with somebody, I end up feeling as though I've devalued what Victor and I shared. Like I've settled for something cheap."

Lucy said, "Maybe you need to raise the bar on what you believe is possible."

"What does that mean?"

"Stop being so prickly," Lucy suggested. "I don't think I really believed in good relationships, love relationships, relationships based on love instead of—" She stopped. "Anyhow, I didn't until I saw you and Victor together, until I saw how happy you both were. Then I believed in it, and once I believed, Greg came along."

"Yes, but he didn't know he'd have to stay up three nights in a row looking for you in a snowstorm." The voice came from the doorway. Greg Lord, Lucy's boy-friend and rescuer, stood silhouetted in the kitchen door frame in Gore-Tex running clothes. But he gave Sabine a wink and came over to rumple Lucy's hair. "Tell you what. I won't make you return the favor today, how's that?"

Lucy laughed.

As Greg headed out for a training run, Lucy said, "Maybe if you believe you can fall in love again, that you can love another man even more than you loved Victor, it'll become possible for you."

"I'll believe it when it happens," Sabine said stubbornly. "And what were you going to say? A relationship based on love instead of—what?"

Lucy shrugged. "I think Mom and Dad just wanted to climb mountains. I'm surprised they didn't give us up for adoption."

"They *wanted* us," Sabine said firmly.

"You think?" Lucy's look was cynical.

Sabine thought with horror of how her own life had changed with Victor's death and how what she often wanted more than anything else was time to herself.

Still, she remembered the pleasure her father had shown in trekking with her and Lucy—and his pride in both of them. Her mother... Well, okay, she hadn't been *as* happy, undoubtedly because a mountaineer who was also a mother was treated differently from a mountaineer who was also a father. She'd been happy in the mountains, however, happy as departure for an expedition drew near. "Look," Sabine told her sister, "our parents loved each other."

"They used to fight."

Sabine stared at her. *She* was the older sister. *She* knew what had happened. "You dreamed that." The remark made her think of Maria telling Joe he'd dreamed his yeti.

"Are you insane?" Lucy asked.

"What are you talking about? I mean, yeah, they'd get grumpy every so often. Married couples argue. Victor and I did, too."

"Sabine, don't you remember?"

"Remember what?"

"He went after her with an ice ax. *And* he threw it at her."

"He did not! You dreamed that," she repeated. What Lucy was saying was as unbelievable as anyone's seeing an actual "Abominable Snowman."

"I did not dream it," Lucy insisted. "It was in China. That one trip. Mom had been on Everest."

Sabine knew the trip. She'd seen the yeti. That was when she'd seen it. In China. But Lucy's claim— "No way. They never got physical like that."

"Oh, yes, they did. *He* did. Don't you remember? You and I were out playing, and we came back to the tents, and Mom was struggling, and Dad was screaming at her. He had her by the hair, and he had an ice ax in the other hand."

And Sabine remembered. *I saw a yeti! Dad, I saw a yeti.* Why had she wanted to tell him, instead of her mother?

Because he'd always listened.

But he wasn't listening that day.

He let go of their mother, and then   "He didn't throw it at *her.* He just kind of tossed it down." There'd been more yelling that night, too. Then it had seemed to be over and done with. "But that was the only time."

Lucy didn't argue with her assessment. "I figure Mom must've had an affair with another climber."

Yes.

That had been it.

How did I blot that out?

Clearly this was the traumatic recollection that had lain buried behind her memory of seeing the yeti.

Her mother had been pretty. Yes, maybe Lucy was right that there'd been a certain distance between her and her husband at times.

"Don't you think they stayed together for us?" Lucy asked.

"No." But Sabine didn't voice the next thought that came to her—that perhaps her mother had stayed with her father simply because he sometimes cared for their daughters, allowing her to climb. And she had to tell Lucy one more thing. "Look, I've heard all the new-age nonsense I want to hear about believing I can love again. I don't even want it. Do you understand?" *I want Victor.*

But did she still? Had the longing changed? If so, what could have made that happen?

Oh, that's a poser, Sabine, she answered herself with an oddly cheerful sarcasm. She couldn't define her feelings for Joe, only knew they were changing, becoming deeper. But she wasn't in love. Maybe she cared more than usual because of the family resemblance she saw, his resemblance to Victor.

"I'm sorry," Lucy said. "You just seem so unhappy sometimes."

Sabine didn't answer, but she felt shame. It was one thing to long for something she couldn't have; it was another to impose her feelings on others, causing them sadness or concern. She said honestly, "I hurt Hart by getting involved with him. It's a great philosophy to love the one you're with, but it doesn't work that easily. Taking other lovers randomly isn't the answer. Love doesn't happen because you make yourself believe. You know that as well as I do. You and Greg are wildly attracted to each other, you have common interests, you share jokes, you're in love. I can't *make* that happen for myself. And if I try, I'll just cheapen myself."

Lucy glanced at her, as though surprised. Abruptly, she said, "Tell me how everybody is. Are we in a mess with shoveling?"

"No." Sabine told her what Joe had done.

Her sister appeared to be biting her tongue.

Sabine looked at the clock. "I've got to go pick up Tori. I'll see you later. Call if you need anything."

"Hey, I've raced in worse shape than I am now."

Sabine knew, and her jealousy returned in full measure. She missed running long distances where the air was too thin. Missed dragging her body up, up, through even thinner air.

But she wasn't going to tell Lucy that.

She was going to pick up her youngest fatherless child, and when Joe Knoll offered to help her with the kids, she would let him. He was no more in love with her than she was with him, and he was too sensible to fall for her, especially if she didn't succumb and become his lover.

But the sale of the property would go through on December twenty first, the winter solstice. And then Joe's year as her housemate would begin.

Already, again, she missed Victor less.

OVER THE NEXT FEW WEEKS, as Christmas drew near, Joe watched Sabine struggling with her children's increased level of excitement and activity. Most afternoons, Finn came out to the shop with him and helped him make sleds or played with pieces of wood. But inevitably, he grew bored and began acting out. So, as the weather cleared and turned cold, Joe took him—and sometimes Tori—sledding on the slope behind the shop, which Sabine said had been Victor's test hill.

One day he arrived at the house to find not Sabine but Karen inside. He told Karen that Finn usually came out to the shop with him at that time of day.

"I guess that's all right," Karen said. "It's nice of you to help Sabine," she added in her girlish voice, the voice that sounded younger than she was. "I looked up your guide service on the Internet."

"It's not mine anymore." But that didn't matter. If she'd been searching for him on the Internet, she could have discovered less innocuous facts about him.

But if she had, she would already have told all of Oro, wouldn't she?

"Which mountains have you climbed?" she asked.

He wasn't sure what answer she wanted. "Truthfully, it's a long list."

"Not eight-thousand-meter peaks. Those are the ones I mean."

He did not like the question and didn't want to answer. First, there were only three on the list. Really, his record was nothing to brag about—even the better part of his record. He didn't know what to say or how to say nothing without appearing rude.

"It doesn't matter," he said. "There are plenty of people who've done more. And they're just mountains." Saying that felt disingenuous. Since when had mountains been "just" mountains to him?

Since never.

"It's nice for Sabine," Karen said, "to have someone taking care of her kids for her."

Joe knew where this was going. "Where are they, by the way?" he asked.

"Maria is at a Girl Scout meeting, and Finn and Tori are both having time-outs in their rooms."

Joe decided not to ask what they'd done. "It's still all right for Finn to come out to the shop?"

"After he has his snack." She nodded at a plate of apple slices starting to brown.

"Shall I come back then?"

"That's probably best. *I* don't like to let them get away with things they shouldn't get away with."

Meaning, Joe surmised, that Sabine spoiled her children and Karen didn't approve. *You're one unhappy female*, he reflected. It had never particularly mattered to him if his girlfriends were people who could get along with other women, but he *could* tell whether or not this was the case.

However, Karen might be able to fill in some blanks for him—if he asked in the right way and was willing to hear the response she gave, which he doubted would flatter Sabine.

"Were you here when my brother died?"

"In Oro, you mean?"

He nodded.

"Yes." Her tone showed some reservation, almost as if she knew or thought things she was reluctant to say— which meant she would say them, given the chance.

"Did you know him?"

"Well, no. I mean, Sabine and I weren't really friends, and Lucy hadn't moved here yet. You've met Lucy, you know that she and Sabine are really different from each other."

Here we go.

"I did see Victor every once in a while. I bought a kick-sled from him, and he was really nice. I felt a bit sorry for him."

This was an angle Joe hadn't heard yet. He lifted an eyebrow and waited.

"He was so nice, and Sabine always had him looking after the kids. I don't know what *she* was doing all that time. He earned the money, as far as I could tell."

Joe said nothing.

"And—" Karen shrugged. "Well, the rest doesn't matter anymore."

"The rest?"

"Oh, I think she got a little tired of being married to someone that much older. It's only natural. She was so young when she married him, she was bound to have second thoughts."

"She seems to have idolized him."

"That's *now,*" Karen told him. "But back then it was pretty clear that they couldn't go on indefinitely. I think she's one of those women who's just determined to be unhappy. She has these three beautiful children, but she'd rather shovel snow than play with them."

Exactly how old was Karen? he wondered. Did she wish she had children of her own and envy Sabine her motherhood? Not avenues to explore. Karen was

Sabine's childcare provider. Little as Joe liked her, Sabine needed her.

I should tell Sabine everything, he thought. *Everything that had happened on Everest. She'll find out anyhow. This woman probably already knows.*

But he liked the new respectability he seemed to have, in Sabine's eyes. How would she see him if she knew what he was really like?

No, not what he was like. Rather how he had once been. *You're not condemned to be like that the rest of your life. That's why you're here, in Oro.*

He decided to steer the conversation elsewhere. "What brought you to Oro, Karen? You—" He smiled. "I hope you don't mind my saying so, but you look like a city girl to me."

"I am." Karen turned her fine-boned profile toward him. "I grew up in Washington, D.C. My father was a physician at Walter Reed."

"He's retired?"

"He passed away when I was fifteen."

"I'm sorry." After a minute, he said, "So, did you always live there?"

"I moved to New York when I became a model."

Joe nodded.

"I'm thinking of going back to the city," she said, "to meet people. You know. There aren't many…opportunities… here."

"It sounds like a good idea," he said, still curious about her reasons for coming to this very small town. "What brought you to Oro?" he repeated.

"Oh, I was engaged to the man who owns the new ski area. Hart Markham?"

Ah. Sabine's lover after Victor's death. So Hart Markham was wealthy, and Karen had been engaged to him.

"What happened?" Joe asked.

"We wanted different things. He treated me *really* well, but I wanted a family. I wanted to raise my kids with good values. And he's…excessive. Everything's about getting the most expensive thing and making the biggest splash, and that's just not how I was raised."

He'd heard Sabine say something similar.

Karen went on. "Also, I like being independent. That's why I got my real estate license, and there's definitely money to be made in Oro."

"Did your brother come here with you?"

"Afterward. He came to help me when Hart and I broke up. I needed to move furniture and such."

"It must be nice to have a family member here."

"Yes," she agreed.

"Were you…upset after the breakup?"

"Well, you get used to being together. It's like we were married, not like the little affair he had with Sabine, which lasted hardly any time. We lived together for five years. I knew I had to get out of the situation if I ever hoped to get the things I really want in life."

"Which are?"

"Oh, children. My university work was all about kids, and I just love them. So, it's hard for me to understand a woman like Sabine who has kids and doesn't take raising them as a serious responsibility."

Joe was tempted to look at the clock, to see how long Tori and Finn had been in "time-out."

"You think she doesn't?" he said.

"I don't think she even *wants* them. Anymore. And she did choose to have them. Some women aren't cut out to be mothers."

Joe had heard enough. "In my opinion, she does a great job. They're wonderful children, and they obviously adore her."

Karen's expression said he was naive. "Well, she's lucky to have you helping her," she replied with a smile. "I hope she appreciates it."

Joe finally glanced at the clock. "I'll come back for Finn in half an hour, shall I?"

"That's fine. I don't really know when Sabine will be home. I imagine she'll stay away as long as she can."

"Why would she do that?"

The voice came from the doorway behind them. Sabine must have crossed the porch soundlessly. Her hair fell in a loose braid, shot with starlight, mussed. Her cheeks blushed from the cold—or from anger?

Joe noticed again how profoundly blue her eyes were, the shade of a fall sky. He wanted to caution her, because she'd said many times how much she depended upon Karen, how irreplaceable she would find Karen.

But perhaps she knew that when the shop and the property sold, she would have money to stay home with her children?

Would she want to? The poison Karen had spread filtered through his mind as he waited for Karen to answer.

Karen said, "I just know you get tired. But you never even rest after shoveling."

Disgust at Karen's dissembling, or perhaps at her own acceptance of it, glimmered on Sabine's face. "Well, I'm home now," she said. "Thank you, Karen. I'll see you on Monday, I guess?"

"You don't need me this weekend?"

Shoveling, Joe knew, was more than a full-time job. But it hadn't snowed since the big storm.

"No," Sabine said simply. "Thank you. Where is everyone?"

Karen repeated what she'd told Joe, gushing, "Tori can't wait to see you. She wants to show you what she did in preschool."

"I want to see it," Sabine replied evenly. She dropped her pack on the table and started for the stairs.

I feel sorry for her, she thought as she climbed the steps. Would Karen be two-faced and hypercritical if she had what she wanted in life, a husband and children? Sabine knew Karen had tired of waiting for Hart to grant her those things and had broken up with him.

She went to Finn's room first, but Tori heard her and yelled, "Mommy!" and came running toward her. Sabine scooped up her youngest daughter and kissed her, then knocked on her son's door. If Karen was watching, or heard Finn shout *"COME IN!"* no doubt she'd have plenty to say about the way Sabine handled discipline, but Sabine was too tired to care.

In any case, she needed the woman's help for only a little longer, and Karen wouldn't do any lasting harm. It was just words with her, and Sabine could withstand Karen's words. She'd had plenty of practice.

CHAPTER NINE

IT WAS CRAZY that he should quail from telling her what had happened on Everest, the event that had lost him his lover and turned him away from the mountains for the first time since Teresa had left him for Victor. Would Sabine refuse to sell him the shop if he told her the story? Or renege on her agreement that he could live in her house? No. Would she say he was not a good influence on her children? No. Was there any law that could touch him here or anywhere, prosecuting him for what was only a crime of conscience? Of course not.

But he wouldn't tell her while the children were awake.

And that night Lucy and Greg came over after dinner. Sabine invited him to join them in sharing a bottle of cognac, which had been a gift from Norah. Joe sat quietly near the fire, listening to the other three talk. Eventually, the conversation turned to Karen.

"She's a bitch," said Greg, pulling no punches. "I can't stand her. Every time you see her, she's got something nasty to say about someone else."

Sabine remained silent, and Joe followed her example.

Anything he had to say about Karen wouldn't be good.

Lucy looked at him. "Have you made any sleds to sell for Christmas?"

"I'm not selling any until—" He stopped. "I need to decide what to call the business. Truthfully, I'm not doing anything till we close."

Lucy turned to her sister. "Well, I guess now is the time. Greg and I want to tell you something, Sabine. And you're family, too, Joe."

Sabine tensed.

"I miss the mountains," Lucy said.

"These are mountains," Sabine answered, as one who refuses to hear what she hears and to understand what she understands.

"The Himalayas. We have an offer to work together at Everest Base Camp this season, and we're going."

Sabine did not ask if they would return to Oro. Once again, Lucy was free to go where she wanted and to be who she liked, an option Sabine didn't share. She had made her choices and now must continue to embrace them.

A mix of despair and envy and rage filled her.

What would she do without Lucy?

And what wouldn't she give to return to the Himalayas herself, as a climber?

And why had Victor died, robbing her of consolation for all she was missing, the life of an athlete?

Finally, belatedly, like a sudden crescendo after a long rest, she recalled the last truth, the hideous truth.

The mountains, the high mountains, the sky mountains, were where people died.

Where her mother had died.

And, although her father had died in Canada, well…it was the same.

Lucy did not intend to stay at base camp. Sabine knew that. She would wait for a chance to guide, so she could summit Everest. All she needed was to get on someone's permit. With Lucy's background, that would be easy. If she wasn't courting sponsors already, it must be only so she could pretend to Sabine that she never planned to climb Everest.

She'll die in the mountains like our parents. Then my whole family...

Victor's death was somehow the worst.

I can't stop Lucy. If she wants to do this, there's no stopping her.

Lucy met her eyes. "You may as well say it."

"There's nothing to say."

"No, tell me I'm selfish and spoiled and care only about myself. That's what you're thinking."

It surprised Sabine to hear this but not that her sister had chosen to say it before an audience.

"That's not what I'm thinking at all."

"Then, you're thinking I'm going to die like Mom and Dad, and it's selfish of me."

"I hope you're not going to die—in any way—until you're about a hundred and six years old."

At the hearth, Joe studied the brickwork, just stared at patterns that weren't patterns. How ironic that on the night he'd intended to tell Sabine about his last expedition on the world's highest peak, this was happening.

Suddenly, he knew it wouldn't be okay with her, that she would judge him for what he'd done—and what he hadn't.

I don't need a judge. There are plenty out there. He

almost followed an urge to get up, say good-night to everyone and head for the shop.

The phone rang.

Sabine peered around for the cordless, but it was beside Lucy who picked it up, shaking her hair out of the way before putting the phone to her ear. "Hello?"

Joe heard a female voice and thought it was Karen's.

"Um, could we talk later?" Lucy asked.

More conversation. Joe's skin prickled. Karen, he sensed, was in full flow about something.

Sabine lifted her eyes to the ceiling.

Lucy listened to the voice on the phone. "In-ter-esting," she said slowly. "I can't really talk right now, Karen."

A question from the other end.

"Yes."

As she hung up, Joe was sure she glanced at him. But whatever Karen had said, Lucy chose not to repeat it.

Joe felt she would as soon as he left the room.

Why not let it happen? Sabine should have no illusions about who he was. She didn't like him, anyhow, even *with* whatever illusions she might have. He rose. "I'm going back to the shop. Good night, Lucy, Greg."

"Do you have an opinion?" Lucy asked unexpectedly.

"About what?"

"Sabine believes that if I work at Everest Base Camp, I'll start climbing again and will eventually die in the Himalayas."

"I'm *afraid* of that," Sabine corrected.

"It's a reasonable fear." Joe didn't want to say more. "No one can do that without seeing death. It's naive to think anyone's immune. But—" he shrugged "—I'm not

sure that's a reason not to do it. If you were my sister— "
he said to Lucy and abruptly stopped, leaving the thought
unfinished.

"If she was your sister, then what?" asked Sabine
sharply, as though his answer mattered to her.

"I would want you around," he said to Lucy, "but I
would realize that it's wrong to put someone in a cage. It's
wrong to prevent people from doing what they love, even
if you believe it will end in disaster. You're loved and
valued, Lucy. You need to weigh your life, your hopes and
dreams, against what might end up being very short-term
goals—with a high penalty for error."

He stuffed his hands in the pockets of his work pants,
frowning at the coffee table.

"I ask because you've done it," Lucy said. "And
because you've seen death."

The remark seemed significant. Karen's phone call? To
confess now would seem… Well, it would seem he was
telling the truth only because someone had found out,
only because he feared exposure.

But there was something he should say. "You also have
to take into account that people rely on each other up
there. You can make mistakes that have repercussions for
your teammates. I don't know why I'm telling you this,
Lucy, or why you're asking. You're an adventure racer, and
you and Sabine are mountaineers. You know these things."

But Lucy looked small, and he recalled that she and
Sabine had been children when their mother died.

She gazed at him. "Have you ever made mistakes?"

"Yes." Suddenly, he was angry. What had happened
was personal, whether or not he was the same as a

murderer, which was what had been said by some people, people who didn't understand.

You should have died yourself, had been the most memorable statement, in a letter from someone grieving and anguished.

Yet he had felt it so little. Only when his lover had said, *I know who you are now*—and left—had he begun to think.

There had been no need to leave the business, although he had. It was just controversy, and it hadn't really sullied his reputation.

"Good night," he repeated and headed for the door.

"HE LEFT A MAN to die on K2," Lucy said. "That's what Karen called to tell me."

"Just once in her life," Sabine said waspishly, "Karen should consider minding her own business. I think the problem is she doesn't have any."

"It was quite a nasty story. His own life wasn't in jeopardy. He just wanted the summit."

"I'd rather hear this from Joe," Sabine told her, surprised she felt that way. "You're just proving you don't belong up there, Lucy. Don't you remember or what? It's different up there. You know it is. Decisions are different, and the only person responsible for the loss of a life is the person who decides to climb one of those mountains."

"You like him." Lucy sounded a bit surprised.

"I like him well enough. He's had some tough times, but he doesn't whine." Sabine didn't know where this defense was coming from, didn't know when she'd begun to respect Joe this way.

Was it because Victor had betrayed him?

A notion occurred to her that she'd rather not examine, but which stared her in the face. Victor had wanted his brother's fiancée, and he had simply taken what he wanted.

And then, in the midst of his marriage to Teresa, had Victor begun to desire another woman? *Her?*

Yet he'd always seemed to respect the bonds of marriage. Engaged wasn't married, and Teresa and Joe had only been engaged.

But, Victor had neglected to mention that to her, not just while Teresa was alive but ever.

Just as he'd never mentioned that he had a brother.

Victor, why did you do that?

She listened for a reply that didn't come, that would never really come. The only reply, the only reply that mattered was that she hadn't known him as well as she'd believed.

"It was a nineteen-year-old kid." Lucy's revelation cut into the brief silence. "Joe should've been looking out for him."

"He was a client?" Sabine asked, more impatiently and less compassionately than was her wont.

"No. Just inexperienced. But he was part of Joe's party."

Sabine ignored it. She hated stories like this. Joe would have a version of what had happened, and other people who'd been there would have their versions.

Karen, needless to say, hadn't been there.

Neither had Sabine.

And in the mountains... *Isn't that part of why you left,*

Sabine? That you didn't like the rules? Or the lack thereof?

Someone, the man who'd lent her the cabin in Minnesota, had suggested that there were aspects of life worth living, aspects she might never know if she continued climbing in the Himalayas. And hadn't she believed she was living a half life, a life that exposed her to a very limited sector of humanity?

But now I could go back. I've seen other things. Done other things.

Risk her life, the life that belonged to her children? She never would. Never.

The thought both satisfied and depressed her.

It also made her wonder again why Joe Knoll had walked away from that sort of climbing challenge—how he'd been able to do so.

"I'll be careful, Sabine. And I'm not *planning* on climbing Everest. This job offer is for Base Camp Manager."

"I know," Sabine said. *And I know what'll happen when the opportunity arises.*

She was sure that Lucy also knew.

THE CHILDREN WERE IN BED when Sabine put on her parka to walk out to the shop. She told herself she'd had too much cognac, and she knew she wanted to blame all her recklessness on the alcohol.

But she'd had very little, and hours had passed since then.

If it's regrettable, she thought, *I want an excuse.*

No, any way she looked at it, getting more involved

with Joe, more intimately involved, was a bad idea, a stupid idea.

But she'd agreed to let him stay in the house.

Lucy was inside with the kids, sleeping or super-sleeping, as she called it, preparing for her biggest training session since before she went missing.

So there was nothing keeping Sabine in the house. Not for hours. If her children couldn't find her, they would wake Lucy. And Lucy would know where she'd gone.

His lights were on downstairs, and as she approached, she saw him sanding the deck of a Minnesota flyer. He looked different at the task than Victor had. Victor had always given the impression that he could do two things with simultaneous perfection—working and listening. Joe looked as though he was having fun. He had music on. As Sabine reached the door, she recognized The Who.

She knocked, and the volume went down before he opened the door.

They looked at each other, and Joe stepped back to let her in.

He studied her face. Had Lucy filled her in on whatever Karen had said? He'd thought of little else since he'd returned to the shop. But he wouldn't bring it up. "How are you?" he asked instead.

"Good," she answered too quickly. "Pretty good, I mean. I don't want Lucy to go. And I wish I was going instead of her."

His wry smile sympathized with her feelings—and reminded her of Victor. What would Victor say if he were here?

He'd probably ask, sweetly, if she'd prefer to stay with him.

And she would have. Always.

It just wasn't an option anymore.

"Did Karen tell Lucy something about me?"

Sabine was surprised. "Are you psychic?"

"I don't have to be. She said she'd looked up my guide service—well, the one I sold—on the Internet. The story is out there."

"I told Lucy," Sabine said, "that I wasn't really interested in hearing about it from anyone but you."

He sat on one of the work stools, staring at his hands. "A young climber named Chris Monegan was with me and two other people on an Everest expedition."

"Everest?" Sabine blinked. Getting the wrong mountain—the wrong country, for that matter—was an almost hilarious statement on the worth of Karen's information.

"I didn't like the conditions, and Pierre—one of the others—wasn't feeling great. Three of us decided not to go for the peak, but Chris was keen to be the youngest person on the summit. He said he wanted to pursue another route—for which he had no permit. We pointed out the illegality, not to mention general stupidity, of the plan. But he got up in the middle of the night and left. You know what it's like up there. Going after him wasn't feasible—one or all of us were likely to die if we did that."

Yes. Sabine saw that at once. The young man had acted alone, against advice, taking his life in his hands. The conditions on the mountain didn't matter. By his choice,

Joe's companion had endangered the rest of the team, who'd already made the safer, more conservative decision. Joe had acted wisely, and it couldn't have been easy.

"Here's where it gets bad," he admitted. "Chris had jeopardized my business position, although this wasn't a commercial expedition. When he disregarded my advice—basically refused an order—I led the others down and persuaded them to pack up and leave without him. He died on the mountain."

Sabine said nothing. She had seen so many things of this nature in the Himalayas. Climbers became ruthless and sometimes made choices that seemed bizarre to others who had never known the thin air of the Death Zone. She had been involved in situations where compassion had lost out to goals that seemed—in the heat of it—to weigh evenly with human life. But the balance was unequal. "You couldn't have gone after him."

"It would've been foolish. The bad part was leaving base camp as we did. When it comes down to it, I was frightened."

"Of?"

"Insubordination I hadn't been able to stop. The possibility of his not dying but being injured, and the loss of life resulting from a rescue attempt. The variables. I wanted to control the outcome, and this was the closest approximation. At first it seemed expedient. But all along it felt like what it was—cowardly and self-interested."

But there was courage in saying so. Sabine didn't know another man who would have been so honest.

If Victor had been a mountaineer, she wondered, if he

had chosen to risk his life in the mountains, would she find any excuse for teammates who'd abandoned him?

"Did you know—" She stopped, not sure she should ask.

"Did I know what?"

"His family?"

He shook his head.

"Did they ever try to contact you?"

"Not as far as I'm aware." He remained silent for a moment. "I was seeing someone. She was with me. She didn't want to leave base camp. Afterward, after she'd learned he'd died, she didn't want to—" He didn't bother to finish the sentence.

"Did you know her well?"

"I lived with her for several years."

Sabine understood the reaction—and the choices—of his lover. There had come a point with Hart Markham when she'd known that he had a mean streak and a curious lack of compassion that would be a problem if he ever took against her for some reason. She didn't trust him, but that wasn't all. There'd been other lacks in him. A lack of depth, for one thing. She'd considered asking Karen what they'd found to talk about for so many years.

But Joe… She wanted to believe that he was deep. And maybe she wanted to believe, too, something at which he'd only hinted—that the tragedy on Everest had changed him, had made him look beyond himself in a way he hadn't since Victor and Teresa betrayed him.

She asked, "Will there be enough stimulation for you here, do you think? Making sleds isn't as exciting as mountaineering."

"We hope," he added, and the darkness in his voice reminded her of Teresa's accident.

"Yes," Sabine agreed but thought only of Victor.

"I don't plan to stop climbing."

Oh.

It became imperative to her that she not love him. *My parents both died in the mountains. My sister is going to die there. Now, Joe... I don't love him. I can't love a climber. I hate them all.*

He asked, "Is Lucy inside with the kids?"

"Yes."

He picked up his sander again. After a moment, he said, "Have you ever had big dreams, Sabine? Being a famous racer like your sister? Or climbing the Seven Summits?"

The question only partly distracted her from the tension going through her body, the tension that had to do with people who loved mountains more than people. She herself was a woman who'd loved people who loved mountains more than people.

"I just want to spin. I love to spin. And I want the freedom to run—long runs, mountain runs. Maybe to climb mountains. But I won't choose mountains over my children." Her voice shook as she said it.

"Any other dreams?"

Bringing the dead back to life? she considered replying.

But she no longer felt that way and was curiously ashamed of the thought. Instead she asked, "What about you?"

"Mountains."

It doesn't matter. I don't love him.

But she was curious. "What were your plans when you married Teresa? For work, I mean?"

"I planned to continue doing this—" he nodded at the sled pieces "—with Victor."

"Are you glad you went to Nepal instead?"

"Yes." He glanced at her. "And I'm glad I came back."

"For a while." With most men, she would not have asked why he was glad to have come to Oro. If it had anything to do with her, she didn't want to know. But she asked Joe.

He studied the wood of the sled deck. His answer had nothing to do with the question. "I'm going to make some snow skates," he said. "You know, like skateboards but for snow."

"Oh, a skateboard on a ski," she said.

"Yes. I'm glad I came back because it's forced me to think of other people and to…deepen my existence. The mountains are a challenge in one way, but there are other challenges."

"I think relationships are a huge challenge." She wished she could bite it back.

"You've never said yours with Victor was."

"I didn't necessarily mean between men and women. Or love relationships, in-love relationships. Friendships can be challenging. Parent-child. My relationship with each of my children is challenging."

He had kissed her once, and Sabine wanted him to kiss her again. But she wasn't sure why. Because of simple attraction? There was an element of that.

To pay Victor back for having lied to her?

This felt like the first time she was putting it into words, even to herself, the first time she believed, truly believed, that he'd lied to her, had intended to lie to her.

"Do you think," she asked, "that Victor ever feared revenge from you?"

Joe raised his head, like a predator scenting prey on the wind. But the prey wasn't her. It was understanding, discovery of something he'd never seen till then. "What kind of revenge?"

She couldn't say what she was thinking. Not yet. She led into it instead. "Say…that you'd return and Teresa would prefer you."

He seemed to consider. Then his eyes lowered to meet hers. "Or you would?"

She didn't deny it.

"I don't know him, didn't know him, well enough to say," Joe answered.

But Sabine realized she now knew Joe well enough to ask what most puzzled her. "Do you have any idea why Victor wouldn't just have told me about you—and about Teresa? There was no real reason to hide it. What he did wasn't nice—I know it as well as you do—but it's not as though you were married. And even that happens. In either case, not telling me was much worse than the offense itself. I mean, not even to tell me he had a brother…"

Joe shrugged, "Maybe he didn't like being reminded that Teresa ever loved someone else."

"Oh, please. She married him. And it sounds as though you were out of their lives after they got married."

"That's true."

"He must have known," Sabine said, to herself as much

as to Joe, "that I'd be more upset by his lying to me than by his st—well, marrying your fiancée."

"Stealing my fiancée? I don't know if he would've perceived it that way. Didn't you ever see him lie to someone to save the person's feelings?"

"Y-es," she said slowly.

"So did I."

"But this lie protected him, not me."

What she was saying troubled Joe. He'd come to Oro expecting that this woman would never have heard of him. But *why* had he been so sure of that? What part of Victor's personality had he understood that explained Victor's being so secretive, secretive to the point of deceiving the person who mattered to him most?

"I think," he said slowly, "that he liked the image of himself as being exceptionally good, as someone who'd make the difficult choice and do the right thing. I don't think he liked remembering that sometimes he chose what he wanted instead. Could that have been it?"

Strange, Sabine reflected. She'd been willing to call it shame. Victor had wanted to avoid the feelings of shame that loving his brother's fiancée had brought.

"He must have believed you were much more handsome, more exciting, than he was," she said. "He must have believed, or told himself, that you could have any woman you wanted."

"That makes it all right?"

"Of course it doesn't. But marrying Teresa, falling in love with Teresa and marrying her, aren't the only things Victor ever did. He *was* a good person."

You sound like you're trying to convince yourself. Joe

didn't say it. Neither of them needed convincing. They were probably the two people in the world who'd known Victor best.

Except Teresa.

So easy to forget Teresa's life with Victor when she'd been a partner, before she had become unwillingly dependent because of the injuries that had changed her.

Joe used to smile, thinking what a merry hell Teresa must have created for Victor with her nonstop flirting, her refusal to sober up or grow up. Then she'd been injured, and there was nothing to smile about. He knew that Victor, too, would have much preferred the first brand of hell to the second.

"You're not at all like her," he said.

Sabine didn't ask who he meant. And she wasn't sure that what he'd said was a compliment.

"You're more mature," he continued.

"It's possible I'm just more boring."

"Well, you're quieter. Don't people say still waters run deep?"

"I suspect men say that when they want to invent a personality for a woman they think is beautiful." She sounded almost bitter.

"Have men invented personalities for you?"

"Oh, yes." She shrugged. "It's a little sad sometimes. Sometimes, someone'll say, 'I know you better than you know yourself.' But really, all that's happened is they've invented some woman in their heads, a woman compatible with an outcome they want, in which she loves him and has his children and they live happily ever after."

"But Victor was different?"

And then she knew. It was like being hit on the head with a hammer—or being forced to look at a photo of something horrifying—or seeing death. It was a kind of death, one she hadn't been able to face with Victor's death. Instead, she'd let her own knowledge die with him and replaced it with something that might be untrue.

"No." She shook her head. "Victor was no different. He invented a wife for himself, too."

CHAPTER TEN

JOE GOT UP to feed the woodstove. This was the first time he'd heard Sabine suggest that her marriage to Victor had been less than perfect. When he glanced back at her, she sat staring thoughtfully at the worktable. Instead of returning to her side, he shut the stove door and leaned against the side of the staircase with his hands in his pockets. "Was there something about you Victor wouldn't acknowledge?"

"It's not that exactly. I don't think it was important to him to know who I really was. He created his own picture of Sabine Ingram. Sometimes it fit. Sometimes it didn't." She considered it herself, trying to get at the root of what she'd just admitted. "For instance, if I'd told him I wanted to climb again—that wouldn't have fit with the picture of me he'd created."

But it was more than that. She tried again to explain. "When I spin and dye and weave, I do particular things with the colors. It's not just what looks pretty. I think about stories. Family tales mostly. I write cards to go with the yarn. I always put a quote from the legend or story that inspired the color combination with each skein of yarn, identical for a dye lot. I do the same for a knitted or woven garment. Victor would generally say something *else* about the stories, something that made them reflect the two of us. And that was all right, but I think a lot of fairy tales are about *women*. About how we grow and change. He liked everything to be the two of us."

Then how had his and Teresa's marriage survived? Joe wondered. "Was he jealous?"

"No. It wasn't like that. And I suppose it's natural in marriage to give up one's own identity for a new identity that comprises both of you. But the new identity should be more than the sum of its parts." Sabine heard herself with horror. *Had* her marriage to Victor equaled more? Now, asking the question for the first time, she felt uncertain.

"Don't worry." Joe seemed to read her mind. "With three kids, I think you qualify."

"That's not what I mean." But then she saw that he was kidding. That he did understand what she'd said.

Joe cautioned himself not to read too much into any of it. Did Sabine's admission about Victor presage a change in her? If it did, what was that to him?

A lot.

Why was it so hard to admit he cared about her? And was he creating her as a fantasy, as she claimed most men did? Or did he love the true Sabine Knoll?

Love.

The idea of loving her, of being in love with her, closed around him. He felt like gasping for air, as though he were in the thinnest air of all.

Joe watched her from across the shop, then abruptly stared at the floor, averting his eyes.

"What?" she asked him, waiting.

He didn't look up. His voice was quiet. "I want to make love with you, Sabine."

Her legs shook. The muscles and tendons no longer seemed connected, as though only bones supported her and they, too, were failing.

This was not what she'd felt with Hart Markham. That whole affair had been so unfelt that she wasn't sure she'd ever been wholly present.

She was present now.

What was more, she was herself, perhaps more herself than she'd ever been with Victor. She was firmly inside her own skin.

And everything she'd told herself about climbers and mountains and death and Victor and who she could love and who she did not love and who she would never love— it all trembled, formed a crack, the kind that prefaced an avalanche, a slide to change the landscape of her life. Joe was of her generation, and he was *like* her; she wanted him, and to love him would be more of a risk than climbing into the Death Zone.

"Yes," she said.

IT DIDN'T MATTER that she'd made love with Victor in the loft. Victor was not coming back.

Perhaps it was a flash of anger at Victor, anger at his desertion that made her so sure she wanted this. Or anger at herself, over what she'd just realized. Who she'd been in his eyes.

She did still love him, did still miss him. But had he ever really loved her? Had he ever *known* her?

He receded in importance. Joe was before her, real and alive....

On the futon, they lay down together, stripping off

outer layers first. They lay on their sides, and she watched his eyes, like and unlike Victor's, sweep over her. She remembered what love with Victor had been like. It had been based on trust.

Illusory trust.

She trusted Joe, too, and felt she shouldn't. Was he a man who would leave her to climb a mountain, meet a woman on the way and take that woman as his new lover?

What was his moral compass?

Was it the top of the mountain at any cost?

She paid no attention to his undressing of her or of himself. He had condoms. That thoughtfulness pleased her—pleased her because she had a distaste for men who wanted to make love without attention to birth control or health considerations.

The union with him was quiet, loving in ways she hadn't expected. His eyes focused again and again on her face. His kisses were leisurely. He said, "I didn't intend this to happen when I suggested my living at your house. Please don't feel that I'll expect this of you."

She had already sensed that; she also knew he wouldn't ask her to compare his love-making to Victor's. He was not immature.

She did not especially want to have an orgasm, though she knew she could have one easily. The intimacy was all she wanted. The way he looked at her, his quiet shuddering against her. She liked what he said afterward, which was, "Want to do it again?"

She laughed and hugged him.

Happy.

The sorrow was distant, lurking behind her somewhere.

He was not Victor. He couldn't be Victor. And loving Joe meant learning to love different characteristics.

Yet it didn't, because somehow love had *happened*. Sabine loved something inside him, some steadiness she felt.

The exterior was fine, as well.

He was tall, strong. She had never in her life loved a man for his appearance alone, but Joe's looks appealed to her.

What would it be like to climb a mountain with him? she asked herself.

She would never find out—not a real mountain. Mount Sneffels, Handies, Uncompahgre, one of the nearby thirteen- or fourteen-thousand-foot peaks. One of those she might climb with him, perhaps with the children.

But no Himalayan climbing. Not together. If she went with him, she would be waiting at base camp as she had when she'd accompanied her parents.

He had never hinted that he intended to climb.

She wasn't going to ask.

But I'm ahead of myself, she thought. *We've made love. This doesn't make a commitment.*

She was surprised at herself for wanting one. She'd never wanted a commitment to—or from—Hart Markham.

He wasn't the one for her.

Is Joe Knoll the man for any woman, though? Is he capable of commitment to anything but climbing?

He'd committed himself to buying the shop and the land. They would finalize the contract that week.

Be content with that, Sabine.

At two in the morning, she walked back to the house.

He had wanted her to stay with him—or to share her bed—but Sabine knew it would be better for the children if she slept in her own bed alone, as usual.

Before she went to sleep, she opened her nightstand drawer and removed a photo of Victor to look at. There was the smile she was used to, all the features she'd loved. Joe was so different. *Victor, what do you think? Is he a good man?*

But she'd answered that question for herself.

Joe was no better or worse than Victor had been.

AFTER SHE'D GONE, Joe lay alone on the futon, awake, still smelling her scent. He had not expected her to make love with him. And he knew it wasn't simply a physical act for her, that emotion was present, that she cared for him, that maybe she was falling in love with him.

He could commit to her, easily. He was monogamous by nature and had never enjoyed having many lovers. They were too easy, too impressed by his having summited Everest or some other peak.

Sabine he liked for herself. He liked her mothering, liked watching her spin, liked her company and her sense of humor.

But an obstacle lay between them.

Her parents had both died in the mountains, and she feared her sister would, too. She had not mentioned, yet, any fear for him, but it would tear her apart if he left on an expedition. Too many people did not return. Those who lived in the mountains often died in the mountains. To stay alive, a climber had to be not only good but lucky.

And no person could gauge his or her own luck.

He wanted to follow her into the house, to climb into her bed, to promise her that she was enough, that he didn't need the thin air.

But he couldn't make that promise.

"SO, HE'S LIVING in the attic?" Karen asked when she arrived to babysit three days before Christmas. It was 6:00 a.m., and Sabine was dressed to meet her sister and shovel some roofs. Though she would soon have money from the sale of the property, she needed to see her shoveling contracts through. Businesses were counting on her to protect their property by shoveling snow off roofs. Old people needed her to shovel their walks and their driveways.

"Yep," Sabine said. She felt more tolerant of Karen than usual, knowing that if she absolutely had to, she could stop asking her to babysit. Joe would help. Or, once she had the money, she could pay another sitter more than she paid Karen.

"So," Karen said eagerly, "are things…?"

Her voice hinted.

Sabine thought of Karen as a friend—but a friend she couldn't really trust, a friend too inclined to discuss her business with other people. Still, her children had already seen Joe kiss her. None of them seemed bothered by it. "We're involved," she answered.

"That's great!" said Karen. Karen who'd been willing to spread news of Joe's sins in the Himalayas. "I'm so happy for you. I know you haven't really been able to get over Victor."

Sabine had no answer to that.

"Do you think he'll, like, keep climbing?" Karen asked. "I know how you feel about Lucy going to Everest Base Camp."

Sabine almost said she doubted Karen really knew how she felt about anything. "It's not a requirement," she said. Because it couldn't be. You could never ask anyone to give it up. A person had to decide on his own, decide he wanted to live, decide not to die in the mountains.

She did not expect Joe to love her more than the mountains.

No one in her life, no one who'd loved the mountains, ever had.

Maybe that's why I love him. Because I know I'll never be first with him.

"Aren't you scared?" Karen asked.

"Of what? He's not going anywhere today."

"Well—just don't get hurt," Karen replied.

Sabine said, "That's not what life's about," and went outside. Victor hadn't been a mountaineer, and he had been taken from her.

THAT AFTERNOON, she and Joe took the children to cut a Christmas tree. Sabine hadn't cut a big tree since Victor's death. She didn't enjoy hanging the ornaments they had chosen together, some of which he'd made. She didn't like remembering the surprises he'd given her for Christmas.

She didn't like missing him.

They didn't choose a big tree this year, either, but it was bigger than any she'd had since Victor died. When they came home, Finn helped Joe test the lights and replace burnt-out bulbs.

They set up the tree in the spinning nook, near the windows, moving the wheels to make room. Halfway through the decorating, all the children got tired of helping and left Sabine and Joe. The television went on, and Maria picked up her spindle and began spinning.

She was learning to spin on a drop spindle. It was harder than using a wheel, but Sabine believed that her daughter would spin more expertly on a wheel if she learned first on a spindle.

Joe took an old glass Santa Claus from one of the boxes. "I remember these," he said, "from when I was a kid."

"There are some more like that," Sabine told him, glancing at him curiously.

"I'll be gone for a few months this spring and summer," he remarked. "It should work out well, since that's downtime for sled sales."

A sudden, jarring change of subject.

This was it then. Much sooner than she'd expected.

"Where are you going?"

"K2."

Shit. "Who with?"

She barely listened to his answers. Two of the team were well-known. Competent, as no doubt Joe was.

"Do you have sponsors?" she asked.

"Actually, I've been writing some articles, and my agent's been talking with a publisher about a book deal."

"What angle?" she asked.

"Why I climb. Why people climb. It'll involve interviews

with other people, too. And, yes, to the sponsorship question."

Sabine didn't answer. Not at first. There was nothing to say. K2, of Pakistan's Karkorum, was a brutal mountain, notoriously dangerous. She almost asked him if he wanted to die.

Instead, she imagined the feel of the hairs on his chest, imagined touching them. By the spring, so many details of his body would be familiar to her. *Then I'll lose him, just like Victor.*

Her reaction stunned her. *She was in love with him.* She was in love with him, and she wanted him to quit climbing mountains so that they could share old age, so that he could be a father to her children.

"Why *do* you climb?" she finally asked.

"For my self-esteem."

Sabine turned to him.

"I've been thinking about it. Victor had unassailable self-esteem. Then I was going to marry this woman I thought was terrific, and she fell in love with him instead. So I had to do something more than he could do. Every mountain I've climbed, I've told myself, *Victor can't do this.*"

"Maybe you could find something else that's good for your self-esteem." She hadn't meant to say it, and she covered her mouth with her hand, trying to recapture the words, the request she should not make and he would not heed.

She heard his breath escape slowly.

She wanted to say she was sorry, to say she knew he'd agreed to take part in the expedition, to say she was behind him.

The words didn't come out.

He turned and the heel of his hand brushed her cheek, a big hand like Victor's, and his fingers combed through her hair. He kissed her.

He didn't tell her he'd come back.

They both knew it would be an empty promise.

CHAPTER ELEVEN

ON CHRISTMAS EVE, Sabine lacked her usual excitement about seeing her children's happiness with their presents. She had knitted Finn a sweater with a Blizzardman snowflake on it. Tori had asked for Barbie dolls, and Sabine had gotten them for her, along with a Barbie boat to play with in the bathtub. Maria had asked for clothes and for beads to string. Sabine had also bought Finn a snowplow to play with outside and had gotten all the children some small metal skiers they could race down piles of snow. She'd bought Lucy a pale-blue fleece jacket she thought would look good with her sister's coloring, and Greg a compass with inclinometer.

She'd chosen two books for Joe. Jonathan Foer's *Extremely Loud and Incredibly Close* and, because she had read it and liked it, Jennifer Jordan's *Savage Summit,* about the first five women to summit K2, all of whom were now dead, climbing. The choice spoke of her own ambivalence. She wanted to inscribe those words about freedom from *Me and Bobby McGee.* Instead, she wrote nothing. Then, on Christmas Eve, she spontaneously went out and spent her entire share of a heavy-snow bonus from one of her shoveling contracts on the same model compass she'd bought Greg, the newest Tracker avalanche beacon

and the fee for a January avalanche safety course, all for
Joe. *I'm in love with him,* she thought almost desperately.

She wished she could turn off her love for Joe as easily
as she could have if he'd shown interest in another
woman. Another woman she would not have tolerated.
But mountains?

It took longer than usual to get the children to sleep.
Finn didn't drop off until eleven and then simply because
he could no longer keep his eyes open.

Joe was out working in the shop, and Sabine went
ahead and arranged the presents, eager to get to sleep
herself. Joe now slept on a futon in the attic. Sometimes
late at night, Sabine joined him there. She had never
invited him into her bed. In the past couple of days, she'd
begun telling herself that this was a form of self-protec-
tion. If her bed remained the place she'd made love only
with Victor, then she would never love Joe as much as she
had loved Victor, and Joe's disappearing into the mountains, to return or not, would bother her less.

He came inside just as she was turning off the living
room light.

He said, "Plug in the tree."

She almost told him she was going to bed but instead,
she turned on the Christmas tree lights and went into the
nook to sit on a pillow.

He had a stack of boxes with him, wrapped in pages
torn from magazines, homemade wrapping paper.

He set the boxes around the tree, and Sabine saw that
each was labeled. He kept out one small package and
handed it to her.

She said, "You want me to open it now?"

"I have more for you for tomorrow."

Wary without knowing why, she unwrapped the package. To her astonishment, it held a handcrafted wooden photo frame, with a photo inside.

They were young, Victor in his early twenties, Joe a child. They hung from the limbs of a sprawling oak tree, and both were grinning, Joe's grin missing teeth.

"Thank you," Sabine said. She didn't know if it was strange for her to love two brothers, strange that Victor had been so much older, strange that he'd never told her of Joe's existence or all of it equally strange. She asked, "Does this mean you've forgiven him?"

"I think I forgave him a long time ago."

"But didn't you still feel angry?"

"I'm not sure I'll never *not* feel angry at that memory."

"Teresa."

"Yes." He hesitated. "But it's not my heart that felt hurt. Well, my heart was hurt by *his* choices. Mostly, it was pride."

"He was disloyal to you," Sabine said. "If I tried to make Greg, Lucy's Greg, love me, that would be disloyalty. It would be an awful thing to do to my sister." She realized what she was saying, that Victor had done an awful thing to Joe.

"But what if you fell in love with Greg? What if, by spending time with him because of her, you came to love him?"

Sabine said, "I'd think I was the unluckiest person in the world. But I'd turn my back on the situation."

"Even if he didn't want to be with your sister anymore and wanted to be with you?"

She considered that. "It's impossible to really know, but I still think I'd pass. What happiness could he and I expect to have together by making Lucy unhappy?"

And what happiness had Victor expected? Hadn't he cast off his brother, for all intents and purposes? Hadn't he made clear that Teresa mattered to him more?

The thought chilled her. It wasn't just that he'd hidden things from her. It was that this one hidden action suggested to her that she hadn't known him at all.

"Fortunately," Sabine said, "I'm not attracted to Greg, and he's in love with Lucy."

"Very fortunately," Joe agreed.

They sat studying the picture. "I'm surprised," she said, "that you chose to give me this."

"It's a copy."

"That's not what I meant."

He cracked a smile but made no comment.

It occurred to her that he wasn't concerned anymore with whether she loved him as much as she'd loved Victor.

Odd how all the safety that had allowed her to love Victor so thoroughly was absent in Joe. She had known, when Teresa was dead and Victor showed interest in her, that he'd want to marry her. For all she knew, Joe Knoll didn't believe in marriage—not for himself. And while she'd foreseen that Victor would be a devoted, attentive and practical husband, she could nearly guarantee that Joe would always love climbing more than her.

She used to cry for Victor's return from the dead, but she no longer said that prayer.

Joe was an open door.

Unfortunately, the door led to the Death Zone.

She almost told him, then and there, that if he planned on going to K2 that spring, they should ease off on their relationship. But she'd never blackmail someone into quitting climbing. If she ended their relationship, it mustn't be with any hope that he would change.

And she *didn't* want to end their relationship. She felt as though part of her had died with Victor but was now reborn.

She would just have to be careful of her heart. She would have to measure her caring for him, not let it out of her control.

"I was wondering," he said, "if on another mountain— The approach to K2 isn't appropriate for it. But sometime, I'd like us all to be in the mountains together."

"So would I," she answered truthfully.

"I want to climb with you," he said.

"I'm out of practice and out of shape. And I don't think I'll climb in the Himalayas again. At least not till my children are grown. But even then—" She didn't finish.

"Do you think it's self-serving?"

"Don't you?" she demanded.

"Oh, yes." He gazed into her eyes for a moment.

It shocked her, as it always shocked her, that he had admitted to a cruel selfishness, a selfishness that would not stop his slow suicide for love or money.

Somewhere, sometime, it would happen. He would die in the mountains.

Anger pulsed through her. Again, she nearly told him she didn't want to be involved with him.

But she'd promised he could live in her house for a year. *Except for the days he'd be gone climbing K2?*

She could tell him that his trip was a violation of the agreement they'd made. If she was insistent, it might save his life for another year.

But freedom was a sovereign right.

It trumped love.

And negated it.

She couldn't say to herself with any conviction that if he loved her he wouldn't go. Because he wasn't wired that way. He had become wired to climb mountains *no matter what*.

He said, "Will you come up to the attic with me?"

"Yes."

THEY MADE LOVE, and afterward she said, "Tell me about the book. The book you're writing. Is it sold?"

"There's some bidding going on."

"Have you written part of it? What do you call that? A proposal?"

"Yes. The topic is why people climb, and it starts with a look at mountains as birthplaces of various religions. Then, indigenous attitudes toward different Himalayan peaks." He caught Sabine's suddenly closed expression. "What are you thinking?"

"I'm thinking," she said at last, "that I have no respect for the sport or the people who do it. I think it's self-serving, yes. And most mountaineers I know become impressed with their own accomplishments to the extent of not noticing the basic human skills they haven't mastered."

She'd said it, and it was out. There was no taking it back, and she didn't want to take it back.

"I've done it, too," she continued. "It's incredible. It's hard, it's amazing. You're trying to do something in which dying is part of surviving. It's a high like no other. The exhaustion, the thought that you really might not make it, the pain, the whole thing, all of it, I loved it. But it's not life. It's just not. It's a way to keep from growing up."

"You sound scared," he said.

"Of what?" she snapped and sat up, then got to her feet and pulled on her clothes. "*I* have a life. Scared Lucy will die? Scared you will? Yes. It's occurred to me. But I'm not telling anyone else how to live."

"You just told me."

"Merry Christmas," she replied coldly, walked to the door, opened it and went down the stairs.

When she reached her own room, she shut her door and lay on the bed Victor had made for them and took his photo out of her nightstand.

Now it was easy to wish him back.

But she wondered whether, if Victor had not fallen in love with Teresa and married her, his younger brother would ever have climbed any mountain at all.

TORI HOVERED over her as she unwrapped the large flat box that was marked, "Love, Joe and Tori." Mindful of her daughter's obvious excitement and trying to keep last night's spat with Joe from hurting this day and this moment, Sabine carefully separated tape from sky-blue tissue paper. From within, she drew out a stretch-lace dress in cloudy shades of gray and blue, and a long white hooded sweater-coat of woven raw silk.

"Now you can have a date!" Tori said. "Like Barbie."

Sabine laughed as she hugged her youngest daughter.

Joe's hand settled on the back of Sabine's neck. "Tori said that if you and I were dating, you'd need pretty clothes." His lips brushed the top of her head.

I can't help it. I can't help it. I love him. Loved him. Wanted him. Couldn't stop—or change—her feelings.

Besides the clothes, he'd give her fiber—raw merino and more exotic fibers. As she opened each package—and there were many—she saw that he understood and respected what she most loved to do. While she refused him a reciprocal understanding.

He'd made things of wood for all the children— something Victor also used to do, though she wasn't sure whether or not Joe knew that. For Tori, he had crafted a closet for Barbie doll clothes, for Maria a jewelry box and for Finn a wooden tank that shot wooden balls and which was Finn's favorite present. He shot balls at Tori's Barbie dolls, and when Tori then made the dolls lie down and rest, to recover from being hit, Finn joined in and made sure they had blankets on them.

But Joe had gone the extra mile. He had helped the children make gifts for Sabine. Maria had done her own. With the sense of responsibility of the oldest child, she had, on her own initiative, knit a scarf for her mother out of a wool the same blue as Sabine's eyes. Finn had made a totem pole, of sorts, for Sabine and painted it with acrylic paints. Tori's gift—besides the clothing, which Sabine would always think of as her Barbie date outfit—was a drawing.

"Karen wanted to help us make presents," Tori said, "but I wanted Daddy to do it."

"He's not Daddy!" shouted Finn. "He's Joe."

"I can call him Daddy if I want," Tori said.

"You're stupid," Finn told her. "You're the stupidest one in Colorado."

Joe said, "No good, buddy. You need to apologize."

"No, I don't!" Finn shrieked.

Joe took Finn upstairs for time-out, and Sabine asked Tori, "Why can't you call him Joe? Daddy is a special word, and he's not your daddy."

Tori fell mulishly silent.

Maria abruptly said, "I miss Daddy."

Sabine didn't respond, not convinced that Maria really remembered anything about Victor.

"He used to take me to town whenever he went. He always took me on sleds. He always walked with me. He always wanted to be with me."

She *did* remember.

"I like to be with you, too," Sabine told her. She sat down beside Maria, on the pillows at the foot of the tree, and put her arm around her oldest child. "I miss him, too," she said. "Do you want to go to the cemetery with me and visit his grave?"

Maria shrugged.

Only as Sabine hugged her did she notice that Joe had returned. How long had he been standing there?

"Daddy," Tori said defiantly and ran to him, as though making a statement.

Joe picked her up. "Tori," he said, "I don't mind your calling me that, but only if it's okay with your mom."

K2, thought Sabine. A daddy who climbs mountains and might not come home....

"It's okay," she said.

Women *did* tie their lives to mountaineers. Women bore their children. Loved them. Waited for them.

Couldn't she?

But Joe might not want that. Their relationship was still new, still untested.

Later, while the children were immersed in *The Incredibles,* Sabine began combing some of the wool Joe had given her, preparing it to spin into worsted.

Joe came and stretched out beside her, his long legs in blue jeans reaching alongside the tree.

He was her lover, and she felt tenderness toward him and too much love, too much for the risks he was willing to take.

He said, "It's really okay with you if Tori—"

"Yes. Victor never even knew she was alive in me. Anyway, that's not relevant. It's fine. You need to realize that people will begin assuming things. You're living here, my daughter calls you Daddy."

"Is what they're assuming true?"

She lay back against one of the pillows, still combing wool. "You tell me. Really, we haven't known each other very long."

"I love you," he said.

He had never said it before. Not in the throes of their lovemaking. Never.

"And I you," she answered.

She felt as though she'd known him longer, as though in some way she'd known him the whole time she'd known Victor and been without Victor and longer than that.

"I'm a very monogamous person," he said.

She didn't say anything. Having mountains for a mistress… Was that monogamy?

He tried again. "You said some heartfelt things last night."

Yes, and she couldn't take them back, couldn't deny that she still believed and felt those things. Except— "I do respect you," she told him. "You're a good person. And I understand the lure of—what you do. But…I don't think I can handle it with much grace, Joe. It isn't something anyone with a family should do. But I guess we're not your family."

"I think you are."

She sighed. "My daughter calls you Daddy. Can you imagine me explaining to her that you died because you were climbing mountains?"

"My grandma and grandpa died climbing mountains."

Neither she nor Joe had noticed Maria approaching. She often appeared silently, a shadow. Something in her face reminded Sabine of Victor, and now she longed for the person whose genes had mingled with hers, the person who had been a true husband, who'd been willing to make the required sacrifices.

But Victor never wanted to climb K2.

Sabine reached for her daughter and hugged her. Maria stared at Joe. "You're a mountain climber, aren't you?" she said.

Joe nodded. "Your mother is, too. Did you know that?"

"My mother doesn't do anything dangerous," Maria answered. "She knows we need her, so nothing's going to happen to her."

Joe studied Maria, wondering why she was telling him this. *Because you called Sabine a mountain climber, why else?* Maria was saying that it wasn't true—that Sabine was her mother, a mother who *wouldn't* climb mountains at the risk of her life.

A striking contrast to Joe Knoll.

He abruptly found himself in the position of other climbers he'd known, who left children, pregnant wives, girlfriends, loved ones behind, who climbed mountains despite the suffering of those people. He had understood the anguish of his colleagues, partners and friends. He had understood what made them do it anyhow.

Now it had happened to him. He had a girlfriend, and she had three children, children related to him, his brother's, his blood. He was enmeshed in their lives and wanted to become more so. Yet he still wanted the freedom to go, to climb and to die in the mountains.

It was a selfish urge, and he didn't know by what right he felt justified in yielding to it.

It's just who I am. I climb mountains. That's what I do.

But didn't he make sleds as well?

"Are you going to die in the mountains?" asked Maria.

This girl did not love him, did not care about him. But what if she began to do so? How could he say to a child that he might die in the mountains? He didn't know how to answer. Even to say *I hope not* would not be precisely true. Where would he prefer to die?

In Sabine's arms?

That was how he was supposed to feel, and he suddenly doubted that he was the man for her.

Why, then, did he feel contentment at the idea of

growing old with her, perhaps having more children or just raising those she'd had with Victor?

"I don't plan to die in the mountains," he said.

Sabine didn't say anything.

She didn't say, No one ever *plans* that.

Joe wished he could know her thoughts, then realized he probably already did. The dangers were inherent, and there was nothing to say about them.

If he continued to climb, there was a good chance that, someday, one of his expedition partners or a wife of someone he was climbing with would come to her door to tell her he'd died.

And in the spring Lucy, too, would head for the Himalayas.

Nepal, not Pakistan. It was unlikely their paths would cross in Asia.

What had happened to him that he could no longer feel, with certainty, that he had an inalienable right to climb high and dangerous mountains, to go into the Death Zone?

He had become Sabine's lover, but he had taken other lovers in the past, and they had not affected his feelings about climbing.

She was Victor's widow, but that, too, seemed immaterial.

In the short time he'd known her and begun to help her, with shoveling, with Finn, with the details of daily life, ever since he'd begun living in the house—in that time, he seemed to have stretched and grown. He found himself becoming someone new.

And isn't that really why you came to Oro?

But he still wanted K2.

Maria asked if she could spin, and Sabine helped her begin on the wheel Victor had made.

If Sabine ever said to him that Victor wouldn't have left her to climb K2, Joe would point out what Victor *had* proven himself capable of.

Marrying his brother's fiancée.

Neglecting to mention to his second wife that he even *had* a brother.

Saint Victor.

Well, Joe was no candidate for sainthood, and this summer he intended to climb the second-highest mountain in the world.

CHAPTER TWELVE

AFTER NEW YEAR'S, as Joe increased production, even hiring Karen's brother, Jason, to help him in the shop, he also began training. When he left on his first training run, Sabine felt the same internal bitterness and resentment she'd felt watching Lucy train. Joe, like Lucy, was free of responsibility.

But when he returned, he came into the great room, where she was spinning. As he stretched, he said, "Do you like to run?"

"I love it," she answered succinctly.

"Would you like me to watch the kids while you go?"

It was that easy. Sabine found herself out on a long road with little winter traffic, taking her first solo run since Victor's death. Her lungs felt ready to burst in the altitude. She sprinted, then walked, chest heaving, then ran again.

As she ran, she thought about the possibility of Joe's death. Dreaded it.

I don't want him to go to K2.

She was almost sick at the prospect, but she could do nothing to stop it, and wasn't sure she *would* do anything if she could.

When she got back to the house, Joe and Finn were

throwing paper airplanes in the great room. Tori was playing with dolls, Maria spinning.

"Thank you, Joe," Sabine said as she sank down on one of the rugs and began to stretch.

"You're welcome. It would drive me crazy," he said, "if I had to watch someone else take off on a run and not have the chance to go myself."

Instinctively, Sabine jumped up and rushed over to hug him. "Thank you," she repeated.

He returned the embrace, and in his arms she felt a safety she hadn't known since Victor's death. Her body, her soul, didn't know him as someone who would leave but simply as the man who loved her, cherished her.

With amazement, she realized she loved Joe in a way she'd never expected to love again.

But he was going to the mountains, the mountains that had killed both her parents, mountains with many avalanches. An avalanche had killed Victor.

"Would you like to do some ice-climbing with me?" he asked. "I bet Karen would babysit."

"Yes," Sabine said, thinking that, like her, Joe seemed to have accepted Karen's presence in their lives as a necessary evil.

They went the next day, driving to an ice park in the next town, over the steepest and most treacherous of the mountain passes.

As Sabine waited in the cold, watching him lead, she reflected that Victor had never asked her to do anything like this with him. They had gone for walks, gone sledding, occasionally skied together, though always cross-country, no backcountry. Victor had not been an athlete. He had been impressed with some of her feats with the kicksled, even when he feared for her safety. He'd never shown overt jealousy over men who climbed mountains or ran ultra-marathons. But she hadn't been doing those things, so there was no reason for jealousy.

Was it true that she and Joe had more in common than she and Victor ever had?

Yes.

She and Victor had made a life in common. She had admired his woodworking, he her spinning. They had shared ideas about what was good for the children, had shared parenting. Occasionally they'd read stories aloud, exchanged thoughts about what was important in life.

To her surprise, she now found her own climbing was still strong. Lifting children gave her some upper body strength, though not necessarily the type that would help her climb. But, she remembered the rhythm she'd learned when she was young. Her body, too, remembered.

The day spent climbing with Joe pleased her. As they walked down to town together, to get espresso drinks, Joe said, "You're good. I knew you would be," and Sabine heard the pride in his voice.

She said, "Thanks for making it possible for me to get out and run and things like that." She planned to visit the gym at the Oro school that night to use the climbing wall there with Lucy and then to lift weights with her sister.

Yet even the prospect of working out with Lucy reminded her that her sister was going to Everest Base Camp that summer.

And Joe to K2.

My whole family will die in the mountains. Can't these people stop going there, stop doing this?

When they got back to Oro, she and Maria spent a peaceful afternoon spinning together, both on spindles. She couldn't help noticing that all her children seemed more secure since Joe had come to live with them.

But what will happen when he goes away?

She could not imagine telling them that he'd died. She still remembered telling Maria about Victor. For Finn, it must have been as though Victor had just disappeared, vanished from their midst.

It continued to snow, more than it had for thirty years. Each month pressed up against an old record.

Every day Joe worked in the shop, then trained. He ran, skied the back country down treacherous Weathertop Mountain and its fellows. Sabine reflected sometimes that climbing K2 could hardly be riskier than what he did in Oro.

But that wasn't true, and she knew it.

He often skied with Greg and wore the beacon Sabine had given him. Since the avalanche class, he, Greg and Lucy had regularly practiced using beacons and probes. Sabine knew of these practice sessions, which were as important as the equipment itself, but had no desire to take part. She used an inclinometer and stayed away from slopes that were steep enough to slide.

On a sunny February afternoon she came home from shoveling to find Karen waiting with a tense expression.

"Where's Joe?" Karen asked, tight-lipped.

"Skiing."

"Mommy, look at my painting," Tori said, tugging on Sabine's sweater as she turned to hang up her parka.

"Oh, it's pretty. I like the ducks." For some reason, Tori had been painting ducks lately. "What did you paint, Finn?"

"Blizzardman making peace with the yeti."

Yetis had been standard fare in Finn's artwork since Joe had first mentioned them to the children.

Sabine could feel rather than see Karen's expression. But now she reinterpreted it.

Worry.

"What's wrong?"

"I don't want to say anything if— I just don't know."

Sabine wondered whether she was about to hear that Joe was having an affair with another woman, someone he skied with, for instance.

"You may as well," Sabine told her.

"There was an avalanche up on Weathertop. Two people died."

"If Joe was one of them, someone would've come here."

"Not yet. I just found out. They had to close the pass there. The sheriff on the other side told me. I'm not supposed to say anything."

Then why did you? The sheriff in the next county had been dating Karen—rarely, because she rarely accepted his overtures.

And Sabine was infuriated on behalf of her children, all of whom had been told how Victor died. "Joe had a beacon," she said.

"So did both of these people. That's why they found the bodies so fast, I guess. The sheriff thought one of them might be from Oro, and they were both men."

It wasn't true. It had nothing to do with her. Joe had gone with Greg and Lucy, and none of them were dead. They couldn't be.

She said nothing to Karen, forgot to thank her for watching the kids. She put on her parka and went outside, forgetting what Karen had just said, letting it fall into a compartment in her mind while other doors opened, doors that went in only one direction. Away.

"SHE GOT IN THE CAR and drove off?" Joe asked. "Where did she go?"

"I don't have the slightest idea. I just assumed she had to work some more. Maybe she's still shoveling," Karen told him.

That was possible. It was only five o'clock. Lucy had gone to Greg's; otherwise, he could ask her where Sabine was likely to be. He said, "Well, I'm back, so I'll watch them till she gets home."

"Who was killed in the avalanche?"

"Two guys from Wyoming." He didn't like to think about it. "How did you hear?"

"Oh. A friend."

He felt suddenly uneasy. "Does Sabine know people were killed?"

"I told her."

Brilliant. He didn't answer. She probably just went out to shovel—or maybe to track down someone who could tell her the identity of those killed. It must have seemed preferable to sitting at home, waiting to hear.

He called her cell phone, but she didn't answer, so he left a message.

It grew dark outside, and he made spaghetti for the kids and called Lucy, who said she'd go look for Sabine at all their usual shoveling sites. At nine, she came over. "I can't find her. Do you think she went down the mountain for groceries or something?"

"She might have."

He put the kids to bed. Maria and Tori both asked where their mother was. Finn did not. Joe told them he thought she'd gone to buy groceries.

By midnight, she still hadn't returned.

He called the local sheriff, who was on duty and came by.

The sheriff's name was Frank Drey. Joe had never met him before, but he seemed to know that Joe was Victor's brother and that he lived with Sabine and that he was her boyfriend.

"It's not like her," Frank said. "I'm going to put in some calls on both sides of the mountain and let the CDOT guys know in case—well, sometimes people go off the road, and we don't find them right away. Doesn't mean she's dead, though, even if that's what happened."

Dead?

No. Sabine wasn't going to die. Not like this and not at her age, leaving three small children as orphans. That wouldn't happen.

He went up to the attic and wondered if the children would come up to see him if they couldn't find their mother. He left the attic door open at first, then couldn't sleep.

But he couldn't sleep in Sabine's bed, which was sacrosanct, the place she never allowed him. She hadn't said why, but he knew. Victor had made that bed. She and Victor had shared the bed.

He tried to sleep on the couch downstairs and finally dozed, then awoke in the middle of the night, knowing she hadn't returned.

IT WAS AS THOUGH she'd vanished into thin air.

Authorities throughout the state were looking for her car, but there were many blue Subaru Legacy Outbacks in Colorado. It was like hunting for a contact lens on a lawn.

No one answered her cell phone.

He and Lucy and Greg spent hours imagining scenarios, most of them triggered by Karen's telling Sabine that there'd been an avalanche and people had died.

But none of their theories held water.

Foul play, the overblown phrase for someone abducting and/or murdering her, seemed least likely of all. What had happened to her car?

From the first, Joe assumed the role of caretaker for the children. He told them no one knew where their mother was, and that he, like they, hoped she was safe. She had driven away the day before, and no one had been able to find her since.

Maria said, "We should pray."

"Fine," said Joe, who thought that their all getting in his truck and driving and looking until they found Sabine was a better option. "Let's pray. You say the prayer, Maria."

They all held hands, even Finn, and Maria said, "Dear God, please bring our mother home safe and sound. Amen."

"Amen," Joe agreed.

"I don't want her to be dead!" Finn suddenly yelled.

Pandemonium ensued, with Finn and Tori both sobbing hysterically, and Joe not saying anything because he couldn't think of anything to say. He hugged them but couldn't bring himself to insist, or even suggest, that Sabine wasn't dead. He didn't know and he'd known too many people who had died.

But nearly all of them had died climbing mountains.

Victor had been an exception.

He suggested reading out loud. He found *The Hobbit* on a bookshelf and began reading to them about Bilbo Baggins and Gandalf and dwarves and an unexpected party.

Tori got up in the middle and began playing with her Barbie dolls.

Maria said, "You're going to take care of us, aren't you?"

Joe looked at her, thinking that if Sabine was dead, Lucy would probably be their legal guardian. He didn't know what sort of will, if any, Sabine had. Yet he thought Maria was asking her question in a very serious, adult way. She was that kind of child. She wanted the truth.

He said, "I'm going to take care of you."

Maria nodded, and he understood that he had made a promise.

SHE HAD BEEN GONE for nineteen days when her car was found in a paid parking lot in Denver's LoDo. No one named Sabine Knoll had checked into any hotel in Denver during the time she'd been gone.

Joe had entertained the hope, once, that when he came to live with Sabine they would cease to hire Karen, Karen whom he now blamed for Sabine's disappearance. She *must* have left that day because of what Karen had said.

Now he relied on Karen to be with the children when he couldn't. Still, because of his dislike of her, he worked on sleds while the children were at school. After picking up Tori from preschool, he brought her out to the shop, where he'd constructed a simple house for her Barbie dolls, not to rival the lavish dollhouse up in the attic, the dollhouse Victor had built for Maria.

He and Tori went together to collect Finn and Maria from school, and then he gave up work for the day to be with the children. Only rarely did he accept the offers Karen continually made. Instead, he confided in Lucy his dissatisfaction with Karen, and Lucy came over to watch the kids so that he could go for an occasional run. He knew that if Sabine wasn't found soon—*how could she be alive?*—he was going to have to look for other child-care options so he could train as he needed to for K2.

But what about his promise to Maria? Hadn't he told her he would take care of them?

Earlier, when Sabine had accused him of selfishness, of being willing to risk his life without concern for others who needed him, her criticism had seemed moot. No one *did* need him. She'd gotten along without him before, and she would again.

Children were different.

Especially motherless children.

He missed her in an appalling way. He kept looking at her idle spinning wheel.

When she'd been gone three weeks, he at last went into her room, not for a quick house-check, not hunting for clues of where she might be, but perhaps to discover who she was.

Even the air smelled like her.

Before, he and the sheriff had made a cursory examination of furniture tops, of drawers, seeking some hint of where she might have gone, what might have happened.

She wrote a diary, and they had looked at it. It was just a chronicle of events, possibly useful for billing in her shoveling business because she'd recorded hours worked and where. It wasn't *personal.*

Now Joe wanted to find something personal. He wanted the essence of why this room and this bed were so sacred to her that she'd never invited him in. Not to lie on the bed with her, not to spend the night.

In a bedside drawer, he discovered a framed photo of Victor. In Joe's eyes, his brother was old. Yet the sunny smile, the charisma, remained. On the dresser sat a box of her earrings. In one drawer were summer clothes, for Oro's brief season of warmth and light. It struck Joe again how little he knew her—and how much.

She was not an emotional person. To him, her long devotion to Victor felt like tightly reined anger—and a way not to be hurt again. A way not to suffer loss.

Two desires danced within him. One was to get past her careful control, to break her out of her self-imposed prison. The other was to protect her from hurt.

So where is she now, Joe?

How could anyone simply disappear?

She had to be dead.

But her car's turning up in Denver gave him hope—illogically, he thought. It had been locked. Inside were gas receipts, though no hotel receipts.

A psychologist who was a member of Lucy's adventure racing team had suggested that Sabine had experienced some kind of psychological break. Perhaps she had amnesia and had no idea who she was. Sometimes people wandered in this fugue state for years, assuming new identities. Sometimes their families never found them.

But it seldom happened.

Still, that was the idea that appealed to Joe, and he clung to it. Karen did watch the children while he helped Lucy and Greg with the shoveling. When he came home one day at the end of February, he saw that all three children were watching a movie while Karen prepared their dinner.

He said he could take over the cooking, but Karen said she was almost done. Then she remarked, "You know, some women do things like this."

"Cooking?"

"No. Going off to start a new life."

Joe lifted Karen's long black sweater from the hook by the door and handed it to her. "Goodbye," he said.

"I know you don't want to believe it," she said, "but she always hinted she'd like to do it."

He held open the door.

Karen put on her sweater and picked up her purse.

Joe waited for her to leave, which she did without speaking. He shut the door behind her.

Sabine would *not* walk out on her children. On him, possibly, but even that wasn't her style.

The phone rang, and he picked it up, expecting Lucy.

"Hello?"

"Victor?"

First thing, he checked the caller ID. It was a payphone with a prefix he didn't recognize.

"Sabine, it's Joe," he said. "Victor's brother." He could barely talk, his heart was pounding so hard. "Can you please stay where you are? And tell me where that is?"

"I'm in Kansas City. I don't know why I'm here. I remember now. I remember Victor's—the past."

"Will you stay where you are and let me come and get you? Or Lucy can come if you'd rather."

"Lucy," she said.

His heart twisted. He'd been left behind, watching her children, doing everything he could for her and for them in her absence, yet now she wanted her sister.

"I don't know. I don't know how I got here…." She sounded odd, shaky, and he was terrified that she'd go back into whatever confused state had led her to that place. He would call the Kansas City police to go to her once he knew where she was. Then Lucy could bring her home.

"Where are you exactly?"

"The Crown Center. I like this coffee place here. I like the windows."

"Will you stay at the coffee place? I'm going to have the police go there, just so someone will be with you while you wait for Lucy. Is that okay?"

"Yes. Bye."

And she hung up.

He realized that unwittingly he had gotten through her barriers, the barriers for which Victor, her undying love for Victor, had always provided camouflage. But Joe had broken through. He hadn't even known till now.

And this was what had happened.

CHAPTER THIRTEEN

SABINE LOOKED NO DIFFERENT when she returned home, except for having lost some weight and seeming unsure of herself. Lucy had taken her to a hospital in Kansas City, where a psychiatrist had advised her to seek more counseling when she got home. He said she'd experienced a fugue state and that she should look for the trigger.

But during the ride home with Lucy in her sister's car, Sabine discovered the trigger.

No puzzle there.

It'd been Karen's announcing that people had been killed in an avalanche—and that one of the avalanche victims might be Joe.

On the way to Kansas City, Lucy had dropped Greg off in Denver so he could pick up Sabine's car. Behind the wheel of her own truck on the drive home Lucy said, "Joe's sure committed to you. He's been taking care of the kids. They're crazy about him."

Were they?

But how was she going to cope if this was how she reacted to news of an avalanche? She couldn't ask Joe to stop climbing just because she had this mental weakness—or simply a history of family members dying in the mountains.

When Lucy drove up to the house, all three children ran

outside. As Sabine climbed from her sister's truck, her children threw themselves at her and all began talking at once, not asking where she'd been but telling her what they'd been doing.

They were changed by more than a month without her. Maria and Finn both looked taller, and Tori's hair was longer and a bit straighter.

On the porch stood Joe, belonging there. He waited like a husband and father.

But I'm the one who'll have to wait.

Yet he *had* waited.

Her heart arranged its arguments, its fears, its histories, and flung them at one another. The war, awaited and then forestalled by her long absence, broke out within her.

With Tori on one hip and Finn clinging to her other side, she walked toward her house as a veteran coming home. But she took her war with her and it also waited on the porch—tall, dark-haired and dark-eyed, the most attractive man she'd ever known.

Save one.

No.

That was no longer true. Another love had cured her of Victor, and she was desperate not to lose this new love. The only way to do that, it seemed to her, was to banish its object. Then the result wouldn't be helpless loss but her own choice. *She* would choose when and how to end the relationship. She, rather than K2 or Kangchenjunga or Nanga Parbat or Annapurna or some other mountain she had never considered that stood waiting to make her a widow.

An again-widow.

Joe took Tori from her and set the four-year-old down, then clasped Sabine against him.

Maybe, she thought suddenly, *he understands now.*

But she was ashamed of that thought. She would never have engineered something like this, and her shame over her weakness, her breakdown, was vast. It embarrassed her to think of her confusion.

That endless search…for her father.

Talking to people and telling them she was looking for her father. All those people who had assumed she was insane because she couldn't remember her own name or her father's or what he looked like.

Going homeless and…well, there were many things. Some of them she could remember; some she couldn't.

She trembled, trying to imagine confessing to Joe the things she'd done. *It doesn't matter, and it won't matter to him.*

They didn't really talk until the children were asleep. Her homecoming had exhausted Sabine, and yet she wasn't ready to lie in the attic with Joe.

Familiar man, hard muscles, eyes so identical and yet so unlike Victor's.

They did not make love. She made no move to take off any of her clothes.

It isn't going to happen, she thought. *Not anymore.*

He said, "Want to tell me about it?"

"No. But I will." She went through what she could recall, which was so incomplete. She didn't remember leaving Oro. At some point, she'd found herself in Colorado Springs. She'd had some cash; the owner of the Oro market had paid her in hundred-dollar bills for half the season's shoveling the afternoon she'd left. She'd bought a sleeping bag at a thrift shop. She recalled asking for money at a church and getting some. She'd stolen food several times, twice left restaurants without paying.

She'd looked for her father, a father whose appearance she couldn't remember, then realized that she was an orphan because her parents had died. She couldn't remember how they'd died, holding only a dreamlike sense that the circumstances had been terrible.

"Nobody...hurt you?"

"No. Not how you mean. I was in a car with a man whose breath stank. Well, all of him smelled. He kissed me, and I kissed him back, but then I left. I got out of the car, and I got on the Sixteenth Street bus. You know, in Denver."

Joe's chest tightened, not in anything like jealousy but just in belated terror. Things he'd been unwilling to imagine now grew real. Too real.

"The most strange and frightening thing was this woman. I stayed with her in this squat. It must've been in Kansas City, but I'm not positive. It's fuzzy. She was crazy, and she'd have these rages. Sometimes she shook me and screamed at me. When I left, these men chased me. I thought she'd sent them." That memory frightened her more than all the others put together. "But...my father came. I know it sounds unbelievable. I must have dreamed it. One of these guys must've been six foot four, but my father was much taller. They all ran, and he chased them. Then he ran away from me."

She saw Joe's face. "It doesn't matter. I'm sure it was some kind of hallucination. I'm supposed to see a psychiatrist. Did Lucy tell you what the doctor in Kansas City thought had happened?"

"Yes. Do you agree?"

"I suppose I do. But it was all so real. When it was happening, I mean. It wasn't like a dream."

Joe waited for her to say she couldn't tolerate his climbing, that she wouldn't be able to stand it.

Instead she said, "Thank you. For everything you've done for the children. They're—attached to you."

Maybe, he thought, this was how it would come. She couldn't let him break the hearts of her children. She couldn't let them love someone who was going to die in the mountains.

Strange that he'd never seen this conflict in his relationships before. But the reason wasn't hard to find. If women showed signs of wanting him to stop climbing, he ended the relationship.

If Sabine asked him to stay home, to forget K2, would he leave the relationship?

He wasn't sure.

Because he assumed she'd never ask. It wasn't her style.

Yet she suffered. Suffering had driven her away for more than a month, not just away from home but away from herself.

He changed the subject, telling her the details of his falling out with Karen. "You can hire her back if you want," he said, "but she trashes you, and I don't like hearing it."

Sabine considered his words.

The temporary ceasefire in her heart was over, the

conflict renewed. If she asked Joe to leave—*you can't; because you said he could live here for a year*—she'd need Karen again. Karen or someone as reliable.

Particularly with Lucy gone.

It was the fact that Lucy *was* going that decided her. Clearly, she needed Joe, needed him for practical reasons, to watch the children, to help, to take up the slack. That need would undermine the relationship. How would she know if she loved him on a day-to-day basis, how would she keep her own passion alive, if he was in her life because she *needed* him? And in the spring, he'd be leaving anyhow.

"I think," she said, "it would be better if you could move out to the shop and set up a shower and kitchen facility out there."

He didn't face her, and that disquieted her, like a warning of trouble ahead.

You needed Victor, she told herself belatedly. And that never undermined your relationship.

Yes, but since he died, things had been different.

"That wasn't our agreement."

"It wasn't our agreement that in the middle of your year in this house, you'd pack up and go climb K2."

"I dislike emotional blackmail."

She weighed the charge. "So do I. That's not what I intend. I'm not trying to get you to change your plans. If you change your plans, that's your business, but it's not what I'm asking. My children love you. If you die, it'll be hard enough for them that they knew you and loved you and you lived out in the shop and for a few months in the attic. But if you were their mother's boyfriend and continued living here until you left for the Himalayas and *then* died—it would be even more traumatic. Please respect my desire not to expose them to the same grief I endured when I was young."

"It couldn't be the same."

Sabine sat up, preparing to stand. "It doesn't matter, Joe. Please honor my wishes in this. I'll emphasize again: I'm not telling you what to do with your life. And I'm sorry to renege on our agreement, but I don't think you're abiding by the spirit of that agreement, either. You're you—you're a climber and a mountaineer. I understand that people can love being in the mountains so much they'll sacrifice everything else in their lives. That's your choice to make. But I can't live with it."

"This *is* emotional blackmail."

"So be it." She stood up.

He said, "You're welcome."

Sabine lifted her eyebrows.

"You thanked me for taking care of your family."

She snapped, "Don't you understand? You make choices. I make choices. It's the way life is. Your choices are your business, and mine are mine. I'm making a choice for myself and my children, and don't you *dare* say another word about emotional blackmail. I've told you I'm not trying to make you change. But neither am I going to continue leaving my heart in the keeping of someone who—" She faltered, unsure how to go on. "Of someone who doesn't value the gift."

"Because I don't want to change who I am for you?"

"Just don't talk," she suggested. "There's no argument you can make that will have the slightest effect. Except to make me angry. Good night."

SHE DIDN'T GO to sleep or even into her bedroom. She went into the great room, lit a lamp to its lowest setting and sat at her traveling wheel. Maria had showed her wool that she'd been carding and combing since her mother went away, her own tangible prayer for Sabine's return.

Sabine had come home. *Doesn't Joe get it?* she thought. *After waiting and wondering himself? After watching the terror of the children?* Because she had no doubt that they *had* been afraid, afraid she wouldn't return or afraid that she'd die, as their father had.

There had been no way of explaining where she'd gone or why. How could any of it be expressed?

But she had told them she'd lost her memory, that she'd forgotten everything. She'd told them it was because she was very frightened. She'd told them it wasn't likely to happen again.

Remembering Maria's serious face, her expression that showed thoughts whirling unseen, Sabine felt her resolve strengthen. It wasn't likely to happen again because she was going to fall *out* of love with Joe Knoll as soon as possible.

IN THE MORNING, she took Maria and Finn to school, then Tori to preschool. When she got back, Joe was nowhere in the house, and the futon and his belongings were gone from the attic. She called Karen. She understood Joe's objections to Karen, but now he was in no position to make decisions about child care for her, and Karen *was* reliable. In Oro, that was something.

"Hello?"

Karen sounded uneasy, almost chilly, as she answered.

"Karen, it's Sabine. I'm back, and—"

"Where have you *been?* I was so worried! And Lucy said it might be my fault because I told you about that damned avalanche. I feel so *stupid* that I did that, Sabine. I'm so sorry."

This was an unprecedented acceptance of responsibility from Karen.

"Well, I wouldn't call it your fault. It's just a sign that the thought of my loved ones dying in an avalanche is terrifying to me," Sabine answered, liking Karen more than she had for quite a while. In any case, Sabine understood the forces that must have shaped Karen. Karen had gone through life being acknowledged as beautiful, and there seemed to have been no hardships in her past to counteract the effects of nonstop admiration.

Briefly, Sabine explained what had happened, admitted that she was going to see a counselor to follow up.

"That's a good idea," Karen said. "I feel bad, Sabine. I forgot about your parents dying in the mountains and Victor dying in an avalanche. You must be half-crazy with Joe going to K2 and Lucy to Everest."

"I'm upset about Lucy," Sabine replied. "Joe's decisions are his own business."

"Why? I thought you liked him!" Karen exclaimed as though being told of some tragedy. "You're such a cute couple."

Sabine kept from rolling her eyes, although she was alone with no one to see.

"Well, he's a mountaineer, and I have three small children. Those two things don't go together, in my view."

"Oh. I can see that. I'm just surprised."

Sabine changed the subject, saying she'd been told Joe and Karen had disagreed on something while she was gone. She asked if Karen would be willing to work for her again. "When summer comes, it won't be as many hours. The sale of the property means I can spend more time with the kids. But I'll still need a sitter sometimes. And I need to finish the shoveling year, fulfilling the contracts to which I've agreed."

"I'm glad to help! I've *missed* the children," Karen insisted.

Sabine hesitated. Somehow, having drawn perimeters with Joe, having said she would not remain lovers with a climber, would not encourage her children to be so close to him, opened other doors of communication. There were problems with Karen, and it was wrong not to address them.

"Karen," she said, "I know I haven't been paying you a lot per hour. I'm in a position to pay a little more now. Say, a dollar an hour more?"

"Oh, that's fine. But I don't do it for the money. I love your children."

Sabine smiled, believing her. "I need to clear the air about something. I feel you don't respect me as a mother—"

"I think the world of you, Sabine."

Which meant exactly what it said—nothing.

"Anyhow, I know—because people have told me   that you have some derogatory things to say about me when I'm not around. I'm going to ask you to please not do that. You must realize it's not good for the children, and I know you love them, as you said." It was her best stab at improving the situation.

"What did people tell you I said?" Her voice seemed to whine with a strange grief, as though she didn't understand how Sabine could get such a strange and untrue idea.

"Joe was particularly upset by your suggestion that I would abandon my children. I have no idea if you actually believed that or if you just needed to say it for some reason, but I don't think he misunderstood you." Sabine began to regret giving Karen a raise, began to wonder why she had. But she knew why. She needed women in her life, women friends, people, a support group. Lucy was going. Joe, as far as Sabine was concerned, was gone.

Yes. She was choosing to befriend a woman who had little good to say about her, yet she'd turned out of her house a man her children loved, who had cared for them during her long confused absence.

But I can't be lovers with a man who's going to climb like that. I just can't. Someday he'll die, and I'll grieve, and my children will grieve, and in the meantime what happiness could there really be?

Karen, on the other end of the line, remained silent. Would she deny that she'd said such a thing to Joe?

"Sometimes," she said, "it just seems like you don't care about them very much. Like, you don't really want them."

Sabine curbed her temper, trying to think who in Oro would be willing to get up practically in the middle of the night to come and stay with her children so she could shovel. For what was, even with a raise considered, very little money.

She hated to waver on everything, but she was an inch from telling Karen never to darken her door again.

There were moments she wanted to be free from her own responsibilities.

There were no moments when she didn't want her children, and she would never forget what Karen had just said.

"Karen, I love my children. I feel put down by that remark. Thank you for taking such good care of them. I'll call you next time I need someone."

"Okay," said Karen, with a hint of worry in her voice, but not worry for a job, more of a dramatic worry about the state of their friendship. "I just feel bad for *you,* Sabine, that you'd rather work than spend time with them."

"I wouldn't rather work. I *have* to work." It was as true now as it had been before Joe bought the business and the land. She had to do some kind of work because it kept her sane. But when the year's shoveling was over, she would concentrate on fiber arts, spinning and making small items from homespun. Scarves, hats, handbags. That she could do while the children were present. Her children had learned to entertain themselves. "And you're right. But this is mother-hood."

"Well, like the Paulys," Karen put in. "You know, they just have one three-year-old girl, but they *always* try to think of what she wants to do, of what she needs."

Sabine didn't want to hear about the owners of Oro's fledgling Internet outfit. They spent a ton of money on their daughter's clothing, bought her more than any three-year-old could want, let alone need, and took her *everywhere.* "Do you sit for them?" Sabine asked.

"They've *never* had a sitter."

Sabine closed her eyes and said she had to go.

Hanging up, she reviewed their conversation. Karen had never backtracked and said that she, Sabine, was a good mother.

How many other people thought what Karen did, that she didn't want her children?

She longed to talk to Joe, but she wouldn't go out to the shop to find him. She had ended their relationship as lovers, and trying to be friends at this point wouldn't help.

Fleetingly she thought of Victor, missing him but also wishing for those horrible days in the recent past when she'd known with certainty that she would never love again. That state of mind had kept her safe for so long.

Not now. Now the more bitter pain came from missing Joe.

But how much more it would hurt to miss him because of his death.

Half-desperate with loneliness, she phoned Norah, who was packing for a three-week Hawaiian vacation and promptly called Karen "that pathetic creature" and opined that the Paulys, who'd *never* had a sitter, were creating a monster.

As Sabine hung up, her eyes stung. In gratitude for the friends she had, dreading the next three weeks without Norah and the coming months without Lucy…and missing Joe.

He'd proven himself more *like* Victor than she would've believed possible. And so many of their differences were a credit to Joe.

Now the more bitter pain in her heart came from the loss of him, not Victor.

But how much more painful it would be if she lost him because of his death.

"I'M GOING OUT to the shop!" Finn announced after his snack.

There was no reason to stop him. He'd gone through his homework folder and seemed to have done a good job on his work. Sabine had helped him with his three worksheets while he ate his snack. He'd been good, so good that she wondered if Joe, in her absence, had created this new balance.

What would be the harm of his working in the shop with Joe? It wasn't as though Joe was his father or Finn was confused about that. When Joe went away in April, Finn would miss him for a time and then move on to other interests.

But what about Tori, who still called Joe "Daddy"?

My fault, my fault. Getting into a relationship too quickly, trusting in things to work out that really weren't workable.

Last night as she'd tried to sleep, she had counted the number of people she'd known who had died climbing or of altitude-related illnesses. She could name twelve—and there might be more, others with whom she'd lost touch. To six of these people she had felt close—family or good friends. Two of them, of course, had been her parents. The rest were more than acquaintances.

Yet part of her ached for the intimacy of expeditions, even those times at base camp with Lucy and one parent or the other. Waiting. Hanging on the news, listening round the radio, sometimes frightened but used to betraying no emotion because that was expected of them.

Lucy had been her best friend for so long, yet Lucy's decision to return to the Himalayas and Sabine's own disappearance had subtly distanced them.

Tomorrow I'll see my counselor.

She would have to go down the mountain to the nearest city, Bolt, which was a college town. The psychiatrist in Kansas City had gotten the name and made the appointment for her using contacts of his own in Colorado. The counselor was named Andreya Frazier. The Kansas City doctor had said that a psychologist would be a reasonable counselor for her; she didn't need medication.

Finn put on his parka and mitts without being told and headed out the door.

Tori, coming in from the other room, where Maria had started spinning, said, "Can I go out with Finn to see Daddy?"

He's not your daddy.

But she'd told Tori she could call Joe that. So many decisions seemed unwise in retrospect.

"I have something fun for you to play with today. Would you like to make a pot holder on a loom?"

"Yes. What's that?"

"A loom? I'll show you." Sabine carried Tori from the kitchen on her hip, thankful that she'd distracted her from Joe.

"Did your mom say you could come out?"

"Yes," Finn answered.

"Good. I need your help, partner." Joe set him to work with a screwdriver, assembling the part of a sled he could assemble on his own.

"Could you make me a really fast sled?" asked Finn.

"All these sleds are fast," Joe told him, thinking of Teresa.

"I mean *really* fast."

"Isn't your sled really fast?"

"Only on the *big* hill, and I was only allowed to go once, *with Mom.*" The last words were spoken respectfully—respect for his mother and for the hill.

"Maybe she'll let me take you down the big hill." Joe immediately wished he hadn't said it. He was surprised Sabine had even let Finn come out to the shop.

All day, he'd thought about his conversation with Sabine the night before. He regretted accusing her of emotional blackmail. Sabine had not asked him to move out so he'd be tempted to give up K2 and other mountains. She'd done it because she couldn't live with a mountaineer, with someone who might die fast, soon, in the mountains.

With someone she believed likely to die.

He had to consider what it would be like for her, for Maria, for Finn and for Tori, to whom he was "Daddy," if he didn't return from K2.

Yet he'd bought property adjoining theirs. He'd bought Victor's business and his shop. Their lives were intertwined. Her letting Finn come out to the shop seemed an acknowledgment of that.

She would allow him in their lives as the uncle of her children. But not, Joe saw, as her lover, her partner, her mate.

Her choice was wise, and he wouldn't fight it.

He only had to fight in himself an urge to cast away the mountains that were at the base of his life, that were his spirituality, his peace, his exuberance, for her. She was, he reminded himself, just a woman.

The mountains were where he found the divine.

IN THE LATE AFTERNOON, which had turned clear and warm, Sabine heard a car arrive outside. She'd been cleaning up after dyeing some wool, and she glanced out the kitchen window.

Lucy.

She was alone, and Sabine felt grateful. She needed to talk to someone, and Lucy was the only one—besides Norah—with whom she felt comfortable sharing her secrets.

Still, ever since Lucy had announced that she was going to Everest, things had been different.

Lucy studied the wool, which Sabine had dyed magenta.

"I like it," she said. "You can't wear it, and I can't wear it, but it's pretty."

Sabine nodded. "I thought it would sell, anyhow. Want a cup of tea?"

They sat down together to drink black tea grown in Nepal. Maria and Tori were upstairs, playing with paper dolls, Maria making dolls and doll clothes for her little sister.

Sabine finally said, "Well, I told Joe to move back out to the shop." After her sister's exclamations of dismay—and some indignation on Joe's behalf because of everything he'd done while Sabine was gone—Sabine explained the problem.

Lucy sipped her tea silently. "You know what's interesting to me?" she asked.

"No."

"That you've completely set aside the big question of why Victor never told you he had a brother."

"It's because he didn't want me to know he'd stolen his

brother's fiancée," Sabine said carelessly, dismissing the observation.

"Did he ever tell you about Teresa's sledding accident?"

"Yes."

"Was he with her at the time?"

"What are you implying?"

"Nothing. Relax, Sabine. I just wondered how it happened."

"He was with her. They were racing."

Lucy had unzipped her coat and left it on the back of her chair, the way she always did. *I'm going to miss her so much,* Sabine thought.

"Tell me what happened. Tell me everything you know."

Lucy had that dog-with-a-bone look and tone of voice that told Sabine she had a theory of some kind. About what, Sabine couldn't guess; what explanation, after all, could Lucy or anyone come up with for Victor's not telling his wife that he had a brother? There was no reasonable explanation but the one she, Sabine, had just given her.

Still, she said, "I can't remember exactly what he told me. It's been so long. He was reluctant to leave her. She was unconscious—at first, anyhow. He had no cell phone or anything like that. Did you ever visit us there?"

"In Minnesota? Just that one summer."

"That's right. We went canoeing. Well, the good sledding run was about a half mile from the house. It was a dirt road, and snowmobiles groomed it in the winter. Sometimes Victor helped groom it because he used it to test sleds. Anyhow, she didn't wreck at the bottom but about halfway down the course. She hit a tree, but not with her head. She flipped, and she hit her head on the snow and on the sled, I think. My understanding is that there was also some brain damage from the velocity of the crash— I can't remember what you call it—her brain being jarred inside her skull?"

"So what did Victor do?"

"He sledded down to the nearest house, told them to call an ambulance and ran back up the slope."

"It must have cost a fortune," Lucy said.

"What?"

"Taking care of her. Hospital bills. The works."

"He took care of her himself."

"Still, I'm sure they didn't let her come home for a while. I'll bet she was in the hospital a good long time."

Sabine tried to remember if Victor had mentioned this. He hadn't, not really, but Lucy was right; with a head injury like that, Teresa could hardly have walked out in a few days. "They had insurance."

"How? He was self-employed. What did she do?"

Nothing with benefits.

"We always had insurance," Sabine answered. "He had private insurance."

"That's not cheap."

It hadn't been. But it hadn't been horribly expensive, either, which it would've been if Victor had used the insurance when Teresa was hurt. Or would it? She didn't know. "We always had a high deductible."

"He must've had money, Sabine. That accident should have ruined him."

Sabine had never thought about this before. His

business hadn't made all that much money. *He must have had an inheritance from his parents.*

In which case, Joe must have, as well.

And if Victor had become his brother's guardian, he would've been in charge of any trust of Joe's. Wouldn't he?

"What did Victor's parents do?" Lucy asked.

"His father was an engineer. He had patents. His mother..." She faltered.

Lucy gave her a sharp look.

"I don't know, but there's a picture of her at her debut...."

His parents *must* have had money. He'd said they'd been thrifty, that they'd done well for themselves.

How could she find out? If there'd been family money, she hadn't learned about it on Victor's death. It hadn't been included in his will. How could that be?

Norah.

Norah was leaving for Denver the next morning and going from there to San Francisco and on to Hawaii. Should she wait to phone her?

Yet if Victor *had* stolen from Joe, had stolen his inheritance, Sabine didn't want Joe to learn of it through a careless word from her sister—or anyone else.

She changed the subject and told Lucy about her recent exchange with Karen and how it had ended.

Lucy listened thoughtfully. "I think she needed someone to say that to her. I don't know why she's so... that way. I keep thinking if she gets a boyfriend she'll change. She really wants children, and it's getting kind of late, so she's critical of other women who are mothers."

Sabine nodded.

"Are you going to be all right when I leave?"

No! "I'll have to be. I want you to feel free to go where you will. It's just—well, what it is."

"I might never climb Everest."

• Sabine noticed how Lucy had progressed from insisting she never would to saying she might not. She changed the subject again. "You two aren't racing this season?"

"Actually, no. We're both taking time to figure out what we want to do. Greg's pretty sure he wants to come back and study and pass the bar." Greg had finished law school but hadn't passed the Colorado bar. This seemed hopeful to Sabine.

"What about you?"

"I'm not sure. I miss Nepal. I might like to do some kind of work there. But that would mean being apart from Greg. There's an organization that works with orphans... I want to do something with kids."

Lucy sounded serious about this, and Sabine felt a ray of hope. It buoyed her.

But behind her joy were new unsettling questions about Victor. And the extent of the secrets he might have kept from her.

CHAPTER FOURTEEN

NORAH ANSWERED her phone.

Sabine hardly knew what to ask, let alone how to phrase the question. "It wasn't in the will—I was his sole heir—but did you know anything about Victor inheriting money from his parents?"

Norah didn't answer at once. "First, no. Second, who gave you that idea?"

"Well—Lucy pointed out something I hadn't thought about. That Teresa's head injury must've been a huge financial drain. I know she continued to see a neurologist. And right after the accident—"

"I hear what you're saying."

"Also, Victor told me his father had patents. At least, that's what I understood. It all seems— He was Joe's guardian after their parents died."

"Did Joe suggest something wasn't right?"

"No, he never has."

"Well, maybe you should ask him."

"Do you know who represented Victor in Minnesota, who his attorney was?"

"I must have the name somewhere. I've never had to contact him."

"Could you—"

"I'd need a reason, Sabine. Besides, I'm not sure we can learn anything. And I can't imagine Victor doing anything illegal. Now, if his parents left things so that Victor was supposed to share with his brother but didn't actually spell it out... Well, it happens. It's not moral or right, but it's not illegal. And it sounds as though the person who'd actually know was whoever handled Victor's father's estate."

"But if there were patents and they continued to earn, you'd know about them. Unless there was something divided between Victor and Joe, and Victor didn't want me to know about Joe..." It all made Sabine's head swim.

Norah was quiet for a moment.

"What?" Sabine said.

"I think you should let it rest. Not because I'm worried about what you'll find out, but because this kind of search can become expensive and time-consuming and can eat you up."

"It shouldn't be that difficult to—"

"It may prove more difficult than you think," Norah broke in. "And at the end of the day, it may change nothing."

"I don't like feeling this suspicion...."

"Sabine, the man is dead. You have a good life, and you have some money. I know you're not doing this because of the money."

"I'm doing it because I feel as though my husband wasn't the person I thought he was. I want to know if I was totally deceived."

"And if you were? If he lied to you about this? If he defrauded his brother? Sabine, you're talking about the father of your children. If you're determined to pursue this, make sure you're prepared to live with the answers you might get."

SHE HADN'T REALLY SPOKEN with Joe since asking him to move out of the house. Three days, then four.

Finally, one morning while all three children were at school, she decided to broach the subject of Victor's money with Joe.

He wasn't working on sleds but immersed in lists of supplies and equipment for K2. Things to Get, Things to Do and so on.

Sabine stiffened, but his occupation strengthened her own resolve, reaffirmed that she'd done the right thing in breaking off their romantic relationship. She could even tell herself that she'd been mistaken to think she loved him.

Had she been mistaken about Victor, too?

She launched into the subject, explaining Lucy's question about how Victor had afforded Teresa's care.

She'd gone no further when Joe said, "I assume with Teresa's money. She had family money."

Of course.

So simple.

There was no reason to ask about their parents' money.

But she couldn't stop herself from wondering aloud, "So he had access to her money after this head injury?"

"Well, I doubt he stole it from her, if that's what you're thinking."

"No, I just wondered. What was your parents' will like?"

He had turned back to his lists. "Victor and I each inherited. My money was held in trust, but Victor could draw on it until I was of age. Actually…" He sank down on a stool and lifted his eyes to hers.

"Weren't there patents?"

"Not that I know of. There were stocks, securities, a house. We moved to a different house. Money got spent at an equal rate from both accounts."

"There isn't any possibility… I don't even know how to ask…."

"What are you asking?"

"He wouldn't have put your money into investments in his name?" She put her hand over her mouth. *Victor.* How could she be suggesting that Victor would do such a thing? "I mean, weren't Teresa's parents still alive? I know her father was. So how much money would she have? I don't think her father gave Victor money. Though I suppose he might have."

"She had a trust fund. She got about twenty grand a year."

"Head injury, Joe. *Think.* Hospital care could have been twenty grand a *day.*"

He set down his pen. "I'm surprised you're asking these questions."

"Why?"

"I'm surprised you want to know."

"Of course I want to know! I want to know who I married, whose children I bore." She studied him. "Don't *you* want to know?"

He seemed to consider. "No. I don't. I don't want to find out your suppositions are right, and even if they are, I refuse to ask."

Her brow furrowed. "I don't understand."

"If he didn't do what you're suggesting, it would make me feel petty to have investigated the matter. I have adequate money. I always *have* had adequate money. Victor taught me skills that have been useful. From him I learned carpentry, woodworking. I never needed to inherit. If he mishandled money he or we inherited from my parents, so be it. It's passed."

"But it—" Abruptly, she couldn't go on. Joe was right. The doubts were hers. Anything she needed to know was *her* quandary.

Joe had peace.

The peace of a mountaineer, which was no peace at all. She'd been out here long enough.

"Okay. Just thought I'd ask." She headed for the door.

"Why?"

"Why what?"

"Why do you want to know?"

"Didn't I just say?" She turned. "He lied to me about you, about Teresa, lied by not telling me what had happened, not telling me…everything. It makes no sense to me in light of who I'd always believed him to be. I thought this answer might explain."

"Would it?"

Would it?

Quite a question.

If Victor turned out to have been the sort of man who'd stolen his little brother's inheritance, would that make her understand him any better? No. Yet now that these doubts had come up, how could she erase them from her mind, how could she pretend she hadn't wondered? How could she *cease* to wonder, cease to ask herself over and over who Victor Knoll had really been?

But Joe didn't want to ask. From his point of view, asking would be petty.

Her perspective was different.

Yet he might be right that she wouldn't learn who Victor was by simply determining *why* he'd never told her he had a brother.

So I have to resign myself to not knowing?

Even after Joe had arrived, after she'd found herself attracted to Joe—and that, she told herself now, was *all* it had been—she'd maintained in her mind and heart that Victor had been an uncommonly good and kind man, that he'd been somehow different from other men she knew.

In what ways, Sabine? In what ways?

Joe was still watching her, no doubt waiting for an answer to his question.

"Okay, it *wouldn't* explain. But I'd know how to feel about him."

"If he stole my inheritance, it would make your marriage something different than what it was?"

No. No, it wouldn't. Victor had loved her, delighted in her, been resolutely *in love with* her.

Nothing would change those facts.

Joe's wisdom in this matter annoyed her. She didn't want to find him wise about anything. She wanted to find him selfish and irrational.

Selfish? The man who dropped everything to take care of your children when you vanished?

I love him.

A sober and sobering thought. One she blotted out.

"Thanks," she said. "You're right." She opened the door

of the shop and went out, realizing belatedly what Lucy's suggestion had ignited in her. An excuse to be near Joe. That was all. As though she could discover something he would find so valuable he'd decide he couldn't leave her to go climb K2.

But I still want to know.

Strange. Norah and Joe had both urged her not to try and find out. So why did it matter to her?

Because I spent four years of my life believing I'd never love another man, that no one would measure up to Victor?

Not completely.

Because there's always been a small part of me that found the death of Teresa convenient?

She certainly hadn't questioned how Teresa had died. She was in love with Victor and he, she'd soon learned, was in love with her, with Sabine Ingram.

No. He would not have killed Teresa. Victor had been proud of his commitment to marriage, and he had *not* been a hypocrite. Perhaps his commitment to Teresa had been so strong *because* she had first loved Joe, first wanted to marry Joe.

That, Sabine could believe.

Could she believe Victor capable of stealing his younger brother's inheritance? Or of mismanaging it?

Neither.

There was her answer, the answer she should live with.

He'd never told her about Joe because he was ashamed of his own conduct in marrying Teresa himself. That fit with the picture of Victor she'd always held. She needed to forget Lucy's questions.

The same way she needed to forget that she'd ever loved Joe Knoll.

HER APPOINTMENT with the psychologist was in a river-stone house that had been converted to offices. Dr. Frazier had the report from the psychiatrist in Kansas City. She said that Sabine could call her Andreya.

Sabine encapsulated what she could remember of her memory lapse, her time away from home, and told Andreya what she thought was the cause—someone she loved possibly lost in an avalanche. She explained that her parents had died, one of a mountaineering illness, the other in the Himalayas while climbing, and her husband had died in an avalanche.

Andreya listened, her expression sympathetic.

Finally, Sabine said, "I'm not sure why I'm here. I guess for a checkup—or I suppose the man in Kansas City thought—well, he thought I should talk about whatever fears led to this."

Andreya shrugged that off. "You've lost loved ones in dramatic ways, one in an avalanche. I think it's natural to have these anxieties. Tell me more about Joe."

Sabine had not intended for it to come out. She said that he was her husband's brother, that he'd been so wonderful caring for her children. "The thing is—" why was she bringing it up? what did it matter? "—Victor never told me about him."

"Told you about him how?"

"He told me his former partner in the sledding business was someone named Joe. He never said Joe was his brother or that he *had* a brother."

She told the counselor the rest, about Teresa, about how Victor's love for her, Sabine, had seemed like a dream come true, about how compatible they'd been and that now she wasn't sure she'd ever known him.

"What are your feelings about that?" Andreya asked.

An interesting question. But she knew the answer. "Like I've been living for something that isn't real. Because I was so devastated by his death."

The counselor's look was deeply empathetic, her blue eyes intense. "And now?"

"And now it's worse."

"If you need to know," Andreya said, "you might talk to people in the town where you and Victor first lived. Did he know any clergy, anyone like that who might tell you more?"

The minister who had married them. He'd been a bit older than Victor, the married pastor of the non-denominational church she and Victor had attended a few times.

"Maybe," Sabine said. "Maybe."

"But Sabine, if you do ask, make sure you really want to know."

It wasn't the first time she'd heard that advice lately.

As soon as she reached home, Sabine dialed information and was soon speaking to the answering machine at the church, which told her that Pastor Jon and his wife were away and would return in two weeks. *He's still there.* And he might know something.

An article about Joe appeared in the local paper the following week. Granted, Oro wasn't a hotbed of news. Celebrities here were, by and large, elite athletes like Lucy and Greg.

But someone had heard that Joe planned to climb K2.

The article contained all the information about the expedition that she'd never sought to learn from him. After dropping Tori at preschool on the Tuesday morning the paper came out, Sabine sat in her car and read it.

The article included a list of the other 8,000-meter peaks Joe had climbed and, in the case of multiple ascents, the number of times each. Manaslu, Everest times four, Gasherbrum II... Some were like the names of old acquaintances or childhood classmates.

Joe, the article said, did not seek to bag all fourteen. "No. I take one mountain at a time. I don't see any reason to climb them all."

His reason for climbing K2?

"It's always attracted me. I'm drawn there. I can't put it more clearly than that."

Sabine wondered how in hell he planned to write anything articulate about why people climb in the Himalayas when he couldn't say why *he* climbed.

She missed Victor.

Ever since she'd spoken with Andreya, she'd found herself missing Victor. Not in the way she once had, with an almost physical longing, a complete horror that they were apart, but because she wanted to talk with him.

She also missed Joe.

She'd explained to Andreya why she'd felt she had to draw a line with Joe. The counselor had commended her for recognizing her own limits. Sabine had confessed that it made her feel better to think of Joe as selfish, an emotional lightweight.

From the article, she learned when he was leaving, which was something they hadn't discussed.

Three weeks.

Just three weeks, and he'd leave for Asia.

What if he dies? Will I regret having stayed away from him?

She stared down the street at the Victorian that housed the preschool and asked herself instead how her children, each of them, would react if Joe died. It was for them, wasn't it, that she'd broken off the relationship?

So she didn't know why, but when she drove home and climbed out of the station wagon, she headed first for the shop.

He was there, again not working on sleds but examining the latest arrivals from UPS—gear from sponsors, a new down snowsuit and more. Sabine felt the excitement of the coming expedition, knew it vicariously because she'd been there in the past. In some small way, she even wished that she was the one going, and the fact galled her.

He glanced up.

She hardly knew what to say to explain her presence. "You're leaving soon. I just read it in the paper."

"Yes."

"Surely you won't try for the summit until later in the summer."

"In the summer, at any rate. We'll see. The summit date always depends on the weather. You know that."

She did. She knew many things another woman might not. Most of all, she knew what it felt like in the Death Zone. The effort of simply moving, of zipping a coat, of putting on crampons. Yes, she knew. She hadn't really forgotten, despite the years that had passed since she'd experienced that altitude. And the last time she'd *climbed,* really climbed?

It had not happened during her marriage to Victor. They had hiked up to some of the local 14,000-foot peaks. But nothing technical. Victor had no technical climbing background. He liked skiing and had done some backcountry skiing, but she and their children had always been more important to him and more interesting than any adventure sport.

If he knew of Joe's decision now, Sabine imagined he'd shake his head, indicating that he didn't understand Joe's choices, didn't understand his thoughts or *him.*

But she did understand, and that was the strange part. She understood. She was sorry about the way Joe felt, but she understood.

Which was what she wanted him to know and couldn't figure out how to say. She tried.

"I don't want you to think," she said, "that I'm judging you. I was— I've been sad. I wish that things were different, but I understand feeling the way you do. I hope—I hope the expedition is successful. I hope you summit, if that's what you want, and come down safely."

He glanced at her, his face seeming angular, handsome, young and old both. "Thank you." He stood, left the box he'd just opened, and came to her. He reached for her.

Sabine did not resist but hugged him back.

A sudden thought shocked her: *Victor never knew the part of me that completely feels and understands Joe's choice.* She said, "I wonder if I would've been disappointed if you'd decided not to go."

"What do you think?"

She shook her head. "I don't know." She stepped back and looked up into his face. "I love you. I just needed to tell you that. We all do. We all want you to be safe and to be happy."

"I'm not sure those things can happen together."

"I wasn't saying we want you to do safe things. We just want…God on our side, so to speak."

He said, "Shall I bring you a rock from K2?"

She shrugged. "The kids might like that."

"It's not what you want."

Her smile trembled. "It would be great," she said.

Joe almost asked if she wished she was going. He didn't because he suspected she wished she could. She stayed behind for her children.

Why couldn't *he* make that kind of sacrifice? What was wrong with him that he couldn't say, *No more mountains?* He couldn't even find it within himself to say, *No mountains after this one,* which would be a lie, a lie that had been told before. No one meant it as a lie at the time, just as an alcoholic who swore he'd never drink again wasn't lying.

Such comparisons had struck him before. He was a climbing addict. Sometimes he convinced himself that at least his was a reasonable type of addiction. He had no trouble walking away from a climb without achieving the summit. Life held many pleasures, though fewer joys, and there was no reason to cut short his future through a determination to make the summit on a given expedition. If he lived, there'd be other expeditions and other summits, something he'd pointed out to Chris Monegan on

Everest—in vain. But that attitude could not compensate for the inherent danger of the sport or the statistics no one could deny.

I'm choosing death, he thought. *I'm choosing that instead of a different life with Sabine and Maria and Finn and Tori.*

The acknowledgment didn't make him like himself. He loved Sabine more than he'd loved other women. He loved her in a different way, a day-to-day best-friend sort of way. She was a grown-up, and not all his ex-lovers had truly been that. Oh, a woman might be twenty-five, thirty or more and still never have grown up. Perhaps the difference lay in Sabine's willingness to admit that her children were more important than her own desires, so she could forego those desires.

Who would she have been had she not married his brother, not borne three children? It didn't matter to Joe Knoll. He dealt in reality. She was who she was, with her own history, her own choices, the consequences of those choices.

Now he held her head, tilted back her head to look into her eyes.

He felt her waiting for him to say he loved her more than the mountains, felt her knowing that he'd never say such a thing.

He kissed her brow at last and released her. "I understand," he said.

Sabine imagined what it would be like to trek to base camp with him—though the approach to K2 was notoriously difficult, days across a glacier, the sun beating down and reflecting back up. She, as a woman in Pakistan, would have to endure whatever liaison officers and porters chose to dish out verbally. If she was Joe's wife, which she wasn't, the situation would be marginally improved.

There would be no great danger in her accompanying Joe to the base of a climb. Her past experience at high altitude had been positive; she seemed to adapt well to the physical challenge.

But it wasn't going to happen this time.

This time, Sabine? Are you planning some kind of future with this man?

She *knew* better than to link her life to Joe Knoll's. She knew better in a hundred ways. Moving out of his arms, she turned to walk out of the shop. "What day are you leaving Oro?"

He told her the date, told her he'd be lending his truck to a friend in Denver.

He's really going. She didn't know why she still half expected him to come to his senses. That was, of course, denial.

"Sabine?"

She paused at the door.

"I love you. You know that, don't you?"

"Not really. I mean, you made love with me, we were lovers. But...I think maybe love is different for you."

Meaning, Joe thought, *that I can walk away from love rather than pay for it by becoming someone else, someone I'm not?*

"Maybe it is," he answered. "Maybe it is, at that."

CHAPTER FIFTEEN

SABINE DID NOT HEAR from Pastor Jon in Minnesota. She
tried calling again and received a busy signal, then got distracted. Every time she remembered to phone, it seemed
to be too late at night.

Her urgency to know, to know truths about Victor that
probably only God could tell her, became less and less important as new loss surrounded her.

Lucy and Greg planned to leave three days before Joe.
Sabine kept trying to quiet a feeling like panic inside
her. She spent time with another mother from Tori's preschool, but the relationship seemed to revolve around
trading child care. Sabine knew she'd miss her sister
terribly. Nothing she could do changed the fact that Lucy
was heading for Everest—*nominally* base camp—and Joe
would be attempting K2. Nothing made these things go
away.

She felt like a woman left behind when others go to
war. She could fight, too, but she had children; she must
stay and protect the home.

She must *be* the home.

Sabine found it to be every kind of nightmare, preparing for this.

Lucy and Greg would be leaving from his house. They

had put his furniture and belongings in storage; most of hers remained in her room at Sabine's house. The night before they left, they both came over to say goodbye to Sabine and the children.

"Are you going to climb a mountain?" Finn asked Lucy as they all sat around the table, eating cookies and milk, a bedtime going-away party.

"Maybe," Lucy told him. "And then I'll come home and climb some of the mountains around here with you. Would you like that?"

"Okay!"

Sabine let the promise of this wash over her, soothing. She liked the idea of her children hiking up peaks of the San Juans. It bore no resemblance to entering the Death Zone, where even to stop and rest meant to creep toward death.

When Lucy hugged her goodbye, Sabine said, "I love you very much, Lucy Ingram. I'm really proud of everything you do. Never forget that." Her eyes were wet, not because she believed this was the last time she would see her sister, but because mortality was always there, the threat to love.

"Thanks," Lucy said, "but what you do is much harder."

Sabine did not argue.

The next day, she awoke with a sense of abandonment, and also the sense that she and Joe were somehow alone on an island of feelings that involved just them. Her feelings were those only he could understand.

As though tuning into Sabine's thoughts, Joe came to the house while Tori was at preschool—in other words, when he knew all the children would be out.

"I want you to come to the library with me," he said.

Part of her wanted to agree immediately to what he asked just to be with him, just to spend an hour with him. Yet she'd spent so much time avoiding him, being distant from him, she couldn't restrain a certain wariness. "Why?"

"I'll have e-mail at base camp. I want to communicate with you, send you reports from the expedition. So you have to set up an e-mail account, which you can do for free."

She nearly retorted that she didn't *want* reports of the expedition, she didn't want to hang on their exploits, on their living or dying. She didn't *care*. She had decided not to care.

But it wasn't that easy. And if he died on K2 and she hadn't granted him this?

"All right."

They walked to the library, and Sabine was conscious of his long legs in his blue jeans beside her, remembering muscle, remembering intimacy. She felt a spasm of agony. The unique bond between lovers had been made between them. Sex had not been casual.

But it's over.

What kind of cold person had she become that she could turn her back on love, on the experience of being in love, being united in love? Had she been hurt so acutely by Victor's death?

Yes.

And I'm not going through that again.

Funny. She kept wishing Victor back—or had for so long—and she would've taken him back from the dead, even if it meant losing him again, being parted from him again by his death.

Do I love Joe less? Or was Victor's death the known, while Joe's, if he died in the mountains, would be the unknown? Each death was different, but they gathered each other up, surrounding her. One death spoke to the others, calling them back to her, pressing upon her.

At the library, Sabine set up an e-mail address at ecologyplace.net. The name she used was *spinster.* For a password, she chose MYVICTOR. She knew that Joe watched her type that password. It was right. She was willing to correspond with him as concerned sister-in-law. She was willing to have him in her life on those terms.

Behind her, Joe said, "Ouch."

She said, "You have mountains, Joe. They're worth it." For a person without family, a person choosing the mountains, they were superb. To climb was to live free, to live for oneself.

She'd had that option once. She'd chosen a family, instead. It was what she wanted.

Joe wanted the mountains. She said, to emphasize this, "It's what you want." Because that was what he'd told her. Why not say it back to him?

But she couldn't bring herself to look at his face.

She knew only that behind her he was very still.

HE SAID GOODBYE to Sabine and the children the night before his departure, telling them he'd be gone by the time they awoke the next morning.

This parting was quite different from Lucy's.

There were cookies and milk to be had, but no one, even the children, seemed particularly hungry for them.

Anxiety pervaded the kitchen.

Sabine spun some alpaca on a spindle while Joe hugged each of the children, answering their questions.

"My teacher," Finn said, "told us it's very dangerous in the Himalayas because up high the air isn't safe to breathe."

"That's not scientifically accurate," Sabine said swiftly. "There's just not much oxygen."

"Is it safe?" Tori asked.

"No!" Finn said.

Joe's lips parted, as though to explain high-altitude mountaineering. He planned to carry oxygen and use it on the descent. He had told Sabine this, and she'd said, *I don't want to hear about it,* telling him, more plainly than other words could have, that she was terrified. She knew the danger, she'd seen the danger, she'd mourned the results of the danger.

"Of course it's dangerous," snapped Maria. She frowned.

Tori said, "But Daddy is a good climber."

Sabine wanted to hit something, break something. She wanted to say, *He's not your daddy, damn it.* But she needed to be civil to Joe, to express love to Joe, because she wouldn't see him until his return.

Which meant that perhaps she'd never see him again.

But civility wasn't what she felt.

Only rage.

She waited for Joe to make some appropriate remark to Tori, some response that would create *distance* between the two of them.

He's the only daddy she's ever known.

"Good night, all of you. I love you all," Joe said. "You're my family."

Sabine bit her lip. Hard. Any words that came from her now would be incoherent. How *dare* he say that, *knowing* she sought to exclude him from *her* family for the emotional well-being of herself and her children.

Instead, coldly, she said, "We love you, too. Have a safe trip." She left the room without touching him, without hugging him, and climbed the stairs, determined not to see him again before he left.

"Will you tuck me in, Daddy?" drifted up from the kitchen.

I'm going mad.

She went to the attic, now partially divested of its essence of Victor, stripped of the presence of Joe, and shut the door. She sat on the floor against the wall, listening, hearing his voice in the halls, hearing him say good-night to Tori, then Finn. There was a knock at the attic door.

Sabine opened it.

Maria came in.

"Are you all right, Mom?" she asked.

"I'm fine. What would you think," she said, keeping the subject off Joe, leading the conversation to a life *without* Joe, "of knitting a summer sweater with some of that pale blue angora/merino I've been working on?"

"For me?"

"Yes. Would you like to knit it? We could work on the hard parts together. You know that pattern you like with the zipper and the hood?"

"And the silver tassels!" exclaimed her daughter.

Sabine heard the front door below close. "Yes. And silver tassels."

SHE DREAMED vividly that night.

It was cold. The place was a resort on a high, windy plateau with a freezing-cold lake, in which no one swam or canoed. Families were there. Maria ran from one building to another, which was a store.

Joe was there.

And Lucy and Greg.

And Victor, though he seemed too busy to talk to Sabine.

Hart Markham was there and Karen and several celebrities.

Then it was time to leave, and there was only one way out, which was to glissade down an icy, watery natural slide into a freezing river, with waves in which ice floated, a turbulent breakup.

Sabine no longer noticed her children.

The slide was inherently risky, but there was no choice. Everyone must go down. Each person must go down alone. She watched the others.

Victor sat, like a child descending a slide "the right way." He seemed safe and solid. He splashed into the river, into its waves, and went across.

Sabine wanted to get to him, but he was so far ahead, so far out of reach.

She watched a bartender she remembered from Minnesota take the slide headfirst, hands pointed ahead. Eventually he emerged from the waves.

Not everyone did.

Joe dove. Headfirst, unafraid, crossing the river strongly, confidently.

Sabine didn't know how to do this. The waves at the bottom seemed lethal. Indeed, some people didn't make it.

She had no ice ax and wished she had one to slow her descent. She sat like a little girl, following Victor's lead, planning to skim across the river.

But the waves were over her head.

She couldn't reach the top, and she awoke.

Joe.

He had dived headfirst into those waves. And he had come out fine. She knew what the waves were. Water always represented emotion, didn't it? Even frozen emotion could not remain static.

Joe had dived headfirst into emotion, into love, into uncertainty. And his way was *the* way.

The only way to face life and loss.

The only way to survive love.

But other ways worked, too.

Victor's had.

She went to her window, to peer out toward the shop in the early morning light, thinking she would see the lights of Joe's truck.

But the truck was gone.

He had left.

The dream memory swept her in.

She had tried to approach the torrent Victor's way, the safe way.

But the water was still over her head, the water still tried to drown her. It was beyond her control.

Love could not be harnessed, managed, controlled.
I was wrong. I've been wrong.

SHOULD HE GIVE UP on his feelings for her? Sabine occupied the back of Joe's mind as he went from car to airplane, to airplane. As he dealt with an appalling amount of luggage—gear for the climb. As he met team members, one of whom, Ross Keyes, shared his flight across the Atlantic.

Ross wanted to talk about K2, and Joe *should* have wanted to talk about it. Ross was uneasy, expressing the kind of superstition that Joe had long since learned to take seriously.

He told Ross, "If you have a premonition you're going to die on this climb and you don't want to die on this climb, then don't go." Joe couldn't believe this thought had formed words in his mouth. In his head was one thing; voicing it was another.

"But I feel like this before every climb," Ross explained.

"Ah." I should stop thinking about her. *She's not in love with me. If she was, she wouldn't have asked me to move out.*

That conviction kept him on his course, urged him to return his focus to what lay ahead.

But would it be any different if Sabine *was* in love with him?

For the first time in his life, he thought it might make a difference. She was so strong, and yet hearing that two unnamed people had died in an avalanche had temporarily broken her. She was not simply a selfish woman trying to manipulate her lover. She had said, *Uniting my life with a climber's is more than I can tolerate.*

So perhaps the question truly came down to what he was willing to sacrifice in his love for her.

To stop climbing was a sacrifice so great that he couldn't imagine a comparable sacrifice on her part.

Ross said, "What about you? How do you feel about this climb?"

They were a team of four. They would rendezvous with the other two members, one Pole and one Brit, in Pakistan. Joe had previously climbed with the British Ian Maxwell. The Pole, Dorek Dolinski, was well-known and well-respected, with six 8,000-meter peaks to his credit. He and Ian had attempted K2 the year before and turned back three times because of bad weather. "Comfortable," he answered at last. He knew himself to be a strong climber, who had been to the summit of Everest four times without oxygen. He usually climbed without oxygen, but what he'd read of K2 had convinced him he'd be smart to carry some.

And not linger in the Death Zone.

It was his most important rule. It was the rule he must not violate.

But if others lingered?

It was not his expedition. It was Ian's.

And for reasons Joe didn't understand, experienced climbers, savvy climbers, again and again made the mistake of staying up high for too long. They decided a day's rest—while their brains and bodies were dying on thin air—was necessary before the summit. Or they stayed at the summit, taking photos or just *being* there.

And sometimes weather caught them.

Mistakes were made by people with too much experience to make them. But everyone was fallible.

Joe talked with Ross about Ross's reasons for climbing, took out his laptop and began writing, began telling the story of the expedition, choosing the present tense for his diary of events.

He wrote:

I have committed myself, but I have never set out to climb a mountain with stronger personal ties calling me to remain, to back out, to stop. I have left behind the woman who is everything I've always wanted in a companion, yet a woman who will not maintain a relationship with a climber. I've made the choice I always make. This incarnation of the choice: I have chosen K2 over her....

HE SENT HER his first e-mail from Heathrow. He had no idea what to say, what she would want to hear. He chose to address it to her and the children, knowing she wouldn't appreciate the children's inclusion but that Maria, Finn and Tori would.

Dear Sabine, Maria, Finn and Tori:
I am in England now. That means I'm still far from the mountains.
Ross and I had a good time on the plane. They showed *Hidalgo*. Have any of you seen it? There are wild horses in it....

The letter was difficult to write. He was dancing around the reasons for heading to the other side of the world. If he mentioned equipment or supplies, would Sabine think he was trying to lure Finn, for instance, to a life of high-altitude mountaineering?

An American going home after a month in Glastonbury photographed Joe and Ross with Joe's digital camera. Joe downloaded the picture and attached it to the e-mail before sending the latter.

Sabine would be angry. She'd ended their relationship as lovers for a reason and had made that reason clear.

In fact, she might not even bother to go to the library to check her e-mail.

SHE WENT two days later and found three e-mails from Joe with pictures attached. The last e-mail was sent from Pakistan. None of the children were with her, and she wondered if she should bring them to the library to read the e-mails that had been addressed to them, as well. Seeing Joe's face smiling at her from the photos made her heart ache. She longed for him in a way she'd never longed for anyone but Victor.

How petty she'd felt typing in the password she'd chosen, MYVICTOR. Shutting out Joe for being himself, for doing what mattered to him.

And Victor was gone.

Because she had Lucy's e-mail address, although Lucy hadn't known Sabine had an address of her own, she e-mailed her sister, too, telling her that Oro was lonely without her.

"Sabine."

Sabine started. She glanced up. Karen stood behind her with a handsome young man. He was tall and very blond, with chiseled cheekbones. They seemed to be a couple. "This is Jack Hellier. Jack, this is Sabine Knoll. I take care of her children sometimes."

"It's nice to meet you." This was a boyfriend. Karen had a boyfriend, and, to Sabine's mind, this could only presage good things.

The library was deserted except for the librarian, so Karen and Jack took nearby chairs and Sabine asked Jack where he was from and what he did. He lived in nearby Bolt, where he worked for the fire department.

Karen said, "Lucy's gone, and Joe's gone. Have you heard from them?"

"Joe. Lucy didn't know about…" Sabine explained about her new e-mail account.

"I bet the kids miss Joe," Karen said. "Finn really looks up to him like a father."

Sabine hissed in a tone she hoped couldn't be heard by the librarian, "Would you want your kids to have a father who was climbing in the Death Zone?"

Karen's look was full of sympathy, this time for Sabine, and Sabine could tell that Karen's distress was real. "It must be hard to know what to do," Karen said.

"No. It's hard to do it." But Sabine remembered her dream. Perhaps Karen was right, after all. Perhaps *knowing* what to do was every bit as difficult as doing it.

Karen said, "Joe seems very responsible."

"Would you call me responsible if I set off to climb K2?"

"Well, no. But you're their mother."

"Fathers don't matter?" Jack said mildly to Karen.

"I meant—" She stopped.

"You just said," Jack told her, "that her kids see him as a father."

Karen looked mildly chagrined.

Spontaneously, Sabine invited them over for dinner that night. "I'll pick up some pizza from D'Angelo's. What do you guys want?"

Jack and Karen engaged in some good-natured bickering over toppings before giving her their preferences.

When they'd left, Sabine turned back to the computer and wrote to Joe, telling him about Karen's coming in with Jack and that she'd asked them for dinner.

She hesitated, then wrote,

I love you, Joe. Sorry to have been a coward about it and about what you're doing. I pride myself on making good decisions for myself and my children, but the right decision isn't easy to see when it comes to you. Be safe.
Love,
Sabine

She reread this letter, considering options that couldn't happen—impossible, in other words. Her flying to Pakistan, traveling to Skardu, crossing the Baltoro Glacier in pursuit of the man she loved... No.

Victor had an easier time of it with me, she reflected as she drove to the preschool to pick up Tori. A woman without children could follow her heart, could fall in love and pursue its natural consequences.

Now she wished she'd communicated with Joe more fully through her e-mail. She wished she could tell him that she was in love with him, that she would be his lover again should he ever return. But if she said that now and if he returned after attempting K2, what would that do to their relationship? And what kind of relationship would they have? What would be the balance of power?

Certain minimum requirements were necessary in a person who would be father, adoptive father, stepfather or any related role to her children. One of the minimum requirements was a basic sense of self-preservation, made manifest in an unwillingness to climb 8,000-meter peaks.

And it would be wrong, she told herself, for Joe to decide not to climb such mountains so that he could be her lover. If he did, he might always hold her ultimatum against her.

Did that mean that the only right solution would be to accept him on his terms?

Or that the only right solution was the one she'd chosen? To just bow out of the relationship, with no hope of restoring it.

"Where are we going?" Tori asked a few minutes later, after Sabine had buckled her into her car seat.

"Just to the library for a few minutes."

"Can I get a book?"

"Yes."

"And a movie?"

"Yes."

While Tori looked at books in the children's section, Sabine returned to the computer and brought up her e-mail account again and began to compose a new note to Joe.

Dear Joe:
I wish you were with me, and I'm looking forward to when you're here again—whenever you can be.
Love,
Sabine

She hesitated, ready to hit Send.

And not ready.

I'm giving in. Why should I be the one to give in?

But she saw her dream again, remembered the people sliding down the icy slide headfirst or feetfirst, remembered that Victor had gone the safe way, while Joe had dived.

Yet Victor was dead.

She pressed Send and stood to see if Tori was ready to go.

SHE BEGAN PACKING up Victor's belongings in the attic, determining which to keep—just a few—which to give or throw away.

But she couldn't deny that she was still *looking* for something. Looking for the reason Victor had never told her about Joe.

I've come up with a reason that makes sense, she reminded herself. Victor hadn't wanted her to know that he'd lured away his little brother's fiancée. Maybe he'd

even feared Joe might return someday to pay him back—
by trying to lure away the woman Victor loved.

If there were financial records she hadn't seen, then
they weren't in any box here. She'd rejected the idea that
Victor had stolen Joe's inheritance.

What she wanted were photos from Victor's and Joe's
childhood. Victor had saved one, and Joe had given her
another. Were there more?

But the secret wouldn't be there. It had to do with
Teresa, since Victor's lie was about Teresa as well as Joe.

It wasn't related to Teresa's accident, since that had
happened later.

*Sabine, why does there have to be a better reason than
the one you found? Maybe Victor privately resented giving
up some dream of his, some dream you never even heard
about, to raise his brother.*

Should she try again to reach Pastor Jon in Minnesota?

But how could he know Victor's heart any better than
she had? Yet Victor *might* have confided in the man.

But once again she looked at the clock and realized it
was after ten in Minnesota.

Victor had not kept many letters. She found occasional
Christmas cards that it appeared he hadn't discarded only
because he hadn't noticed their presence among his belongings. None of the names meant anything to her, and
only one had a personal message, something about hoping
the sweaters fit. Sabine wondered if the sweaters had been
for Victor and Joe, for Victor and Teresa or for someone
else altogether.

What he *had* kept, what he'd cared enough to keep in
their own box, were cards from Maria and the cards

Sabine had made with Finn's handprints and footprints on them and his one- and two-year-old efforts at art. Cards for Father's Day, birthdays, Christmas, Valentine's Day, preschool projects, Preschool art.

And cards from her. They'd never been apart to write letters to each other, but he'd kept her cards—all of them, as far as she could tell.

She found no similar tokens from Teresa.

He hadn't thrown them out right after her death. Perhaps he'd gotten rid of them when he and Sabine moved here from Minnesota.

There was an index card. On it, Victor had scrawled May 3, 1986.

That was all.

That date… When did Victor and Teresa get married? Sabine thought it had been that year.

Instinctively, she knew what the date meant. It was the day Joe had walked out of Victor's life. She could check with Joe, but she was nearly certain she was right.

Had Victor been angry that Joe hadn't been more forgiving? Had Victor wondered why, after all he'd done for Joe, Joe should begrudge him this one thing?

So difficult to know what had been going on in the head of a man who'd never kept a diary.

In the bottom of the box, something had slipped under one of the flaps of cardboard. A photo of Teresa Young, beautiful, unharmed, her red curls frothing around her face as she grinned, her chin smooth and strong over the neck of her Icelandic sweater.

And another index card.

Victor's writing but not, Sabine thought, his words:

Why are you so resentful and crestfallen? If you do well, you can hold up your head; but if not, sin is a demon lurking at the door: his urge is toward you, yet you can be his master.

Her own background in theology was weak, but surely this was from the Bible. Where? She decided to recopy the quotation and take it to the library with her. There was a chance the librarian would know. Or she could look on the Internet.

And at the bottom of the box, a letter in an envelope, addressed not to Victor but to Teresa. The postmark was 1987. It was from Joe.

CHAPTER SIXTEEN

Dear Teresa:
In two words—not interested. I have said goodbye
to my brother and to you. Does Victor know what
he signed up for yet? I never thought I'd pity either
of you; now I'm sorry for you both. You, because
you're never happy with what you have, Victor
because he traded his honor for you.
Joe

SABINE CONSIDERED the letter from every angle. Joe wasn't
interested in...*what?* He'd said Teresa was never happy
with what she had. Had she become unhappy with Victor?
Had she wanted Joe back? If so, the fact that this letter was
among Victor's things meant he must have known.

But the statement that he'd said goodbye to both of them
seemed to imply that someone had attempted to reach out to
him; certainly, it seemed as if Teresa had, one way or another.

She told the children she felt like going to the library.
The afternoon was nice, so she and the girls walked while
Finn accompanied them on his bicycle.

The librarian was named Sandy and had lived in Oro
all her life. Sabine felt vaguely intimidated by her,
although she wasn't sure why. But she approached her,

nonetheless, showing her the quote. "Would you know where in the Bible this occurs?"

Sandy squinted at it and shook her head. "I couldn't tell you."

While Sabine waited to get on a computer, Norah came in. She'd been back from her trip for more than a week and had been over to see the children twice, relieving some of the loneliness Sabine felt without Lucy.

Sabine showed her the quote.

Norah put on half glasses and read it aloud. Then she raised her eyebrows and handed the paper back to Sabine. "My dear, it's from Genesis. God speaking to Cain when Cain is upset because God preferred his brother's gift. But *prior,* of course, to Cain's slaying Abel. Apparently, the counsel didn't sink in."

Sabine discovered she couldn't tell Norah where she'd found the card—or what else had been there.

Poor Victor. The quote implied that he'd believed accepting Teresa's love would be wrong, yet he'd chosen to do so. If she'd then been unfaithful, turning back to his younger brother... Finally, the sledding accident.

He'd never spoken of these things, except when he'd told her he didn't think Teresa's accident was a punishment for anything.

She decided that as soon as she got home, she'd try to call Minnesota again.

When she was able to get on the computer, she found no e-mails from Joe. There would be none until they reached the satellite phone at base camp, which they were sharing with another, larger, expedition.

Nonetheless, she wrote him an e-mail, feeling trivial as she asked, Please tell me if Victor ever made any effort to reconcile with you and if so, how you responded.

But even as she wrote, she had a strong feeling about the answer.

Victor *would* have tried to make peace. And if there'd been no movement on Joe's part, eventually he would have steeled himself and written off the relationship.

That must be the answer.

Shame would not have made him hide his brother's existence from Sabine. But if Joe had refused—especially if he'd refused repeatedly—to make peace with him...

Still, why not say, *My brother and I had a falling out. We don't get along?*

Had it seemed so appalling to Victor to admit that he'd stolen his brother's fiancée or fallen in love with her or been seduced by her or simply married her? Any version would have done.

Victor, why didn't you tell me?

With a fervor even more intense than her grieving desire for the husband she would never hold again, she longed for one last conversation with Victor, to ask this one question. If she knew, it would free her. If she knew, perhaps she could let Joe, when and if he returned from K2, sleep in the bed that Victor had made, sleep there with her.

Was there any living person who could tell her the answer? Sabine wondered. Could Pastor Jon?

When she reached home, she looked up the number and dialed it.

He answered, "Pastor Jon."

Sabine quickly told him who she was and that she wanted to talk about Victor.

"I am *so* glad you called. We couldn't make out your phone number on the machine's message. I didn't know where you were calling from, and caller ID didn't give a number."

"My home number isn't listed. I'm sorry. I wanted to know…"

And she told the man who had presided at her wedding to Victor. She told him of Joe's appearance, of her astonishment that Victor even had a brother. "Did *you* know?" she asked.

"Oh, yes." A pause. "I married Victor and Teresa, too."

And then it came, the kind of answer she hadn't really hoped to receive. "I counseled him to tell you everything. He sympathized with his brother in Joe's pain at Teresa's and Victor's marrying. He blamed himself completely."

Relief flowed through her. This sounded like the Victor she'd always known.

"I believe he was afraid. Afraid you'd think he couldn't be trusted in your marriage because of his betrayal of Joe. Afraid that if you knew the truth, you wouldn't marry him. Then, he was afraid of your reaction if he told you everything later. He held you in such high esteem. He felt guilty for the relief he experienced at Teresa's death. He felt undeserving of your love."

Sabine asked more questions, asked until she was satisfied with the answers. These answers convinced her, finally, that what Victor had done in concealing Joe's existence was less out of character than she'd feared.

They ended the conversation with her promise to send

a photo of the children and many thanks to the minister for new insight into Victor's conscience. Pastor Jon had spoken with Victor on this subject not once but several times and had urged him to trust in Sabine's love. But Victor had been painfully afraid of losing that love—in part because he believed he deserved to lose it.

It was only that night, when Sabine lay alone in the bed of her marriage, that she realized what she'd been doing by obsessing over the mysteries involving her dead husband.

She was avoiding thoughts of the man who was crossing the Baltoro Glacier on his way to climb K2.

She was avoiding images of what her life would be if he was lost to her forever, like his brother.

JOE HAD WALKED along the rows of photographs at the Hotel K2, studying faces of legend and faces he had known, faces of friends and acquaintances who had died.

Four had died on this mountain. Four of his friends. Plus three acquaintances.

Now, crossing the glacier under a merciless sun, protecting his face from the reflection off the ice, carrying his own load, feeling the altitude less than some, more than others, he imagined his face on the wall of that hotel.

He imagined another kind of photo. Of himself and Sabine and Maria, Finn and Tori. He imagined a photo of Finn on his shoulders atop a Colorado peak, one that he and his brother's son had climbed together.

Why should the image of the solitary, hardened mountaineer continue to attract him, to call him?

What do you want out of this, Joe?

It wasn't the *having done* that drew him. It was the doing, the climbing itself.

There are other challenges, Joe. There are other climbing challenges, challenges less deadly.

And wasn't it a challenge to stay alive, to live as a family man, to raise children, to keep a marriage together?

Wasn't that the challenge of an *adult?*

They stopped during the heat of the day and pitched their tents. He joined the others in Ian's tent. While they planned, discussed filming, Joe remained quiet.

I'm not going on. I'm not going to do this.

He would go to the base of the mountain. He would provide support for the expedition, trek to the first two camps, but no higher. Even there, he needed to take care with himself, as though he was taking care of something borrowed, something that belonged to someone else.

He didn't tell Ian until they reached base camp.

The words came neither naturally nor easily. "I've decided to give the expedition what support I can from our first few camps. But I'm not going for the summit."

Ian's young face—the face of a person perhaps too young to lead such an expedition—fell. He rocked back, hugging his knees to his chest. "Problems with Ross?"

"No. Not at all. I— There are children in my life now, my brother's kids." He hated himself for prevaricating. While what he'd said was true, it was more true that he was in love with Sabine, that he wanted to marry Sabine, that he wanted to build a life with her, that he was ready for the sacrifices that life entailed. Integrity made him say more. "And their mother. She's…" He didn't finish.

Ian had seen the one picture of Sabine that Joe carried.

Joe had taken it before he left and had a small print made to carry with him. She wore her hair in two braids, and her smile was shy and pure and seductive at once.

"She's beautiful," Ian remarked. "But women are just women, Joe. Mountains are…" He shrugged, as though forfeiting the argument. "It's up to you. I can't try to talk you into this. And I'm sure we can pick up a climbing partner for Ross here. Things get shuffled around. Teams shake up and split up. And of course I'm grateful for your support at the lower elevations."

Joe noticed that Ian seemed to be suggesting that his decision not to go for the summit had to do with doubts about his capacity to achieve it. *Lower elevations.* Ian had to know that the altitude—or, specifically, Joe's ability or inability to perform well at high altitude—was not behind his choice. He wondered if there was subtle pressure in the remark.

It didn't matter.

Finally, he was at peace. He checked his e-mail and found several notes from Sabine. Sabine, asking questions about Victor, about whether Victor had ever tried to reconcile with him.

He answered that one quickly: Yes, he tried. I was young, Sabine, and not very forgiving.

Had Teresa, she wanted to know, ever wavered after she'd married Victor?

Joe had never discussed this with a soul, never wanting Victor to find out. But Victor was dead. Yet he didn't want to describe Teresa's transgressions in an e-mail.

He tried phrasing it different ways, and all the time, in the back of his mind, was the issue of how to tell Sabine, *whether* to tell Sabine, that he'd decided not to attempt the summit of K2. Would she believe him? How many climbers wrote home such promises only to go forth anyway, sometimes to death? Sabine knew the answer to that as well as he did. But his own resolve was more than words. He understood that because of the comfort that had settled upon him.

Rather than anticipating the climb, he anticipated interviewing other climbers at base camp, anticipated writing about the mystery that was high-altitude addiction. Rather than thinking about summiting himself, he looked forward to providing help to the expedition lower on the mountain, along with their base camp manager, Pam Brighton.

He tried again to answer the question about Teresa: She wrote to me, wanted to meet.

He didn't add, *Just the two of us.*

Apparently Sabine had seen the letter he'd written back to Teresa. Joe couldn't remember the content of that letter, but undoubtedly his answer to Teresa, whatever words he'd found for *No,* had told the tale. Yes, Teresa had wanted him—or, rather, wanted excitement. She wanted him and Victor *both* to love her.

So Victor had gotten his hands on that letter.

At least he knew then, Joe thought, *knew that I didn't betray him.*

But it pained him that Victor had learned of Teresa's unfaithful heart, and that fact surprised him. He'd never *wanted* Victor to know, which was why he'd sent the letter back to Teresa's secret P.O. box instead of to the one she and Victor shared.

But how was it, why was it, that he'd obviously wanted to protect his brother?

Victor.

What would he say to his brother, if the dead could hear?

Victor, I'm in love with Sabine. Hope it's all right with you.

No, not that.

Victor, I'm sorry I didn't accept your peace offerings. I'm sorry I didn't forgive. I said I'd forgiven, yet I wanted nothing to do with you. I'm sorry. I should never have let a woman get in the way of our relationship.

Perhaps that.

He took a photo of base camp with its many tents, downloaded it to his computer, and told Sabine which tents belonged to which expedition, told her of looking forward to meeting and talking with other climbers, seeing old friends.

He did not put in writing that he wasn't going for the summit. It would be better to tell her after the fact, to tell her when he was on his way home, and that was still months away.

When he'd sent that e-mail, he saw another from Sabine. In this one she related her conversation with Pastor Jon from Minnesota.

Victor again, Joe thought as he read.

Yet at the end of the e-mail, she wrote, You've helped me move on, Joe. Things are better now.

THE HAT ARRIVED in June. It was made of brown worsted, a fine yarn that he knew she had spun. Close-knit, close-fitting, practical.

In case he hadn't understood her blessing, the small piece of paper within, a piece of paper decorated with crayon by Tori, bore the message: *To keep your head warm up high. Love, Sabine.*

It fit perfectly, and he wore it the following day from base camp, skinning up to advanced base camp on skis, continuing to Camp One and then Camp Two, the highest he had intended to go.

But he felt strong.

He felt so strong, so satisfied—both relative terms, because there was no feeling truly *strong* at that altitude— that he *knew,* knew he could make the summit *and* descend safely. The descent was the trick on this mountain, on most of them. Having the willpower that overrode everything else so that one did not linger in the Death Zone.

Briefly, he was guiltily glad he'd never told Sabine he wouldn't go for the summit.

She had given her blessing, and it was on his head, soft and warm.

He would at least help fix ropes above Camp Two; he would do that much for his teammates. He was acclimating well. Ross had developed a cough that Joe suspected he would have till the expedition's end.

Joe spoke to him in the tent that afternoon, when Ross arrived at Camp Two. "Do you feel okay about doing this?"

Ross had been paired with a new climbing partner, a British woman named Lisa Jones. She had some good climbs behind her but little high-altitude experience.

"What is okay? It's a crazy thing we do, isn't it?"

Joe didn't disagree. A sudden yearning for the summit

had cut through the peace he'd known in his decision *not* to go for it.

"I just need some rest," Ross said. "Last night, the snoring…"

From the next tent—a Russian climber who they all joked would cause an avalanche some night.

Joe himself slept like a rock. In the morning, as he gathered the ropes, Ian joined him. "Change of heart?"

"Just thought I'd help you up higher. No use Ross expending more energy than he needs to."

"As long as he acclimates."

"I think that's happening."

Ian said, "So you're going to Camp Three."

"You don't want help?"

"I want you to come to the summit. That's why I invited you in the first place."

For a moment, he saw himself there and saw himself as one of those who'd summited K2, the savage mountain, and lived. He *could* do it.

Then the image faltered, wavering.

It was such a solitary picture. The picture of a man who chose mountains over people.

Over life.

"I think I can help more down here," Joe said.

Ross dragged himself over. He'd been sipping tea in the tent. Now he was dressed, crampons on, ready to climb.

Joe led. From below, Ian filmed them with a digital camera and digital movie camera.

Two pitches.

The rhythm of crampons and ice ax was familiar, comforting. Difficult labor. Joe relaxed into it, the breathing and concentration taking over, blocking out everything else. As he set the new ropes, he discarded old ones, tossing them down crevasses or elsewhere, out of the way of climbers who might be confused when coming upon them.

Joe jerked away from the wall just as he heard an indistinct cry from below.

He tried to arrest his motion with the ice ax, to minimize the impact the rope would take and the possibility of protection popping free of the ice.

The rope caught, something caught, and Joe looked at where he was—off-route and twenty meters below where he'd been—then searched for Ross.

The rope had snagged around a lip. Joe called, "Ross!" Nothing.

And there was no option but to climb, to get back on route, then downclimb to where Ross must be.

He started, but the slow pace that had seemed acceptable two minutes earlier no longer was. Where was Ross? He should be clipped onto the rope. Joe was almost sure that Ross had fallen—or been hit by rock- or snowfall?— almost sure that was what had pulled Joe off the wall.

It was an hour and a half before he was able to secure another rope and descend to where he thought Ross must be. The lines of the route hid him from Joe's view until not far above the last pitch.

Exhausted, weary as he would not have been at a lower elevation, Joe found his friend hanging from the rope, unconscious. What was more, he could see no reason for the unconsciousness, no obvious sign that he'd struck his head, for instance.

His first reaction, human and appalling, was that he himself would not die because of this mishap. And Ross *was* alive, though in obvious danger from cold.

I have to get him back down to Camp Two.

Someone was bound to be up soon. Ian and Dorek had said they planned to start climbing not long after Joe and Ross. So where were they?

Descending *with* Ross was the only answer. Joe was strong enough. He roped Ross to him and took extra care tying in to the next length of rope. The altitude that had seldom been a problem for him fought him now in his efforts to rescue a teammate.

He felt as though Sabine was watching over his shoulder. If she could see him, would she say, *I told you so?* The unexpected happened, one unexpected thing, one factor left out of calculations, and then the danger doubled, tripled, multiplied exponentially.

He considered leaving Ross on the rope and getting others to climb back up for him, but that presumed Ross had time and that others could absolutely, definitely make the climb. Until he saw Ian and Dorek, he couldn't be sure of that.

He'd descended about twenty-five feet with Ross when he saw a figure on the ropes below and recognized Dorek's green snowsuit. Joe yelled to the Pole that Ross was hurt, unconscious. He continued descending. Then Dorek and Ian were able to take over guiding Ross down. Ian, hearing the news, had radioed base camp for medical help.

At Camp Two, Joe heard, almost through a fog, as Ian said, "It's HACE. Look at his pupils. We've got to get him down."

High Altitude Cerebral Edema.

Climbers from a Japanese team were also at Camp Two, but Ian and Dorek and Joe, between them, felt able to take Ross to base camp. Their base camp manager had already ordered a helicopter, but that didn't mean they would count on seeing it.

Joe felt the numb disbelief that always overcame him in the midst of climbing emergencies—particularly those that looked like unstoppable fatalities.

Ross could not be dying.

Ross could not be in a coma, which was how it looked.

Why hadn't he, Joe, seen the symptoms earlier?

But that's how it can happen, Joe, fast.

He saw himself doing a task he'd done only once before, notifying family members of the death of a fellow expedition member. He was the logical person to go to Ross's mother, because Ross was American, as he himself was.

Instead of Ross's mother, he imagined Sabine. He imagined having to tell her about the death of a full-grown Finn.

I can't do this. I can't do this anymore.

How ironic that he'd decided not to go above Camp Two, yet had broken that promise to himself and then…

Would anything be different if he hadn't volunteered to fix ropes? His intention had been for Ross to get some rest at Camp Two. But Ross had ended up following.

This is a nightmare. He was fine. He was fine.

Sabine would hate him for climbing this mountain at all, for taking this risk, for having a part in someone else's death.

He recognized that assumption as untrue and irrational, but he couldn't escape the feeling that Ross's death was now inevitable.

I can't stay here all summer. Not now.

Ian would probably prefer for someone else, a climber in the area where Ross's mother lived, to take the news to her. He wouldn't want Joe to leave. Oh, Ian would make a show of deliberating, of deciding whether or not to go on. But finally, *for* Ross, supposedly, they would continue.

But Joe knew he was leaving.

Everything was draped in a pall now.

ROSS BECAME somewhat conscious just above base camp.

Joe said, "We're taking you down, buddy."

And if the helicopter didn't arrive, he, Joe, would carry his friend down the Baltoro Glacier. For High Altitude Pulmonary Edema and High Altitude Cerebral Edema, descent was the first response.

The helicopter did not come, and Joe told Ian, "I'm taking him down." It wasn't quite dusk, but he had known people to die while waiting for a helicopter, and the object now was to descend with Ross as quickly as possible. Ross was not yet lucid, and Joe felt certain he would improve at a lower elevation.

"Are you coming back?" Ian asked.

Joe stared, his mind full. Ian should help him take Ross down. Dorek should help. But neither had offered. Both knew the difficulty of the long march, and neither would jeopardize his own summit bid by helping.

Possibly someone from another expedition or a porter, someone, would accompany him and Ross. Joe was exhausted, but he knew that if he was going in the other direction, if he was going for the summit, he could keep moving. This was more important than any summit.

The base camp doctor, an Australian, was giving Ross oxygen. Joe's teammate's eyes looked clearer, better, than they had.

"I'll take him down," Joe said, "if he needs to go."

"I think he'll be able to go under his own power, with some help."

Joe felt himself smile.

CHAPTER SEVENTEEN

SHE'D HAD NO e-mail from him for fifteen days.

He hadn't said he was starting for the summit. She searched the Internet for news of K2, but Joe's expedition was not as high-profile as many others. She didn't know how to get hold of him. Would anyone *tell* her if something had happened?

Yes. His friend Ross would tell her.

What if *both* were dead?

But Sabine didn't think he was dead.

She met with Andreya and told the counselor she'd had no message from Joe, no message in more than two weeks.

"Is there some way you can find out if he's all right?"

"If there'd been a death on K2, there'd be news of that on the Internet. So he's not dead."

"Right."

Sabine sat back in the upholstered chair in the therapist's office. "I'm going to stay with him."

Andreya stared.

"I mean, if—when he comes back, I'm willing to be with him. To be his lover."

"Sabine, isn't that too much of a compromise for you?"

"No. I love him. He's the man I love, and I'm willing to sacrifice security, certainty. There was nobody in the world more stable, more safe, than Victor, and he died. I just can't control life and death. Joe is the man I want."

Her therapist nodded. "It's good to know what you want," she said, quietly.

I want him, Sabine thought. *And I want him home.*

JOE'S TRUCK WAS PARKED in the drive outside the shop when she returned from her therapist's. Karen and Jack had taken the kids with them to the Oro Summer Carnival. They'd planned to spend the day there and weren't back yet.

Sabine didn't park at the house but drove straight to the shop and parked behind him.

The door opened, and he stood there, and it seemed incredible to her that once she would have preferred to see Victor—that she would have preferred anyone to this man.

He lounged in the doorway of the shop with lazy grace, his hair a little too long, uncombed. He wore jeans and a blue T-shirt that she remembered.

"What are you doing here?" she said, and her voice cracked, her mind disbelieving what her eyes saw.

"Decided not to summit. I was going to spend the expedition at base camp and Camps One and Two, but then Ross got sick. So I helped him down."

Sabine squinted at him. She felt her eyebrows draw together in skepticism.

"You *decided* not to summit?" She wished she could take the words back so they didn't sound so...doubtful. Or worse.

Joe rubbed his arms. He'd come home prepared for her to take him back, prepared to see her gratitude at his change of heart—for it was more change of heart than sacrifice. He hadn't expected this rough welcome.

"God, I'm sorry," Sabine said, shaking her head. "I

don't know what I'm saying." She walked closer to him. "Can I hug you?"

He reached for her, wanting their embrace to heal the rift. "Thanks for the hat," he whispered. "I wore it a lot."

"Good. It fits?"

"Perfectly."

They went up to the loft, where he'd opened the windows. He discovered he couldn't put into words why he'd decided not to climb K2. He said lamely, "I don't know. It seemed so…pointless. All about me. Then, when Ross was in trouble…"

He related everything that had happened, including Ian's asking if he planned to come back after helping Ross down.

"I realized I don't feel the same about it as I used to. I don't feel okay about people deciding a summit bid is more important than the life of a friend. It's hard to see, sometimes, how I ever did feel that was okay."

Sabine told him about the dream she'd had.

Joe cracked a smile. "So how are you going to go down the slide?"

She eyed him. "Maybe I'll watch and see what you do."

He laughed and hugged her. "Where's the rest of my family?"

She told him about Karen and Jack. "Karen seems *much* happier."

"In other words, she has something to think about besides what's wrong with you."

"She's been one of my best friends since you've been gone. Not on a par with Norah or Lucy, but I really would've been lost without her, Joe. And she's not finding fault as much as she used to."

"Like I said, she's probably too busy."

Sabine saw his mouth twitching.

She said, "Want to come up to the house? Are you unloaded?"

"Not unpacked. But yes."

He took her hand as they made the short walk to the house, releasing hands only as they entered the kitchen.

But then Sabine tugged on his hand again, leading him into the bedroom she'd shared with Victor.

"I'm invited into the sanctum?"

"Yes," she said. "Though we might want to create a new sanctum. Together."

They lay on the bed, gazing into each other's eyes, talking.

"What's going on with your book?" she asked. He'd gone to contract with a publisher months before.

"Still in progress. I'm planning to interview some Colorado climbers, and ask the kids at the climbing wall why *they* like climbing."

"Is the publisher content?"

"They're very pleased. They said this'll make the book different from what they've seen before. They like the idea of including kids and distinguishing between different types of climbing."

Sabine's eyes narrowed in mock threat. "You wouldn't be thinking of teaching *my* kids to climb."

"I'm thinking of calling them *our* kids. And…yes, actually."

Sabine grinned. "Good."

He kissed her lips for the first time in so many months.

SHE SAID, "You know I feel something I never thought I'd feel for any man again."

"Passion?"

She shook her head. "There *is* that. But you're my best friend. That's what I mean."

"And you're mine." He paused a minute. "I never expected that would happen *ever.* Lovers are lovers, friends are friends. But when you wouldn't make love with me anymore, I discovered that what I was going to miss most was your friendship. I love your children, Sabine. I meant that, when I said I want you to think of them as *ours.*"

"I already do." She rested her head against his chest. "Why didn't you go for the summit? Really. What made you think differently about it?"

"I realized that at the end I'd just be standing at the top of a mountain alone. It didn't seem like something that would change the world even a little bit. It also seemed sad."

"I didn't think that way about it. I didn't think of it as sad. I know what it's like to want the summit, Joe."

"But you've taught me to want more. Maybe Victor taught me, too. Sabine, I understand why he took Teresa— why he went ahead and let their love prevail over loyalty to me."

Sabine raised her head to look at him.

"He was *young* when our father died. So he never had a chance to be young. Instead, he had to raise me. And he did it, and he never let me know if he resented it. He was mature. So, I think when Teresa came along and wanted him and he wanted her, I think he said to himself, 'I'm going to take this. I deserve this.'"

Sabine thought that over. What Joe said made sense.

"But he felt guilty," she said. "I e-mailed you about the things I found. The things Pastor Jon said. And that Biblical quote, God talking to Cain before Cain kills Abel.

He was feeling guilty. He may have surrendered to his emotions, but he never believed what he did was right."

"I should've forgiven him, Sabine. I mean, *really* forgiven him. I've always said that I forgave him, but I wouldn't talk to him, wouldn't see him, wouldn't make peace with him."

"Did he often try?"

"In the beginning, he tried a handful of times. After Teresa's accident, he stopped."

Sabine nodded.

They heard a car outside, and they slowly got up, and went into the kitchen.

Finn raced in first. Without a word, he ran to Joe and hurled himself into his arms.

"Daddy!" yelled Tori.

Maria stood watchfully in the doorway as Karen and Jack came in. Introductions were made, but Maria still didn't greet Joe.

Finally, when Jack had said, "I'm sure you all have lots of catching up to do,"—which Karen, Sabine thought, would have taken much longer to say—and the couple had left, Joe approached Maria.

"And how are you?" he asked.

"Fine. Did you climb the mountain?"

He shook his head.

"Did you bring us rocks from the top?" demanded Finn.

"He didn't *go* to the top," Maria told him. She looked at Joe. "I made you a present. To go with your hat." She went into the other room and came back with a neck gaiter that she'd knit for him. Sabine had explained that scarves weren't practical for climbers, that they could get caught in the ropes.

"They're not from the top," Joe said, "but I did bring rocks from K2. I brought rocks for everyone."

"Where are they?" Finn shouted.

"Out in my pack. Shall I go get them?"

"I'll come with you," Tori said. "Carry me."

Joe picked her up and said, "How about the rest of you wait in here?"

"I want to come!" Finn insisted.

"Finn," Sabine said softly. "Just wait."

"I'll be quick," Joe promised.

SABINE SLICED CHEESE and apples for snacks, and before she was done, Joe had returned, bearing a small blue nylon sack with a drawstring.

"I got these at Camp Two," he told the children, who crowded around the seat he'd taken at the end of the table, "which is a lot higher than Mount Sneffels or Uncompahgre Peak or any of the big mountains around here." He handed a rock to each of them.

Maria examined hers thoughtfully. "This is really from K2?"

"He said it's *not*," Finn said.

"He said it's not from the *top*," Maria snapped back.

"It's from K2, and it's not from the top," Joe agreed.

Tori stared at hers, then lifted her eyes to Joe. "What else did you bring me?"

"Tori," Sabine said, suppressing her mortification, "that's not polite. Say thank you for what Joe brought."

"Thank you." Tori's mouth drooped.

Joe fished in the sack and took out two silver bracelets, one for her and one that he gave to Maria. He gave Finn a pendant on a strong cord. "For Blizzardman," Joe said.

"Thank you," Maria told him. "I like my bracelet, and I like the rock."

"You're welcome."

"Doesn't my mom get a rock?" Maria asked.

"I told him I didn't want one," Sabine interjected hastily. She set the cheese and apples on the table.

Finn grabbed three apple pieces and four slices of cheese and stuffed them all in his mouth at once.

"I did bring her a rock, though," Joe said.

"Let's see it," Finn mumbled, mouth full.

Joe withdrew a jewelry box from the bag and reached for Sabine's hand. He pulled her down onto his lap and placed the jewelry box on the table.

"Let's see it!" Finn said again.

"It's a wedding ring," Tori predicted before the box was opened.

"Of course it's not," Maria said. "People give engagement rings before wedding rings."

"He and Mommy are married," Tori decreed.

"They are not. You're stupid," Finn told her.

Joe met Sabine's eyes. She saw the question in them and shrugged, smiling.

He said, "How would all of you feel if this box contained an engagement ring? Would it be okay with you if your mom and I got married?"

"You're already married," Tori insisted.

"You're stupid," Finn told her again.

"Finn," Sabine said in a warning tone.

Joe held his hand down tightly on top of the box.

"Let's see it!" Finn said for at least the third time..

Joe shook his head. "I'm waiting."

Finn dropped his head slightly. Then he muttered, "I'm sorry I called you stupid, Tori."

"Thank you."

Joe glanced at Maria, at all the faces avid to see what was in the box.

"Are you going to answer him?" Sabine asked.

"It's okay," Maria said. "It's fine."

Joe held the box toward Sabine and opened the lid to reveal the ring.

It glittered, with stones in shades of black, green and pale aqua. They winked from their gold setting.

"Try it on," Joe said.

"It's a princess ring," Tori declared.

Sabine removed the ring from the box and passed it to Joe, giving him her left hand.

He slid the ring onto her finger, where it fit smoothly and snugly. The top stone was large, a blackish green. On each side were stones in green, then small aquamarine gems.

"*Now* you're married," Tori pronounced.

"Black emerald," Joe said, "peridots and aquamarine, all from Pakistan."

Finn laughed suddenly. "You *did* bring her rocks."

Maria said, "It's pretty."

Sabine said, "Yes."

"What's that?" Joe asked. "Did you just say you'll marry me?"

"Yes," Sabine repeated.

"I told you they're not married," Finn told Tori, "stupid."

HARLEQUIN *Romance*

A family saga begins to unravel
when the doors to the Bella Lucia
Restaurant Empire are opened...

The Brides of Bella Lucia

*A family torn apart by secrets,
reunited by marriage*

AUGUST 2006

Meet Rachel Valentine, in
HAVING THE FRENCHMAN'S BABY
by Rebecca Winters

Find out what happens when a night of passion is followed
by a shocking revelation and an unexpected pregnancy!

SEPTEMBER 2006

The Valentine family saga continues with
THE REBEL PRINCE by Raye Morgan

www.eHarlequin.com

HRBB0706BW

If you enjoyed what you just read,
then we've got an offer you can't resist!

Take 2 bestselling love stories FREE!

Plus get a FREE surprise gift!

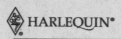

HARLEQUIN®

American ROMANCE®

American Beauties

SORORITY SISTERS, FRIENDS FOR LIFE

Michele Dunaway

THE MARRIAGE CAMPAIGN

Campaign fund-raiser Lisa Meyer has worked hard to be her own boss and will let nothing—especially romance—interfere with her success. To Mark Smith, Lisa is the perfect candidate for him to spend his life with. But if she lets herself fall for Mark, will she lose all she's worked for? Or will she have a future that's more than she's ever dreamed of?

On sale August 2006

Also watch for:

THE WEDDING SECRET
On sale December 2006

NINE MONTHS NOTICE
On sale April 2007

Available wherever Harlequin books are sold.

Stability is highly overrated....

Dana Logan's world had always revolved around her children. Now they're all grown up and don't seem to need anything she's able to give them. Struggling to find her new identity, Dana realizes that it's about time for her to get "off her rocker" and begin a new life!

Off Her Rocker

by Jennifer Archer

HARLEQUIN®

Next™

...ble August 2006

...el.com

#1362 A TEMPORARY ARRANGEMENT • Roxanne Rustand
Blackberry Hill Memorial

All Abby wanted was to spend a quiet summer filling in at a small hospital in the beautiful Wisconsin woods before going back to teach nursing. But this temporary arrangement is far from quiet. Especially since single dad Ethan has the only vacancy in town.

#1363 THE HORSEMAN • Margaret Way
Men of the Outback

When Cecile meets Raul Montalvan—a mysterious Argentinian—she knows she has to break her engagement with a man she doesn't love. Not that she really expects anything to happen with Raul—because as attracted as they are to each other, she can't help but sense his reasons for being in the Outback are not what they seem....

#1364 BEACH BABY • Joan Kilby
A Little Secret

Nina Kennerly has a full life, but she's always regretted giving her daughter up for adoption and losing her first love, Reid. Now her grown daughter has found her—with her own baby girl in tow!—and Nina may finally have a second chance at the family she always should have had.

#1365 FAMILY AT STAKE • Molly O'Keefe
Single Father

Widower Mac Edwards's twelve-year-old daughter has spun out of control. Now he's in danger of losing custody of her. The one person who can help keep his family together is Rachel Filmore—the woman he once loved...and the woman who broke his heart.

#1366 A MAN OF HONOR • Linda Barrett
Count on a Cop

Heather's father was a bad cop, which is why she'll never depend on a cop again. Out on the streets, helping runaways, she's forced to accept Officer Dave McCoy's protection, but she'll never trust him. Not until he proves where his loyalty truly lies.

#1367 REMEMBER TEXAS • Eve Gaddy

When marine biologist Ava Vincent accepts a job in Aransas City she has no idea her estranged brothers live there, too. Ava ran away as a kid and carries a secret so shameful she believes no one can ever forgive her. Yet when she meets Jack Willi... a widower with a troubled son, she discovers she wants to have a f... Still, she can't believe anyone can accept her past, much le...